To Live in Peace

By the same author:

The Life Situation
The Long Hot Summer
Proofs Of Affection
A Loving Mistress
Rose Of Jericho
A Second Wife

As Robert Tibber:

No White Coat
Love On My List
We All Fall Down
Patients Of A Saint
The Fraternity
The Commonplace Day
The General Practice
Practice Makes Perfect

Juvenile:

Aristide

To Live in Peace

Rosemary Friedman

For
Renate & Martin Zimet

Copyright © 1987 by Rosemary Friedman

First published in Great Britain in 1987 by
Judy Piatkus (Publishers) Limited of
5 Windmill Street, London, W1

British Library Cataloguing in Publication Data

Friedman, Rosemary
  To live in peace.
  I. Title
  823'.914   [F]   PR6056.R49

ISBN 0-86188-596-1

Phototypeset in 11/12½pt Linotron Garamond by
Phoenix Photosetting, Chatham
Printed and bound in Great Britain by
Mackays of Chatham Ltd

What do I have in common with Jews? I have hardly anything in common with myself.

                                                    Kafka

What a tragic story is the history of the Jews in modern times! And if one tried to write about the tragic element, one would be laughed at for one's pains. That is the most tragic thing of all.

Heine

Chapter One

Whenever Rachel gave her name, Klopman, in the antenatal clinic, she was aware of a *frisson* that passed between herself and the clerk behind the counter. When her name had been Shelton, conjured by her grandfather from Solomons, she had not, as often as she was required to identify herself, been made conscious of a difference which was impossible to quantify but had resulted in the expulsion of the Jews throughout the ages from so many countries of the world. They had been persecuted if they were poor, resented if they were rich, were the objects of opprobrium in both religious and secular societies, and to the Third Reich responsible for an economic depression for which the punishment had been the gas-chamber. Since the emergence of the Jewish State, antisemitism – blamed at various times on the need for scapegoats, ethnic hatred, xenophobia and religious bigotry – had acquired a new and 'respectable' image, changing its name to anti-Zionism, a euphemism heard more often since the day, one month before Rachel's wedding, that three Israeli armoured columns had rolled purposefully into the Lebanon.

Patrick's father had referred to the event briefly in his wedding speech. 'We are condemned for not fighting,' he said, 'and we are condemned if we fight.' He was right of course. The Jews of Europe had been accused of not rising up, although Rachel had yet to hear of the threatened passengers of a hijacked plane, in a parallel situation, indicted of the same crime.

The war in the Middle East, two months old now, which many had expected, Israeli-style, to be over in days, had had a curious effect. It had forced diaspora Jews to take a stance, set them at each other's throats. To their horror, on their honeymoon, Rachel, the hawk, and Patrick, the dove, had found themselves on opposing sides. 'Operation Peace for Galilee' was, according to Rachel, Israel's response to fourteen years of terrorist warfare – avowedly dedicated to her destruction – launched from Lebanese soil. To Patrick it was an obsession of inept rulers and vain military men who were running a nation created by moralists and dreamers. In the interests of harmony the subject was, as far as possible, avoided.

Fortunately Rachel had other matters on her mind, not the least of which was the child she was carrying, whose movements in its aqueous nest were a source of never ending astonishment and pleasure to both herself and Patrick. She had experienced the first of these beneath the marriage canopy. Rabbi Magnus had just proclaimed them man and wife, delighting vicariously in the forthcoming kiss, when Klopman junior had, without warning, made his presence felt. Rachel, almost dropping her bouquet, had put a hand to her belly, causing an expression of alarm to cross her mother's face, and felt with amazement the inapt protrusion through the lace of her dress. It was as if the baby had waited for the ceremony to be completed, as if he had bided his time, as if he knew.

She was sure that he would turn out to be an exemplary child, cooperative and manageable, that there would be none of the alarums and excursions of rearing that beset her sister Carol, and that she and Patrick would set a new and enviable trend in the art of parenthood. There was nothing to it. Take pregnancy. Carol, who was in the midst of her fourth, would regale Rachel with tales of indisposition and matinal nausea, while her sister-in-law Sarah, who made the hat-trick, had in the first trimester clung on to the child she was carrying only by the skin of her teeth. Rachel, who was certain the whole thing was in the mind, had never felt better. Her son, for she had never had any doubts that this prize-fighter, this acrobat who made his existence so manifest within her, was anything but male, took his cue from his host. Unless the subject of the Lebanon was broached, Rachel was a model of serenity – a state which she hoped would communicate itself to the foetus – acquainting herself with every *nostrum* of pregnancy in the absence of her mother, whose departure to New York with Maurice Morgenthau had brought Rachel closer to her sister Carol, with whom previously she had never had much in common.

Keeping her options open, Kitty had not sold the flat. Widowed now for two years she was ambivalent about Maurice Morgenthau. She had agreed to go to New York with him, to live in the apartment that he used as his studio, but there had been no talk of marriage. Rachel, remembering her father and the special bond that had been between them, hoped there never would be. Her brother, Josh, said her attitude was selfish. Carol, who had met Maurice only briefly at Rachel's wedding, wasn't sure. She was living in Kitty's London flat (an arrangement which had worked out most conveniently) with her three children who were on summer holiday from school, while her husband, Alec, remained in Godalming to care for his patients and supervise the renovation of the Queen Anne house they had bought there. Rachel found it strange to go into her mother's home and find Carol – who so resembled her – as beautiful in her pregnancy as Rachel knew from the family records Kitty had been. Rachel's condition seemed to have overlaid her features with an unattractive mask.

'How could you have married me?' she'd say to Patrick in the mornings, examining her unfamiliar features, the novel contours of which confronted her from the mirror.

'You trapped me into it.'

'What if I don't get my looks back?'

The question was rhetorical. Patrick's regard for her had grown stronger with the marvel of each successive month. He practised sensual massage as he had been instructed at the clinic and took photos of her gravid body with its shadowed planes, contact sheets of which – 'Rachel with Child' from a hundred miraculous angles – he passed round the family, profoundly shocking Carol.

'You don't look at the mantelpiece when you're poking the fire,' Patrick said.

Rachel stood still. It was the first time she had heard Patrick make a joke. His father made jokes. Herbert Klopman. He was renowned for them, cynicism covering the feelings he was unable to express. She could hear the ring of her own father's voice in her ears repeating the family aphorism, which had been handed down, concerning apples which did not fall far from trees.

'Klopman,' the clerk repeated Rachel's name, isolating her from the Wheatleys and Frasers, the Stylianides and the Obodos. She was happy with 'Rachel' (she had been called after her maternal grandmother) from the Hebrew for 'ewe'. She liked the names, lyrical and poetic, derived from scriptural objects: Leah, a gazelle; Zipporah, a bird; Jonah, a dove. Rachel's son would be named Sydney after her father who had not lived to see him. They would have to find a derivative, something more contemporary, to go with Klopman, which, according to Patrick's grandmother, had originated when the first census was taken and Jews under the Austrian Empire had been required to provide themselves with Germanic names. Those who had not objected to the decree had chosen Blumenthal (Valley of Flowers), Rosenberg (Rose Mountain), Bernstein (Amber). The Orthodox, unwilling to dehebraise their names, had been at the mercy of spiteful officials by whom they had been saddled with Eselkopf (Ass's Head), Stinker, Lumper, Fresser (Glutton), Elephant and Weinglas.

Rachel's own recent name change, Shelton to Klopman, had, she supposed, brought to the surface her ambivalence about her Jewishness. She was not observant, as her father had been and as her mother and sister still were. She did not go to synagogue, cooked bacon and eggs for breakfast and disregarded the Sabbath with its injunctions. Even so, looking round the waiting-room at the polyglot mothers in their various stages of gestation, she realised that she was not as others, and like Israel herself aspired to be like the whole world yet to be apart.

Unlike Patrick's background – his father had been more concerned with producing an accomplished professional than an accomplished Jew – Rachel's had been steeped in religious values. When she went to college, regarding her parents' lifestyle as alien, she had felt herself to be Jewish but not uncomfortably so. As a freshman she had gone along to the Jewish Society but found that the *mise-en-scène* was a replica of the parental home on Friday nights and that she had nothing in common with the members. The following autumn she became involved in the Students' Union; but it wasn't until her final year that she became increasingly disturbed by, and could no longer ignore, the activities of the far Left, who passed resolutions equating Zionism with racism, and put forward provocative views in their official handbook which roused ancestral voices in her, forced her to take a stand. Now it was the war in the Lebanon which led her to reappraisal.

Unlike her father, and Carol who had always followed blindly in his footsteps, Rachel – as far as Judaism was concerned – was uncommitted. She could no more identify with her sister than she could with the *Hassidim* (with their long black coats and side-curls who walked the streets of Stamford Hill or toured the suburbs with their *mitzvahmobiles*), or the Anglicised practices of Reform and Liberal congregations who recited the liturgy in the vernacular and summoned women to the Reading of the Law. Sometimes she had difficulty in identifying with herself. There had been heated discussions with her father – which upset Kitty, disturbed the equilibrium in the home and ended invariably in deadlock – in which Rachel challenged as outmoded the need for organised religion. Wasn't it OK, she argued, to be a good individual, someone who didn't hurt anybody? Not hurting anybody, Sydney said, was not good but merely not bad. To be a worthwhile person involved the active pursuit of good. It was not enough to refrain from abusing fellow human beings, one must intercede on their behalf. Jewish law – unlike secular laws which were almost all negative, forbidding criminal acts – demanded positive action: to give charity, silence gossip, visit the sick. Involvement was required which, to be effective, needed (like political parties and other social systems) organised operating procedures of laws and ethics. Ideas such as Rachel's were the product of woolly mindedness and were not sufficient to create responsible people and a moral world.

It was easy for Sydney. Like Tevye – the Jewish Everyman created by Sholem Aleichem and popularised in *Fiddler on the Roof* – he seemed to have an intimate and personal relationship with his Maker, a direct line to God. The pious milkman had prayed three times a day, understood his history and the meaning of continuity, yet had little interest in the outside world and no particular measure of parental insight.

In the *shtetls* of eastern Europe there had been a pattern to existence, of tradition, of oppression. Life had dictated the terms which must now be redefined. In Anatevka they were born, married and died within the community. Today there were choices. Get blue eyes and assimilate; intermarry as her brother Josh had done; opt out of Jewish life but identify by means of token *barmitzvahs*, a smattering of Hebrew words and nostalgic foods the tastes of which had persisted from the ghetto; join anti-Jewish causes in a process of self-destruction.

The State of Israel itself had not solved the problem but at least, although there were political and religious rifts, there was a Jewish ambience and to be a Jew did not require, as it did in Britain, affirmation.

There had been no necessity, until now, to give these matters too much thought. But what about her son, hers and Patrick's? Was Jewish consciousness to be maintained, and if so how, and to what extent? What acts would they teach him of Jewish significance? Prayer? Language? The basic tenets of tolerance and righteousness in human relationships? The older Sydney had been a firm believer in inculcating children by example. Rachel wondered how much of an example she and Patrick would show their son. She could see that the future held problems other than merely the safe delivery of her child but these she would face as she came to them. At the moment she was devoting her entire attention to the manner of his birth.

Chapter Two

'She's going to have it standing up,' Kitty said, holding Rachel's letter in her hand. 'Did you ever hear of such a thing?'

Maurice was painting at his easel, sombre strokes of grey and burnt sienna, slashing at his past with charcoal and with slate.

'It's the most effective method of pain control,' he said, pausing to half-close his eyes. 'The supine position compresses the veins, starves the uterus of blood, makes the contractions more painful and prevents the force of gravity from helping the baby's head along. It was first used by Louis XIV's mistress so that His Majesty could keep an eye on the proceedings.'

It was not a topic Kitty could have discussed with Sydney. Maurice went back to his canvas. 'Immobilising the mother prolongs the labour.'

Kitty averted her eyes from the painting. She no longer looked. All around the walls, ten deep, were stacked the outpourings of Maurice's daily therapy in which he was both analyst and analysand. When first she had come to New York – staggering under the August heat, that struck like a cobra as soon as one went outside, and the enormity of her own decision to leave her home and live with Maurice whom she scarcely knew – she had looked, had stood by bereft of words as he demonstrated his obsession.

Canvases in which there was no light and little life; crushing invasions of space as stark forms with the just discernible features of human beings clawed a breathing space on barrack bunks; forced marches, and cattle trucks in which the beasts were human; the distribution of the bread and the crucifixion on the wire; heads which were all eyes; eyes which were all dead; the grisly ballet of the leaps for air in the ovens; a misery of little children; a landscape of bones. After the first time she had averted her eyes, not focussing on the sludge and the slime of Maurice's canvases in which he said the things he could not say, which were his mute cry, his silent scream, his unsung song.

He had met her at the airport. All the way across the Atlantic she had been terrified that he would not be there, and so appalled at the temerity of what she was doing, that had she had the power to do so she would have gone into the cockpit and asked the pilot to turn back. The realisation of the step she was taking, and the suddenness with which it assailed her, overlaid her views on flying and to her own astonishment she quite forgot to be afraid. Having had seven hours of voluntary incarceration in which to consider the matter she had come to the conclusion that her arbitrary decision, to leave her home and family for Maurice Morgenthau and New York, had been made on the swell of euphoria which followed Rachel's wedding and bore no relation to how she might have acted in a more contemplative mood.

To all appearances she hardly knew Maurice. She had met him on holiday in Israel – her first proper trip in the two years that she had been widowed – and between that time and Rachel's wedding had corresponded with him. Through his letters, poignant and articulate, Maurice had painted his history for her, his childhood in Germany, his existence in the concentration camps which he alone of all his family had survived, his new life in New York as a physician and his retirement since which he had dedicated himself to portraying the unique horror of his wartime experiences in paint. On airmail paper, the tenuous friendship forged in Eilat had prospered. Maurice for the first time shared his past, and Kitty found the sympathetic ear and practical solutions she had lacked, since Sydney's death, for the daily problems which beset her. She should, she told herself on flight BA 175 to New York, have left it at that.

It was the excitement, she thought, of seeing Rachel off on her honeymoon that had led her to accede to Maurice's suggestion that she come to live with him in New York. He had two adjoining apartments and he had offered to move his painting into his living quarters, leaving the studio for Kitty. A more permanent relationship had not been discussed. The decision had something to do with her own flat, which seemed so empty when she came home after the wedding, although it was a long time since Rachel had lived there; something to do with her sister-in-law Beatty, whose husband, Leon, had died in hospital while Beatty was at the wedding and for whom Kitty now felt herself responsible; something to do with Freda, her other sister-in-law, and her husband, Harry, who were always ringing her up for one bit of advice or another; and Mirrie, Sydney's younger sister, who was demonstrating signs of senility; and her nephew Norman, who by the look of things would be getting married himself soon to the South African Sandra and would no longer be dining with her twice a week; something to do with Carol, who was coming to stay for three months and would be bringing the children and chaos into Kitty's ordered life while the house in Godalming received its face-lift; something to do with her son, Josh, and his wife, Sarah, who was also expecting a baby and, under Kitty's guidance, hoping to become a convert to Judaism before the child was born.

Maurice, how romantic he was – Sydney, loving and caring had never been romantic – had tied a knot in the fronds of the flowers he had sent her when he came to England for the wedding, the Bedouin way of saying: I love you. 'Later on, is coming by his very dear one. If she does nothing, she is turning him down. If she opens up the knot . . .' Kitty had opened up the knot.

The family, horrified, had tried to dissuade her.

'A lot of silly nonsense,' Beatty had said, snivelling into her handkerchief when she got up from her week of mourning. She had visualised a new life for herself in which she would see more of her sister-in-law, Kitty, chumming up – although they had never been close – two widows, for shopping expeditions, and holidays in Bournemouth or Majorca. 'Who do you know in New York?' she said.

Her younger sister-in-law had been more honest. 'What will I do without you?' Mirrie said. Mirrie had given up work now; sometimes she was unable to remember what day it was, or if she had turned off the gas. Kitty commended her to Beatty who would have time on her hands (although the two sisters had always been at each other's throats) and to her brother, Juda, who had never bothered with her but was now head of the family. Juda had offered to have Maurice 'investigated' but Kitty, less than politely (she couldn't think where she had got her unaccustomed courage from) told him to mind his own business. Carol was put out ('I thought you'd be looking after the children while I had the baby'), and Rachel furious: 'That old man!' 'You hardly spoke to him,' Kitty pointed out.

The women of the Ladies' Guild were dumbstruck. She heard them whispering among themselves and felt that they regarded her with new eyes in which there was an element of jealousy, as if she had metamorphosed suddenly into an amalgam of Elizabeth Taylor and Sophia Loren. They treated her gently, like an invalid. 'Are you sure you know what you're doing, Kitty dear?'

Of course she did not know. But with the advent of Maurice, a new dimension had come into her life which enabled her, uncharacteristically and late, to step forth into the unknown, to take a chance, to try.

She had waited until Rachel came back from her honeymoon, golden and bursting with Greek food and her child. 'You're being really stupid.' Rachel's eyes were uncompromising, 'You'll hate it in New York.' Inside, Kitty had found the audacity to laugh at the role reversal. For so many years she had been the parent, advising, cautioning. 'He's probably after your money,' Rachel offered as a Parthian shot.

'It's time you started living for yourself,' Maurice had said. 'The children have their own lives. They can manage without you. Give it six months. We'll see how we get on . . .'

She had bought her ticket, packed her case, said goodbye, tearful and choked, to the family who took advantage of her, to the children who liked her to be there, to her friends in the synagogue and neighbours in the flats, and the widows with whom she played bridge and who looked at her with disbelief, and to her grandchildren whose possessive arms almost made her weaken at the last moment.

Josh took her to the airport. The last time they had done the journey was when she had been going to Eilat where she first met the enigmatic Maurice with his flat cap and zippered jacket. This time it was different. Already the enthusiasm was wearing off. She wondered what on earth she was doing, with not a soul that she knew, sitting down to pass the time with coffee and a Danish pastry in the early morning tumult of the International Departure Lounge.

In the plane, setting the seal on her commitment, she had altered her watch to New York time as the Captain announced the route – Northern Ireland, Labrador and Boston – that would be taking her to

Maurice. Hemmed into the window seat Josh had secured for her, covered with the mauve cellular blanket and, plugged into the red plastic headset, trying to concentrate on the film, she realised how much already she missed her family and how very dear to her they were, the importance of one's own flesh and blood which was more, so very much more, than the sum of its parts. Several hours later, after she had filled in her landing card and gone with her sponge-bag to the confined toilet to freshen herself up for Maurice, the First Officer's voice – 'We are beginning our descent for New York' – brought home to her the significance of the step she was taking. The landing at Kennedy, ill-timed and bumpy, had been the beginning of a dream from which she had still not woken. She did not need telling to remain in her seat until the aircraft had stopped and the seatbelt signs had been switched off; the 747 had become her home, her limbo, and she was terrified of moving.

With one ear on the public address system which announced that she could retrieve her baggage from carousel number five (her lucky number, perhaps she would be lucky), she selected, as she did in the supermarket, the shortest and fastest moving queue for immigration. Standing behind the yellow line until it was her turn to approach the uniformed black woman ('One person or family group permitted in booth at a time'), she peered through the glass, vainly searching the alien faces in the customs hall for the familiar sight of Maurice. With her passport unequivocally stamped and having lied about the purpose of her visit – which was neither strictly speaking business nor holiday – she had asked a well built man, no older than Josh, if he would mind helping her with her luggage, but he ignored her, as if she had not spoken, and she knew that she was in New York. Having neither contraband, vegetables, birds nor bird's eggs to declare she had passed, with her swerving trolley, unchallenged through the green channel.

Maurice, waiting anxiously, was in his shirtsleeves. She hardly recognised him without his flat cap and zippered jacket which was the image of him (despite the handsome figure he had cut in his tuxedo at the wedding) she carried in her mind. The expression on his face when he caught sight of her, as if with his own eyes he had witnessed the coming of the Messiah, dispelled the doubts and the agonies, the vacillations and the weaknesses of the last days. When he put his arms round her and his cheek against hers, wordlessly, she had the impression that for the first time since Sydney's death, after which she had wandered directionless in the wilderness, she had come home.

For some reason she had not expected Maurice to have a car – MM 200 – certainly not a Mercedes. Sydney, even so many years after the war, would not buy anything that was overtly German. Not because he thought he could achieve anything by boycotting German goods but because he considered it wrong for Jews of his generation, which had suffered so grievously at the hands of the Nazis, to display any symbol so incontrovertibly associated with their martyrdom.

As they adhered strictly to the fifty mile per hour speed limit on the Van Wyck Expressway – eight lanes of traffic – passed Jewel Avenue and Flushing Meadow, which sounded more romantic somehow than Shepherd's Bush and Hammersmith, they were overtaken by blue-rinsed grandmothers, men in vests, and bearded elders in trilby hats, at the wheels of Chevrolets and Pontiacs and Buicks (which seemed to go on forever), and Kitty tried, so that she could later describe them in a letter to her children, to formulate her first impressions of New York. Beneath the puffed clouds in a turquoise sky they followed the signs, brown on white, to Manhattan. 'Welcome to Queens', and 'Liberty Avenue' with its lush trees and clapboard houses, 'Soul Food' and 'Chicken and Ribs'. 'New York City Ice Skating'. Debbie and Lisa would have liked that. 'Catch a Hit Yankee Baseball.'

'Yankee Stadium,' Maurice said, pointing out the concrete circle.

At the traffic lights a diminutive youth in a tattered shirt smeared the windscreen with a sponge at the end of a stick. Maurice put the washers on and gave the boy a quarter.

The temperature in the purring car with its tinted windows gave the lie to the fact that outside, according to the last illuminated sign, it had reached the nineties. The news on the radio broadcast the latest developments in the Israeli siege of Beirut:

'. . . despite calls for a cessation of hostilities Israel has violated the ceasefire and there is sporadic shelling in West Beirut. Israeli Defence force tanks have moved into the central area close to the Green Line and have prevented UN observers from reaching Beirut.'

'They've been cut off for a week,' Kitty said.

'The siege is to prevent food, water and fuel from getting to the strongholds of the PLO. Unfortunately everyone suffers in the inter-

ests of nationalism,' Maurice replied. 'Flags. Emblems. Passports. Anthems. Israel's no longer a model for western civilisation, some sort of *wunderkind*. She's just like the rest. "If you will it, it is not a dream," Herzl said, but I think the time has come to wake up.'
'I keep thinking about the women and children . . .'
'Israeli planes distributed leaflets urging civilians to leave the area. There are escape routes open. Thousands already have.'
'They don't tell you that.'
'They've got the fire brigade reporting. Kids from the networks with their inevitable sympathy for what they feel to be the underdog, who come crashing in when there's trouble anywhere, making simple divisions between the "goodies" and "baddies". The less informed they are the more sensation and violence minded they become, photographing the same streets of damaged houses which the Israelis were probably not responsible for anyway.

'They'd be amazed if you told them that in 1947 the United Nations proposed that there was to be a Jewish state and for the first time ever an Arab Palestinian state. The Jews accepted the offer: the extremist Arab leadership wanted all or nothing. It got nothing, and the Palestinian refugee problem was created. That in 1948 *nine hundred thousand* Jews had their property confiscated by Arab governments and were driven out of Arab countries. That the Palestinian Liberation Organisation has never been used to liberate the Palestinians at all, but to keep them in misery, discriminating against their own people, depriving them of human rights . . .'

Maurice pressed the button, truncating the newsreader. 'Not that I condone this war. It's doing inestimable harm to history's impression of Israel which is lying and deceiving for the first time. Frankly, I think Prime Minister Begin has taken leave of his senses.'

'I'm glad Rachel can't hear you,' Kitty said. 'She gets hysterical.'

'Tempers are running pretty high here. The antisemites – anti-Zionists they call themselves now – are crawling out of the woodwork.' He put a hand on Kitty's. 'War is a terrible thing. But there are worse things. Don't let's talk about it, Kit. Tell me how you've been.'

Talking to Maurice was like finding sanctuary. In London she had been surrounded by people, but they had their own problems, none of them more than superficially concerned with what Kitty Shelton had on her mind. The children were good, nothing to complain about there, but she was aware of a look, glazed and faraway, that came into their eyes when the conversation got round to topics that did not immediately concern themselves. It was the same with her bridge circle. The four widows brought their own problems to the table and laid them down with the trumps on the green baize card-tables in the various flats, but each marched to the music of her own drummer and could not hear the other's tune. Maurice listened, as he had in Israel when the confidences had come tumbling out. He did not say much but he gave Kitty's outpourings, trivial as they may have been, his undivided attention, and could, she swore, have taken an exam in the altercations she was having with her landlord who wanted the tenants to pay for the installation of new central heating boilers before the onset of winter; in the state of the portfolio bequeathed to her by Sydney; in Rachel's refusal either to move from her council flat or to make any practical preparations for her forthcoming child. If Maurice could not provide the solutions to her problems at least he provided the sympathy. It was what she wanted. What she missed. Everyone needed somebody. She wondered if the yearning for the soulmate she had lacked since Sydney's death had been worth the transition to New York.

Her previous impressions of the city had been gleaned from the television – '49th Precinct' and 'Starsky and Hutch'. She had been unprepared for the relentlessness and volume of the traffic, dumbfounded by the oscillating mass of multi-ethnic, summer-clad humanity in perpetual motion in the sizzling streets, overwhelmed by the tottering menace of the preposterous buildings, and doubted the wisdom of her decision – despite the comforting presence of Maurice – before she reached his flat. Apartment. She had to remember to say it. There was so much to remember. So much that was new.

She did not know what she had been expecting, she had not really thought about it. As she wrote the address, East 85th Street, on her letters to Maurice, she had not had any clear picture in her mind of where he lived. Seeing the elegant striped canopy which stretched from the doorway of the building, across the wide pavement, to the kerb, Kitty had at first thought that Maurice must be taking her to an hotel. When the doorman, short and swarthy in his neat grey uniform, rushed out to take her cases and greeted Maurice with a 'Hi, Doc!' she knew that he had not.

'This is Joe,' Maurice said, introducing him.
'Hi, Mrs Shelton.' Joe proferred a hand. 'How y'a doing today?'
Kitty was surprised that he had addressed her by name. There seemed no end to the surprises.
'Joe knows everyone on the block,' Maurice said with pride, 'including the man who runs the numbers. Anything you want to know about the Yankees or the Mets, ask Joe.'
Kitty had a vague impression of a smart foyer – 'All visitors must be announced' – with a red carpet, gilt bamboo mirror, porter's desk and ornate lamps on either side of a silk-covered sofa.
'I got the bagels,' Joe said, going up in the smooth elevator, 'and some blueberry pie.'
It was Joe, who as Kitty was later to learn came from Puerto Rico, who had helped Maurice prepare his studio for her and had carried the melancholy accumulation of paintings to Maurice's apartment across the hall. The studio consisted of one large white-painted room with polished boards covered with vivid oriental rugs, at one end of which was a low bed with an American Indian throw-over spread, and at the other the pale and gleaming surfaces of a high-tech kitchenette. Louvred doors led off the room to a walk-in closet and a stripped pine bathroom. On a chrome and glass table, which served as a room divider, was an arrangement of flowers in a pottery crock such as Maurice used for his brushes.
Maurice and Joe watched as Kitty picked up the card: 'Welcome to New York. And to my heart. Maurice.' She could not say thank you. Could not breathe. She rushed to let some air into the room although it was cool, hammering at the glass.
'Double windows,' Maurice said, 'we don't open them.'
It was one of the things she had had to get used to: the fact that she was fifteen floors up with a view only of the apartment building across the street and had to rely for ventilation upon the noisy mechanism of the air-conditioning which kept her awake at night; the confines of the studio when she had been used to space; and above all, the heat. You shivered in the buildings and died in the streets. The blistering city was an inferno.
Maurice's apartment was high-ceilinged, harking back, Kitty thought, with its large dark furniture, its book-lined walls, to central Europe. He had rolled up the rug at the window end where he had

placed his easel, and worked surrounded on three sides by his canvases stacked face to the wall.

In the kitchen, with its *Bauhaus* table, Joe took the bagels from a brown paper bag and, opening Maurice's cupboard, put them on a plate. He seemed very much at home.

'Coffee?' Maurice, his hand on the steaming glass jug in the coffee machine, addressed Joe.

'I already had.'

Joe set the pie, topped with the dusky blueberries Kitty had never seen before, in its fluted baking-foil case on the table.

'Enjoy,' he said to Kitty, and to Maurice: 'You want anything, Doc, you call.'

'He looks after me,' Maurice said when he'd gone. 'Anything you need, ask Joe.'

It had all been too quick. That was the trouble with flying. Your body was transported while your grey matter was still packing its bags. Kitty could hear herself speaking to Maurice, answering his questions, filling in the weeks since Rachel's wedding, but she felt that she was imagining her presence in his apartment and that she would shortly wake up in her own bed to find that it had been a dream. Outside, the orange ball that was the sun shone fiercely but Kitty's internal clock told her that it was time for bed.

Maurice took cream cheese and pale Nova Scotia salmon from the refrigerator. Kitty drank the coffee he poured out for her and toyed with the food.

'I can't believe you're really here,' Maurice said.

'Neither can I.'

He cut a slice of pie and put it on her plate. 'From the *patisserie* on Madison. People come from all over town.'

He wanted to please her. Had arranged the studio with Joe, bought the flowers and the pie, wanting everything to be nice. He could see that she was dropping.

'You go to bed too early, you'll wake up too early.'

He turned on the radio, tuning into the news from the Middle East. She guessed that he listened to every bulletin. '. . . Prime Minister Begin has informed Secretary Shultz that Israel has accepted the proposal for a multinational peacekeeping force to enter Beirut . . . Shlomo Argov, the Israeli Ambassador to Britain, whose attempted assassination purportedly sparked Israel's invasion of Lebanon, has been flown home from a London hospital . . .'

Kitty wondered what she was doing three thousand miles from home sitting next to this strange man. She put her fork down on the blueberry pie and felt her eyes close. Maurice took her by the hand and led her across the hall. In the studio he shut the blinds, fussed with the lights.

'There's a house phone if you need anything.' He showed her which button to press. 'Call any time, I don't sleep.'

'You're very kind,' she said, as if to a stranger.

She went with him to the door, with its safety devices and its spy-hole.

'Lock two turns,' – Maurice said, demonstrating. 'Use the chain. Don't open to anyone. And Kitty . . .'

She raised her heavy eyelids. She must either sleep or weep.

'It'll be okay.'

She wished she could be so sure.

'In the morning it'll look better.'

She hoped he was right.

From Maurice's flat across the hall she could hear the unfamiliar accents of the newsreader: '. . . an eye-witness report . . .' accompanied by the sound of gunfire and of ricocheting shells.

Chapter Three

'Mrs Klopman!'
'Ms,' Rachel said.
'Mrs' made her feel like her mother (of whose present behaviour Rachel did not approve) from whose mould – inadequately equipped to deal with the very different world she found outside – she spent her life, unlike Carol, struggling to escape. As far as Rachel was concerned, Kitty had always been middle-aged, middle class and predictable, occupied with the nurturing of others to the extent of neglecting herself. She had devoted her life to the well-being of her children and supporting the goals and ambitions of a husband (defining herself as relative to him) who allowed her to spend herself in the onerous running of his household while referring to her as his 'queen'. Often Rachel had needled her, accused her of never having an opinion of her own, of not thinking for herself; she had hovered around the light of his lamp, a pale shadow of Sydney, treating her husband deferentially and accepting his natural dominion over her.

Kitty's only interests outside the home and her family had been her charity work – Soviet Jewry and Israel rather than Vietnamese boat-people – about which she had countered Rachel's allegation that Jews only look after their own with the acerbic retort that when non-Jews made such accusations – which Rachel was parroting – what they actually meant was that *only* Jews look after their own. Her mother was always busy, lame dogs and the less fortunate, preserving the fabric of the family of which Sydney had been the uncrowned king. Even after his death, her mother's life had continued along the same lines as before. She had worked for the synagogue Ladies' Guild, cooked for her nephew Norman and for Josh, providing the time honoured dishes into whose mysteries she was initiating Sarah, knitted for the grandchildren. Maurice had come as a shock. Rachel had seen him as an interloper, disliked him on sight, could not understand her mother's enthusiasm for the elderly European with his enigmatic demeanour, his foreign accent.

Kitty had dropped her bombshell at the celebration dinner she had arranged for Rachel and Patrick on their return from honeymoon. Carol and Alec had come up from Godalming for the occasion. They had had the pink beach at Skiathos (cicadas in the olive trees, the smell of thyme and warm grasses) and the sunstruck white of Hydra with Kitty's cold borsht – in which Sydney had always liked her to serve a floury hot potato – and the air, land and naval bombardment of West Beirut over the chicken which had been roasted (the neck stuffed separately and sliced) for family gatherings for as long as Rachel could remember. Over the years the bird had fallen into natural divisions. Rachel liked the leg, Carol the wings, Josh the breast, Sydney the thigh and Kitty, disregarding as usual her own preferences, taking what was left with the addition, if she was lucky, of the parson's nose. Rachel deplored her attitude, as she had her mother's habit, when her father was alive, of no matter who was at the table serving him not only with the choicest morsels but first.

In his father's absence it was Josh who took preference, who sat in his father's place in the walnut armchair with its tapestried seat and ball and claw feet, the seat in which Sydney had been sitting when he'd had his first fit, precursor of the cerebral tumour which was to kill him.

'The Security Council – has admonished Israel to withdraw her troops to the old lines,' Josh had said, by way of conversation. 'I heard it on the radio coming along.'

'Pity,' Rachel said. 'They should let them just get in there and finish the job.'

Josh applied himself to his chicken. He felt personally discomforted by what he considered both uncharacteristic and unjustified aggression by his co-religionists.

'What good has it done us? Israel should go to war only when there's no alternative.'

'You know very well the Israelis were responding to PLO terrorist attacks on civilian targets, which have been escalating since 1968, and to their occupation of the Lebanon which they used as a base to attack Israel.' Rachel said.

'Still no excuse . . .'

'They didn't try to assassinate the Israeli Ambassador in London?'

'Argov was a pretext. The invasion must have been planned for months.'

'Do you really think Begin *wants* to put the lives of all those Israeli soldiers at risk?'

'What about the Lebanese? The women and children who are getting killed?'

'If you took the trouble to open your newspaper you'd have seen General Sharon's statement that no nation on earth, or any other army during a war, had so deeply considered – to the extent of impeding their own progress – the question of avoiding civilian casualties, which was their prime concern. Every one was regretted, every one was a tragedy . . .'

'Regrets won't bring a single one of these children back to life.'

'You know very well that most of the casualties occurred because the PLO deliberately put their guns next to homes and schools . . .'

'Don't get so excited,' Kitty said.

'. . . they set up anti-aircraft bases round clinics, put their artillery on the roofs of hospitals, crates of explosives . . .'

'I'm not denying . . .' Josh began.

'. . . and boxes of ammunition in the cellars of blocks of flats, and the people have to sleep on top of all that! If Israel cared nothing for civilian lives they could have finished the job long ago.'

'10,000 dead! 40,000 wounded! 600,000 homeless!'

Rachel put down her knife and fork. 'If you're going to talk rubbish . . .'

'Rachel!' Kitty said.

'Where does he get his figures?'

'The Red Cross,' Josh said.

Rachel picked up her knife and pointed it at her brother. 'I presume the news hasn't reached Bayswater that those figures came from the Palestine Red Crescent which, by a curious coincidence, is headed by one Dr. Fathi Arafat, brother of the celebrated Yasser Arafat, who just happens to be the chairman of the PLO you seem so fond of, whose

Covenant specifically dedicates it to revolutionary violence, the annihilation of Israel and the Israelis, and of anybody else who gets in the way.'

'For the last time!' Kitty said.

'Let me finish. He knows perfectly well that those figures he quotes have been discredited by both Arab and Israeli sources.'

'That's enough!'

'There couldn't possibly have been 600,000 homeless because the *entire* population of the area which came under Israeli control was only 510,000 and the true figure was nearer to 20,000, all of whom are being cared for and hoping eventually to return home. . . .'

'You're brainwashed!'

'Shut up both of you,' Alec said, 'you're upsetting Carol. She's pregnant.'

'We're all pregnant,' Rachel said.

'I wondered who swallowed that Israeli propaganda,' Josh said.

'If it's proganda you're after what about the PLO, who have hired western professionals specifically to convince reporters that they are a moderate, non-violent, reasonable and democratically representative body, and to inflame public opinion by giving the impression that the Israelis are "intransigent", cruel, bigoted, destructive and racist, given to indiscriminate bombing and the killing of civilians in residential areas?'

'Which is precisely what I was complaining about.'

'Those reporters have been selected, paid, seduced and corrupted by the PLO.'

'According to Israel.'

'It's well known! They bribe them, give them a good time, and provide them with accreditation cards. Those who won't play are forced to leave or are beaten up. At least two have been murdered.'

'Bullshit!'

Rachel stood up. 'I'm going home.'

'Sit down,' Kitty said.

'I'm not staying in the same room. . . .'

'I've got something to say,' Kitty said

Rachel was half-way to the door.

'I'm not telling you until you sit down.'

Rachel glared at Josh.

'Come on Rache,' Patrick said.

Rachel sat down with her back pointedly to Josh. She looked at Kitty presiding over the carcass of the chicken from which Carol, who like her mother had never liked discord, was nervously picking scraps.

'I'm going to New York,' Kitty said.

'Good idea,' Rachel said. 'After all the work you put in for the wedding.'

'New York in August!' Josh said. 'That's when they have the greatest increase in the crime rate. It's to do with the high temperatures. They all go crazy.'

'She needs a holiday,' Carol said.

'Who said anything about a holiday?' Kitty said. 'I'm going to live with Maurice Morgenthau.'

'That old man!' Rachel said.

'You're getting married again?' Josh was stunned.

'I didn't say so.'

'You can't just shack up with him,' Rachel said.

'I thought it was all right these days,' Kitty said, 'I seem to remember. . . .' She looked at Rachel and Patrick.

'That's different,' Rachel said. 'You know very well.'

'There's no explicit prohibition of premarital relationships anywhere in the Torah,' Sarah, who had been studying the subject, said.

'I'm not going to "live" with him,' Kitty reassured them. She explained about Maurice's two flats and saw her children exchange glances with each other as if she had suddenly become unhinged and must be humoured.

'You'll be back for the babies,' Carol said complacently, meaning her own, and reminding Kitty of her responsibilities.

'Give it six months,' Maurice had said.

'Have you thought about what you're doing?' Josh, wearing his head of the family hat, asked.

'*That* Maurice is on to a good thing,' Rachel said.

They had all tried to dissuade her. Josh with reference to the memory of his late father, and Sarah on the grounds that she depended on Kitty's support for her continued initiation into the rites of Judaism and her imminent conversion. Alec, on behalf of his wife, that Carol needed her mother and relied upon her; Carol, that her children would be deprived of their grandmother. Rachel herself had been angry with her mother and had not troubled to hide her antipathy to Maurice whom she had met only for a moment.

'He's after your money,' she said to Kitty.

'Don't be ridiculous.'

'How do you know?'

'He's had a medical practice in New York since he qualified and has no family, he must have plenty of his own.'

'He's looking for a housekeeper.'

'He's managed without one until now.'

'What does he want then?'

'Perhaps he loves me,' Kitty said.

Rachel considered the proposition. It was as hard to consider one's parents in the light of physical desirability as it was to imagine oneself growing old.

'You don't love him.'

Kitty said nothing.

'Do you?'

'I don't know,' Kitty said. 'I'm extremely fond of him.' She thought of Maurice and his letters which had challenged so many of her previously held convictions. 'He has opened up new worlds.'

'If he loves you so much why doesn't he come over here?' Rachel said. 'He strikes me as extremely egotistic!'

'There has to be a break,' Kitty said. 'I'm contemplating a new life not simply a continuation of the old.'

'I suppose he doesn't realise that you may be needed here. That you have three new grandchildren on the way. That Carol's expecting you to look after Debbie and Lisa and Mathew, that Sarah relies on you. He's encouraging you to be selfish.'

'To live my own life.'

'For his ends. You'll be absolutely miserable all on your own in New York.'

'Have I been so happy here without your father?'

'We've all done our best . . .'

'I'm not complaining.'

'I'm only thinking of your own good.'

A phrase from the past came into Kitty's head: 'Paternalism is the worst form of tyranny.' Rachel had used it to her father on more than one occasion.

'I appreciate your concern,' she said.

There had been no moving her. Rachel, unaware of the trepidation with which Kitty regarded the whole affair, had been amazed at both her mother's apparent firmness of purpose and her own reaction to Kitty's decision, from the consequences of which she felt she must protect her. Maurice Morgenthau, from what Kitty had told her, seemed a poor candidate, as far as his religious affiliations were concerned, for her late father's shoes. If his anchoretic state were to be believed there would be no loving family to replace Kitty's own waiting for her in New York. Rachel did not acknowledge that the rationalisations with which she so vehemently opposed Kitty's plans might be camouflaging her own unconscious wish that, when the child she carried was born, she wanted her mother to be there.

The fact that both her sister Carol and her sister-in-law Sarah were also pregnant, and that their children were all expected within a short time of each other, did not impress her. Rachel's world, to her astonishment, had become circumscribed by the unique fruit of her own womb. The embryo, inconsiderately, had materialised four months before their wedding, when she and Patrick had been planning their trip round the world. There was never any question of which should be sacrificed. Deprived of her preoccupations with the travelling plans – they were to have gone overland to India and thence to Australia (where Patrick had a cousin), Africa and Brazil – Rachel's horizons had become bounded by her own physiology, which was playing such extraordinary and wondrous tricks, and that of her baby.

There was no book on ante- or post-natal care she had not read, no theory she had not examined on the emotional, marital, sexual and social aspects of pregnancy. In the interests of her child's future health and the ideal structure of his bone formation – which would determine his physical beauty – she regulated her diet (eschewing everything but wholefoods and healthfoods) and resorted, only when necessary, to homoeopathic medicines. Her anthropological research had revealed that the majority of peoples gave birth in some kind of upright position, most commonly kneeling, squatting or sitting, and were encouraged to move around during labour. There was to be no private consultant, such as Morris Goldapple who had delivered Carol's three children (flat on her back in the 'stranded beetle' position) orchestrating *her* confinement and intervening medically for his own convenience; no home delivery, such as Sarah had opted for, traditional in her family which considered hospital a good place to be only if you were ill. After exhaustive investigation Rachel had discovered a relaxed and compassionate maternity unit which encouraged active birth together with the use of endorphins – the body's own mechanism for pain relief – had no set rules for conduct during labour and considered every baby a special case. She had elected to give birth vertically with her arms round Patrick's neck.

Looking round the waiting room with its plastic cyclamens in hanging baskets, its notices: 'Step by Step to Bathtime' and 'Please make sure your children are not left unattended at any time during your visit'; its free handouts concerning milk and vitamins and the activities of the Laleche League; the attendant fathers deep in old copies of *Mothercraft*, she was amazed that what seemed no time at all ago her only concern had been the concept of a God – which Protagoras ignored, Socrates revealed and Plato placed in the realm of ideas – and whether she would pass her philosophy exams, and now she was lining up for the eternity stakes. With an empathic exchange of smiles with the other prospective mothers, rendered bovine by their fecundity, she made her way to the cubicle with which over the weeks she had become familiar, where the Midwifery Sister was waiting with her blood-pressure machine.

'Mrs Klopman.' The girl smiled.

Rachel climbed up on to the bed.

'Ms.'

Chapter Four

Kitty had an urgent need to empty her bladder and could not find a lavatory. It was a recurring dream. She was in a crowded theatre with Sydney and at the interval hurried away promising to be back before the bell. She climbed the stairs – red carpeted with brass rods – to where she thought she had seen a door marked 'Ladies', which turned out to be a private box occupied by several security officers waiting to check her baggage who looked at her in amazement and directed her to the street. She left the theatre and ran along the pavements, pushing aside the crowds in her urgency. There was so little time and Sydney would be waiting, worried. Down Regent Street and along Oxford Street as far as Marble Arch. A woman with a slippery green Marks & Spencer carrier told her helpfully that there was what she called a 'convenience' in the Edgware Road. At Marble Arch there was a demonstration, a marching column carrying banners which Kitty could not read. She met it head on and, fists flying, fought her way through its ranks, heavy army greatcoats getting into her mouth and threatening to smother her. She managed to extricate herself but lost her handbag with her passport in it and her front door keys. There was no ladies' lavatory that she could see. The butcher, whom she sometimes frequented, was in his shop serving a queue of women. Kitty waited patiently while he instructed a housewife in front of her in the art of ox-tail stew but he kept putting rabbits in the pot and Kitty wanted to tell him that they neither chewed the cud nor had cloven hooves and that she would report him for selling meat that was not kosher, but no words came. Suddenly she was on a ledge with the pigeons, high up on a skyscraper, and had to work her way gingerly along the parapet to reach her destination. Down below the street undulated. She climbed in to the building through a tall window and to her relief found a queue of women standing docilely in line. She tried to explain to them that Sydney was expecting her back – he always got so agitated when she was away for any length of time – but they just smiled and she had to wait her turn for the one cubicle guarded by an overalled attendant, who looked suspiciously like her sister-in-law, Beatty, holding a filthy piece of towel. The queue moved slowly, seeming to take days. After each customer the attendant cleaned the toilet bowl in slow motion with polishes and sprays, although by the time it was Kitty's turn the pan was overflowing with detritus and the floor flooded, and there was no way that she could relieve herself.

She awoke to find herself in bed but she did not know where. She got up hoping to find a bathroom and recalled suddenly where she was. New York. She made for the open door through which she could see the pine-panelled bath. First things first.

Back in her bedroom, her room, she remembered there was only one, she looked at her watch. Two a.m. which was really seven, her normal breakfast time. No wonder she was hungry. She opened the blinds. Outside it was dark, the lights in the tall buildings like so many illuminated postage stamps. Maurice would still be sleeping. In the cupboard at the kitchenette end of the studio she found instant coffee, a packet of Hi-Ho crackers, some Land O Lakes Sweet Cream Lightly Salted Butter and a jar of Smuckers grape preserve. She opened the cooker out of curiosity. The rotisserie and baking tray were wrapped in transparent bubble pack and had never been used.

She was shivering in her nightdress and examined the heater on which she could see no means of adjustment, although Sydney, she was sure, would not have been so foolish and would have known immediately how it worked. She was about to give up when her fingers encountered a panel within which there was a battery of buttons marked 'hi', 'lo', 'duct', 'fan', 'vent', 'air', 'warm', 'cold', 'boost', 'on', 'off', 'exhaust', 'comfort range'. She had always seized up in the face of anything mechanical which offered more than two options so she slid the panel shut again and wrapped herself in her dressing gown.

She managed to make some coffee but there was no milk in the fridge. A packet of 'non-dairy creamer' contained a white powder which she swirled into her cup. She thought about leaving a note for the milkman and then perhaps not, she couldn't imagine him climbing fifteen floors and then having to go back for a raspberry yoghurt. She felt strangely detached, alone in her head, and imagined it was the effects of the time change.

She began unenthusiastically to unpack her cases but the clothes seemed to belong to somebody else and were unfamiliar. It was too much of an effort. She took the blue imitation leather writing case which her granddaughters, Debbie and Lisa, had given her as a going away present and climbed back into bed.

'Dear Rachel. . . .'

Although she got on well with Josh, who was so like his father, and Carol, in whom she so often saw with uncomfortable clarity herself, it was Rachel, headstrong as she was, with whom she had the most rapport.

'I am writing this at seven o'clock our time, although of course here it is only two in the morning. The flight was uneventful, and I was so excited I quite forgot to be afraid. I sat next to a nice young man who was travelling to Poughkeepsie (he collected the plastic cutlery for his camping holidays). He asked me why I was going to New York and it was difficult to know what to tell him. It sounded ridiculous for someone of my age to say I had a boy-friend (gentleman-friend?) so I pretended it was a business trip and he said what business and I muttered something about fashion and started to get myself all tied up.

'Why *am* I here? I ask it now of myself. A bit late perhaps, I hear you say, but I followed my instincts which have always stood me in good stead. You probably won't understand, I remember thinking *my* mother immune from the heart-searchings which plague young people, but since your father died I have felt like a lost lamb (sheep!). I know you thought I was all right because I had a cheerful face and managed to carry on doing all the things that I had done when he was alive. The difference was that when we were together the activities had some meaning, but for the last two years I have done everything mechanically, as if I was a robot which had been programmed, and I was afraid to stop being busy because then I might have to face myself and the empty landscape of the future. I had several roles – mother, grandmother, friend, neighbour, committee woman – and I tried to play them, changing one hat quickly for another to avoid the confrontation with what lay underneath the activity. I know that I appeared to be functioning properly but in actual fact I was outside myself, watching myself live.

'It's funny how I can say all this to you on paper and not face to face? In this strange room, in the limbo of the day/night, I feel that of the three of you I want you, Rachel, to understand. I am not being disloyal to your father. No one can ever take Sydney's place and you know it. We were childhood sweethearts and grew up together and had a very special relationship. I know that you saw your father as rather stern and authoritarian at times but believe me, Rachel, he only had your interests at heart and wanted nothing more than for you all to be happy and good and caring human beings. He *was* uncompromising but he applied the same strict standards to himself that he expected of you so I don't think you really had anything to complain about. There will never be anyone to take his place. This does not mean that I must live for the rest of the life God grants me by myself. I know I wasn't alone, with you and Josh and Carol, and Addie, and Beatty and Mirrie and everyone else around but *inside* I was alone. It wasn't until I met Maurice in Israel that I felt for the first time that someone was relating to me as me, Kitty Shelton, not wearing any of my hats.

'You can't see why I have to stay for six months? About the babies. Of course I want to look after Debbie and Lisa and Matthew while Carol is in the Clinic. Of course I want to be there when Sarah gives birth to Josh's first child. Above all I want to be with you, my baby, when you have yours. But if I'd stayed, Rachel, or came back without giving New York and Maurice a chance, I would be sucked in again to my life on the periphery of things, chopped in little pieces, at everyone's beck and call, to be returned – when you'd all finished with me – to the emptiness of my own flat with only my memories and the television for company. I have to give this a try. Do you think I like it, so far away from you all?

'About Maurice, I realise that he seems an old man to you (I'm not so young myself), but there is something between us, both in the flesh and on paper, which we both immediately recognised as important. It's almost as if I'd known him all my life. If I hadn't felt that there was something strong here, something compelling, something worth pursuing, would I have come all this way? I'm not crazy. Although just now instead of sitting here in this strange room with none of my familiar things around me and the air-conditioning driving me mad, I long to be back in my own bed, my own room where I put out my hand and know just where everything is. I'm not pretending New York will not be an effort – God knows I'm no Columbus – but what sort of a life is it to sit around waiting for the next instalment of "Dallas" or a visit from the grandchildren like the other bridge widows? I am going to live again. Or try. Of course I love you all. I think I love Maurice. Don't laugh, Rachel, the emotions don't age. . . .'

When Kitty awoke for the second time, although the sun was streaming into the room through the window on to the writing-pad which had fallen to the floor, the room was icy. She looked at her watch, struggling to gather her mental and physical whereabouts. It was morning, New York time, and she had been writing to Rachel, and judging from the number of pages which had spilled out across the floor, at unaccustomed length. She had never been much of a letter writer, communicating regularly only with a distant cousin in Greenock – who was now in an old people's home – and was surprised at her nocturnal loquacity. It was Sydney who had done most of the writing, when writing there was to do, most of the talking really, while she got on with raising the family and her voluntary work. Collecting up the close-written pages she wondered if Rachel had perhaps been right, that with Sydney to think for her she hadn't bothered to think – throughout her married life she had scarcely dared an opinion, believing with Sydney in a united front as far as the children were concerned – and that there were unplumbed depths in herself.

All that was past now anyway. Sydney, with his uncompromising views, was gone, and of his children only Carol in Godalming ran her household in accordance with tradition. As far as her own life was concerned Kitty carried on as she had been used to but there had been erosions, which Sydney would not have tolerated, in her performance of the precepts which seemed somehow to be lacking in significance now that he was no longer around. Maurice of course, although the son of a Frankfurt rabbi who had perished along with every other member of his family as a result of Hitler's 'Final Solution', was an atheist. This would have bothered Sydney more, she felt, than the fact that she might be in love with him.

The emotions do not age. She had written it in her letter to Rachel, and it was true. When she considered Maurice there was a quickening of the pulse and a sensation of joy indistinguishable from that which she had felt as a young girl for Sydney. There had been no other men. How anachronistic it seemed now when to be on one's first husband after more than a few years seemed rather quaint and lacking in initiative. She shuddered sometimes when she thought of the offspring of the next generation, a rag-bag of odds and ends with an assortment of parents or petrie dishes from whom they were supposed to derive some vestige of stability. She felt profoundly sorry for all the little AID and IVF mites who would be running around, and although she sympathised with the women unable to have children – she'd had to listen to her sister-in-law Frieda on that subject all her married life – she didn't hold with tampering with the innermost mysteries of nature even if it were for the benefits of technological progress. What about the violation of children's rights, orphaning them by using frozen sperm and eggs, deceiving them about their paternity?

In the Jewish scale of values every innocent human life was of infinite worth, one human being was worth no more or less than a million others, and there was no justification for their sacrifice, *in vitro* or out of it, on the altar of science. She was glad that she'd had her family, her children, before the ingenuity of the scientists had presented so many options. According to Rachel the sum of scientific knowledge was doubled every eight years and man acquired as much new knowledge in this time as he had accumulated over all the millenia of human inquiry and discovery in the past. She'd soon forget all that when she had a child of her own to look after although Rachel was convinced that other than feeding it now and again she would be free to pursue her other interests, just as she had always done.

Kitty hadn't disillusioned her about motherhood; the broken nights – when one must always be listening for the child's call, the child's cry – the practical demands (their inescapable dailyness and unavoidableness) and the necessity of meeting them; the sapping of the energies, the whittling away of the resources until one's entire world became invaded, bounded, by a tiny defenceless, facsimile human bundle. She would have liked to make her youngest daughter a present of more than half a century of experience, to pass on to her the knowledge that having children altered the whole texture of reality, changed the shape of the world, but Rachel had to find out for herself, that much Kitty had learned.

She put the letter on the table to finish later and wondered whether she should put on clothes appropriate to the external heat or the internal chill to face her first New York day. She showered (once she had worked out the complicated vagaries of the unfamiliar plumbing) and dressed, not crediting the sun, in a warm skirt and sweater, and although she should have gone at once to tell Maurice she was awake, unpacked her cases and arranged everything, with the precision she had learned from Sydney, in the walk-in closet which was large enough to accommodate the wardrobe of a film star. She hadn't brought too much luggage, hedging her bets she supposed, the size of her suitcases demonstrating her doubt about the new life she was contemplating.

She buttoned the blouses and shook the skirts on their hangers to remove the creases, aware that she was procrastinating. It was no longer any good wondering if she should have come, wishing she were in the familiar comfort of her home with Addie Jacobs in the flat across the way. She was here and she was hungry. She picked up her handbag, unlocked the double locks of her front door and crossed the Rubicon of the hall.

The emotions do not age. She might have been a girl at the door of her lover. Her mouth was dry. She read the white slip on the door: 'M. Morgenthau', Morning Dew. She adjusted the waistband of her skirt – her body was still swollen after the flight – and pressed the bell. When there was no reply she relaxed her prepared smile. Had Maurice gone out, abandoned her? Was she perhaps still dreaming? She raised a hand to ring again. The door opened.

A cadaverous man wearing a tee-shirt, slacks and a sun visor opened the door.

Kitty stared at him.

'Mo,' he said over his shoulder, 'she woke up!'

Chapter Five

She didn't know what she had been expecting, certainly not the three strange pairs of eyes that appraised her from Maurice's sitting-room. There was the tall thin stranger who had opened the door, stooped and sinewy. What remained of his hair was grey, as was his moustache, and a bald brown dome like the top of an egg showed above the sun visor. A stout man, almost as wide as he was tall, his paunch straining at a yellow shirt and spilling over a pair of violet trousers, sat in an armchair next to Maurice's easel, clutching a carrier bag. A third visitor, in a red track-suit, dark and unshaven, held a pile of newspapers. They were all staring at her as if she were a thing from another world.

Maurice came from the kitchen holding a coffee pot.

'We play poker Tuesdays and Thursdays,' he said apologetically to Kitty, his glance taking in his three companions. 'They couldn't wait.'

'Six months he's been talking about you,' the fat one said. 'Kitty this, Kitty that. We helped him fix the place up.'

'Herb Bograd, Mort Zuckerman, Ed Benedetti,' Maurice said, starting with the fat man. 'Herb had a column in the newspaper *Gourmet Cuisine in 15 Minutes*.

'No one cooks any more,' Herb said. 'In New York people don't have time to open a can.'

'You should try his stuffed mussels . . .' The man in the track-suit began when he was stopped by a look from Maurice who went on with the introductions. 'Mort Zuckerman. Neurosurgeon. Retired. We're all retired. This is Ed Benedetti, one time Professor of Literature . . .'

'We met,' Ed said.

'. . . at Yale. Now runs an Adult Education Class at NYU.'

'Hi, Kitty,' they chorused, as if schooled by Maurice.

'Did you sleep?' Maurice said.

'Until two, your time, then I wrote to Rachel.'

'How's she doing?' Mort said. 'Did Patrick get the psychiatric internship?'

Kitty stared at him.

'They know all about you,' Maurice said apologetically.

'He's been a different man,' Ed said. 'You could never get a word out of him.'

'Let it all hang out on that easel,' Mort said.

'"The dark night of the soul".' Ed nodded towards the half finished canvas depicting an old people's transport – the ill, the crippled, the dying – on its way to Theresiendstadt, in mud brown and in grey.

'He never speaks about it,' Mort said.

Kitty looked round the room. 'I have many acquaintances but few friends,' Maurice had written in one of his letters. This bizarre poker-game, this ill-matched crew must, she thought, sensing the intimacy which filled the room, furnishing it with camaraderie, have been the few.

'I'm fixing coffee,' Maurice said. 'We waited.'

Herb opened his carrier bag. 'I bought the *croosants*, and some back rashers. I thought you might be . . .'

'She'll eat *eggs*,' Mort said pointedly. 'Did you bring eggs?'

'Eggs I've got,' Maurice said. 'How do you like them?'

Kitty realised that it was lunchtime as far as her stomach was concerned, and despite the crackers and the grape jelly of the small hours she was starving. They piled into Maurice's kitchen where they seated her at the head of the table. Herb got busy with the frying pan at the hob.

'Straight up or over-light?'

Kitty realised that he meant the eggs and wondered what fat he was frying them in. 'I'm not fussy.' She decided not to make too many enquiries. Mort poured coffee into her mug.

'I'm a widower,' he said to make her feel at home. He took out a photograph which from the look of it seemed to live in his pocket. A woman with bleached hair and blue eyes, with a crack across her cheek from the crumpled paper, smiled at her. 'Bright's disease. Six years ago.'

'Martha took off when the kids left home,' Ed said morosely. 'With the philosophy professor. My best friend as a matter of fact. I didn't remarry.'

Herb said nothing. Later Kitty heard from Maurice that he had lived for years with the drama critic of his newspaper who had taken his own life in a fit of depression.

'Anyone hear the news?' Mort asked.

'Pictures of Sidon,' Herb said. 'Lebanese women waiting in line for water, wandering around the rubble of their houses. Reminded me of Europe during the war.'

Kitty couldn't imagine the rotund Herb as a soldier.

'I was a cook,' he said as if he had read her thoughts.

'Your Begin thinks it's still 1940,' Ed addressed Mort, 'running after ghosts. He thinks he's the new Jesus Christ or something. You'd think that every bomb they drop on Beirut lands on the head of some terrorist.'

'The arms dumps *are* in the camps,' Mort said.

'That gives us the right to kill civilians because they weren't smart enough to get out? Where did we get to be so cynical? You know who's a terrorist? Menachem Begin's a terrorist. A terrorist with the world's best armed forces at his disposal, for his own use. Because 1,500,000 children were murdered by the Nazis, does that give him the right to bomb Beirut? You know what he's doing? He's not only sacrificing Israeli lives in a war that doesn't officially exist, occupying West Beirut in an invasion that doesn't exist, more important he's killing the moral integrity of a wonderful people. Who's going to feel sorry for a victim who creates his own victims? Ask Mo if he wants to bomb Beirut.'

'What do you do with somebody who won't negotiate?' Mort said. '"No peace with Israel, no recognition of Israel, no negotiation with Israel".'

'Women and children you don't bomb . . .'

'You got war, you got suffering,' Mort said, 'And we don't get any favours for TV. You'd think the Israelis were a gang of thugs.'

'They made up the pictures?' Ed asked.

'OK. Let me ask you something. Where were the cameras for the last seven years when the PLO were terrorising the Lebanese Christian community? Where were the camera in Afghanistan, the Falklands, Iran and Iraq . . . ?'

'Do me a favour!' Herb said. And to Maurice. 'You want to give me the plates?'

'Why did Israel enter Lebanon in the first place? I'll tell you. Number one to get the PLO out of the second country they'd nearly destroyed. Number two to ensure adequate security for the northern settlements of Israel . . .'

'The principle of militiary necessity does not excuse the massive destruction of buildings,' Herb took the plates from Maurice. Mort shook his finger. 'Over 10,000 commando raids have been carried out against Israelis, not to mention the murders in London, Paris, Athens, Madrid, Washington. The hijackings, bombings, kidnappings by the Baader-Meinhof, the Red Army Faction, the Japanese Red Army, all trained and financed by the PLO . . .'

Herb snorted. 'The eggs are up.'

'. . . when the assassination attempt was made this year on Shlomo Argov, outside the Dorchester Hotel in London, the Israeli Airforce – not unreasonably – attacked two known terrorist bases in Beirut without a single civilian casualty. The PLO began a twenty-four-hour attack on Kiryat Shemona and Nahariya, *civilian targets*; they set the whole of Northern Galilee alight. Only then was 'Operation Peace for Galilee' launched.'

'It's enough already,' Maurice said, opening his freezer which to Kitty's surprise seemed to contain nothing but loaves of bread. 'We've got company.'

'Maybe I don't want to eat breakfast with an antisemite,' Mort said, spreading jelly on his toast with the same knife he had used for his eggs.

Herb pointed his spatula. 'Because I don't endorse every move Israel makes, that makes me an enemy?'

Maurice put four slices of bread into the toaster. 'Don't listen.'

'It's the same at home,' Kitty said. 'Rachel and Josh aren't speaking.'

She ate her eggs and the wheat toast Maurice piled on to her plate, marvelling at her appetite, and listened to the conversation, like a shuttlecock, going back and forth across the table as it had in London and was surely doing in Melbourne and Johannesburg, in Montreal and Brussels. 'Don't you agree, Kitty,' Herb said, topping up her coffee, 'that until Israel recognises the legitimate right of the Palestinians, including the right of self-determination, there *can* be no lasting peace?'

They were asking her opinion, waiting for her reply concerning the Palestinians. They were all waiting. Mort, as if she were a politician about to issue some important statement, Ed with his fork in mid-air, Maurice with an expression of what she strongly suspected was adoration. Busy, first with Rachel's wedding and later with her plans to come to New York, Kitty had not really had time to analyse her own reactions to the conflict in the Middle East. Whatever the rights and wrongs of the situation she had a sneaking suspicion that the Jews, who had a long history of being persecuted, should somehow behave better than others. In any case she did not feel that the Palestinian question was ever going to be resolved by killing Palestinians. War, as far as Kitty was concerned, was defined in derelict homes and orphaned children rather than in terms of right or wrong.

'Let the Arab leaders recognise the rights of the Palestinians,' Mort said, without waiting for Kitty to answer. 'Jordan is also Palestine, even though, like Israel, it happens to be called by another name. What I'd like to know is how the 600,000 Arabs who ran away in 1948 became *4 million* "Palestinian" refugees. I'll tell you. They're migrants, needy souls of other nationalities, who've gone to the camps for shelter and have become human weapons in a holy war that will never end. And you know why? Because ever since 1948 the "refugees" and their descendants have been used for political purposes – the Lebanese government actually forbids the rebuilding of Palestinian houses anywhere in the country – they force them to be refugees, to live in camps, because they want to keep their hatred directed against Israel!'

Kitty had to pinch herself. Yesterday she had been Carol's mother, handing over the flat to her eldest daughter and the children, concerned with finding sufficient sheets and clearing away her more precious knick-knacks from the path of Mathew, who at three was into everything, and not twenty-four hours later here she was on the other side of the Atlantic sitting in Maurice's kitchen with a group of men, discussing the political situation.

Ed got up from the table and took his dishes to the sink. 'Why don't we take Mort to the park and try to knock some sense into him?' he said to Herb.

'It's too hot.' Herb was on his fifth piece of toast. Kitty looked up in time to see Ed giving him a conspiratorial wink. Herb wiped his mouth with the back of his hand and shot up like a little rubber bullet. 'Oh, sure, sure. You coming Mort?'

'There's enough hot air in here.' He looked from Maurice to Kitty. 'OK. I just remembered. I have to go to the library.' They clustered by the door. Like a comedy act, Kitty thought, Ed so tall, Herb so short, Mort in his scarlet track-suit. Herb produced a gift-wrapped parcel from his carrier-bag, holding it out to Kitty. 'We want you to have this.'

'A small token,' Mort said.

Ed smiled shyly: 'From the Friday Afternoon Club.'

Before Kitty could thank them they were gone, leaving her alone with Maurice. Remembering that the poker game was Tuesdays and Thursdays she said: 'Why the Friday afternoon club?'

Maurice looked uncomfortable. 'If you assume you're going to live to be seventy, seven decades, and think of each decade as a day of the week starting with Sunday, then the four of us are on Friday afternoon. Aren't you going to open it?'

It was a book, the collected stories of Bernard Malamud. At home people gave her flowers and bath salts and chocolates. There was an inscription on the fly-leaf. 'Enjoy the Big Apple', signed 'Ed Benedetti, Herb Bograd and Mort Zuckerman'. Kitty was overwhelmed by the welcoming gesture of Maurice's friends, her transmogrification. To her horror she felt her eyes fill with tears.

Maurice led her to the sofa from where she could see the wretchedness of his easel. He put a hand on hers. 'It's going to be all right, Kitty. We'll take it one step at a time.'

Chapter Six

'Mrs Klopman,' the houseman said, looking at Rachel's notes.

'Ms,' Rachel said.

As usual the reiteration of her married name made her feel vulnerable, as if she were personally inviting upon her head the heaped blows of two thousand years of persecution.

The houseman, according to the badge on his white coat, one Dr Goldberg, looked up from his notes and, unbeknownst to the Midwifery Sister whose skin had the hue and patina of milk chocolate and whose name was Patel, recognised Rachel whom he had never met. The unspoken acknowledgement of their shared background, their common fate, disturbed Rachel as much as did the thoughts which made their way unbidden into her mind following the pronouncement of her name. She was not like her father-in-law, Patrick's father, whose entire horizon was bounded by things Jewish and by Jews. In the mornings, no matter what was taking place elsewhere in the world, he searched his broadsheet for news of Israel or domestic items involving Jews. In the evenings, on his TV screen, he picked out Jewish actors, comedians, politicians, analysing the proportions in their veins of Jewish blood. Applying the same standards he scanned the book reviews (Jewish authors), public opinion polls (the Jewish vote), the Honours Lists (Jewish accolades), and the obituary columns (Jewish deaths). Notwithstanding this obsession he was not, Rachel observed, a practising and observant Jew as her father had been but was possessed of what he himself called a 'Jewish heart', assessing others according to whether or not they supported Jewish charities and unable to decide whether or not he liked them until he had ascertained their views on Israel.

Patrick considered that his father's parochial attitudes, searching for Jewish involvement in the least likely places, had been a contributary factor to his own rejection of Judaism. Neither he nor Rachel, despite their upbringing, lived a Jewish life. When they crossed the threshold of the Klopman house in Winnington Road it was as if they entered a country for which there was no longer a visa in their passports, as if they trod upon alien soil. Since his childhood, according to Patrick, his mother had been an embarrassment to him, stifling his identity both as an individual and as a Jew. From his first days at prep school there had been notes excusing him from swimming or gymnastics every time he sneezed, setting him apart. Later on she had always been coming to see the headmaster on one pretext or another concerning Patrick's prowess. She had worried when he had put his name down for a university (notwithstanding the fact that it was Cambridge) which would take him away from London and her jurisdiction, and when, before going up to it he had set out overland to Turkey, she had slipped a cheesecake into his rucksack.

On the face of things he had long ago disentangled himself from the stranglehold of his mother's affections but her solicitude had left its mark. If Patrick did not eat (although now it was spare-ribs rather than salt-beef) at regular intervals he became anxious and ill-tempered. If he shivered he believed he was coming down with 'flu. He worried about Rachel if she was late home, and fussed over the child she was carrying. It was hardly surprising, Rachel said, considering the neuroses which were the birthright with which his mother had endowed him, that he had opted, as his medical specialty, for psychiatry.

Rachel associated herself neither with Herbert, with his Jewish jokes and 'spot the Jew' fixation, nor with Hettie and her obsession with the nutritional well-being of her family, more appropriate to the days when starvation was a constant threat. Whence then stemmed her unmistakable feeling of rapport with the white-coated Dr Goldberg whom she had not set eyes upon until this moment? She was not religious, had cast off as anachronistic and burdensome the shackles of orthodoxy imposed upon her by her late father, and on her visits to Israel she had felt herself to be a stranger – more at home in

France or Italy – and had certainly not experienced the sensation, claimed by others, that she had come home.

While she lay, white-shrouded on the bed, watched by the pool dark eyes of Sister Patel who with her kind were shamelessly exploited to shore up the crumbling infrastructure of Britain, as her own antecedents had that of the garment industry, Dr Goldberg checked on the progress of her pregnancy.

'Everything seems to be fine,' he said, as if the embryo carried by Rachel were no different from those of the other women in the antenatal clinic. 'Any problems?'

Rachel smiled. She was not nauseous like her sister Carol, plagued by every minor complication of her condition like her sister-in-law Sarah. She was Ceres, an earth mother, would drop her children like puppies, after which she would proceed on her own two feet, unaided, to the postnatal ward. She took a letter from her handbag and gave it to Dr Goldberg.

'What's this?'

'A list of my wishes for when I go into labour. I don't want there to be any mistakes. I want to remain upright, to be delivered without an episiotomy, to breastfeed on an unrestricted basis and to keep the baby with me at all times.'

'You're a very aggressive young lady.'

'Assertive,' Rachel corrected him. 'I'm not attacking anyone. I'm merely expressing my views. I don't want other people to take decisions for me. To run my life. There's one more thing – I don't want to be electronically monitored.'

Dr Goldberg looked doubtful. 'There could be a slight increase in risk to the baby. . . .'

'What about the risk of allowing technology to replace loving human contact – which will be provided by my labour partner – in the place of birth?'

'Will that be all?'

'For the moment.' Rachel swung her legs over the bed.

'Three weeks then, Ms Klopman,' Dr Goldberg said.

'See you,' Rachel said.

'Not me. I'm off to the Middle East tomorrow.'

'Israel?'

'Lebanon.'

Rachel stood still with her mouth open. Sister Patel wanted to hurry her out of the cubicle, there were other patients waiting.

'They need volunteers,' Dr Goldberg said. 'I feel I have to do something.'

'For the Arabs?'

'I feel no compunction about supporting justice for the Palestinians as much as for the Jews. There is an Israeli people and there is a Palestinian people and we must respect their identity if we want them to respect ours.'

'Dr Goldberg!' Sister Patel said.

'I'm coming.'

'I'm not suggesting one mustn't care about the *Palestinians*', Rachel said, 'most Jews are not insensitive to the feelings of those who have been cruelly misled into believing that they are entitled to still more land. I'm talking about the *PLO*, who have robbed the Lebanese of sovereignty in their own country.'

'And now they're being murdered by the Israelis!'

'Whom they welcomed with open arms after six years of anguish . . .'

'Dr Goldberg, please!'

'The tanks and guns found in Lebanon so far,' Rachel said, trying to look dignified in her white hospital gown, 'are enough to equip an army of a quarter of a million, Dr Goldberg. We are not talking about Israel's prestige in the world – we are talking about her life!'

Disturbed by Dr Goldberg and his views – he was as misguided as Josh – Rachel decided to take the rest of the morning off from her Uncle Juda's art gallery where she was working until her child was born. She would have coffee with Carol whose head was not bothered by political issues and whose horizons were conveniently bounded by her children, extant and expected, and her home.

She found Carol and Sarah at the kitchen table on which there was a ring cake made by Carol, identical to that which her mother had been turning out for as long as Rachel could remember, and a half-finished letter, which Carol had been writing to Kitty in New York.

Chapter Seven

Kitty had never seen so many books. Sydney had had a glass-fronted bookcase in the hall in which he kept his sets of dark blue Festival Prayer books lettered with gold (one for himself and one for Kitty), his Pentateuch with its commentary by a former Chief Rabbi, the three volumes of the Laws and Customs of Israel (everything from Rules of the Morning Prayer to the Laws concerning certain forbidden foods, the customs surrounding birth, and the precepts concerning death), a Maimonides reader which had been his father's, and the dark blue volumes of the Jewish Encyclopaedia.

Maurice's books – which provided him, he said, with the company and spiritual presence of the best and greatest of the human race – climbed from floor to ceiling in both living-room and bedroom and spilled out into bookshelves along the corridor. They were written in Yiddish (Sholem Aleichem and Mendele Mocher Sforim), German (Heine – who with Mozart, according to Maurice, brought man closest to the ultimate mystery of the universe – Goethe, and Schiller, as well as the twenty volumes of *Der Gross Brockhaus*), and English (late Middle Ages, Renaissance and Reformation, and Rashi and the Christian Scholars), and touched upon the fields of literature, religion, sociology, psychology, medicine, history and ethics. Apart from Cora, the twelve stone maid from Atlanta who came once a week to clean (and would not let even a cup of coffee pass her lips before pronouncing grace) and flicked a desultory feather duster over their spines, he did not like anyone to touch them.

He had in his sitting-room a complicated looking music centre with giant speakers which flanked his easel though no television

(Maurice said he was very particular about whom he let into his room) but he bought one with a remote control switch for Kitty so that she could operate it from her bed. He wanted to buy her everything. She had only to ask.

He was, he told her, a rich man. He had worked all his life, had no extravagances other than his library and his music, no one on whom to spend his money when he was alive, no one to leave it to when he was dead. His loneliness – he cared for few people other than Herb and Ed and Mort, had nobody – seemed strange to Kitty who had spent her whole life surrounded by family. Everything seemed strange. It had not been easy. She had been in New York for three weeks and there had been moments when she had taken out the return ticket Josh had insisted that she buy and fingered it longingly; moments in her studio, a world away from Rachel and Josh and Carol, away from her friends and relations, that she had sat down and unashamedly wept. There were times when she thought she must have been out of her mind when she accepted Maurice's invitation, a little deranged by the excitement of the wedding, and others when she imagined that late in life a new Kitty had not only been born but had taken wings.

She was, she knew, Rachel was always telling her so, a creature of habit. At home she was used to having her flat exactly as she wanted it and for her life to proceed, as it had unchanged for many years, according to routine. As far as housekeeping was concerned, before her arrival Maurice had not bothered. On her weekly visits Cora vacuumed as the fancy took her – taking care to keep out of Maurice's way – sprayed silicone polish indiscriminately wherever she saw a surface, took Maurice's personal washing down to the machines in the basement and sent out the laundry. When there was dry cleaning to be done or shoes to be repaired (Kitty was amazed that they came back polished) it was Joe who arranged it, hanging the clothes in Maurice's closet as they were returned. The German restaurant on 86th and 2nd kept a window table for him at lunchtime and he did not need to ask the waitress, who had been serving him for years, for his *sauerbraten* and red cabbage with its tennis ball of potato dumpling. When he did not feel like going out Joe fetched a sandwich – shrimp salad or liverwurst – from the corner deli.

'A strange way to live,' Kitty thought, and tried in as non-intrusive a way as possible, to make a more comfortable domestic life for him, hindered only by the fact that Maurice was as set in his ways as she was in hers.

While Maurice painted, catching the morning light, Joe, whose fund of knowledge was invaluable, took Kitty under his wing. He directed her to the nearest Post Office (Gracie Station) where she seemed to spend much of her time (although Joe would gladly have taken the letters for her), the public library on 79th Street from which she borrowed books and gleaned recipes from *Gourmet* magazine – and the local shops. From the technicolour display in the Paradise Market on 83rd Street (run by Koreans who had, according to Joe, revolutionised the New York fresh fruit and vegetable trade), Kitty – eschewing the unfamiliar rhutabagas and spaghetti squash – selected red onions and Boston curly lettuce and delicious vineripe tomatoes and Simka plums in an effort to supplement Maurice's diet, and thought longingly of her High Street greengrocer's where they picked out the choicest produce as soon as they saw her coming and greeted her by name.

At the kosher butcher's (not so different from the one at home) Lennie and Charlie in their *kappels* were fascinated by her foreign accent and initiated her into 'Hanging Tender' and 'Kolichel', to their frozen 'Franks 'n Blankets', and razor thin slices of 'Beef Fry' about which she did not disillusion Maurice who thought that it was bacon.

She shopped daily at Gristedes on Madison with its 'specials' of Solid White Tuna and Sara Lee Pound Cake, and Bremen House where she bought Maurice his Bergarder Blue and German cheese and Bobka, and weekly in the giant Food Emporium where the aisles were unfamiliar, she didn't know a soul and was jostled right and left by impatient New Yorkers who never seemed to look where they were going. From the cornucopia of goods on offer she loaded her trolley and was amazed to find that unlike in England the goods were not only packed for her but delivered to her door.

At first she ventured no further than a few blocks either way of Maurice's apartment building but she soon grew tired of the windows of Bolton's Designer Clothes at Discount Prices, and Venture Stationers (the manageress of which came from Israel), and Mr Mad Rags, and David's Cookies, and Maury's Children's Shop, and Little Bits (where she kept her eyes open for bargains for her grandchildren) and in a brave moment of decision, remembering her coordinates –

85th and Madison – as Mort had cautioned her, took the bus downtown where she had never seen so many greeting card shops, so many matching sheets and comforters and towels, so many derelicts wandering the streets among the smartly dressed women or so many ordinary people walking along muttering to themselves.

She moved slowly, battling against the heat – which seemed to rise suffocatingly from the pavements and from the subway vents in the road, taking in the snarled up goods vans ('The Messiest Department Store', 'Nice Jewish Boy Moving Company' and 'The Pickle Man – Our Pickles Make You Sexy'), the summer sale bargains displayed on Adèle Rootstein models, the impressive towers of single titles in the thriving markets of the bookshops, the corner newspaper and hot-dog stands, and looked into passing countenances reluctant to believe that amongst them there was not a single one that she recognised. Once she stopped off for a pair of shoes expecting it to be like Golders Green where you sat with your foot raised on a little stool and a nice young man or woman listened sympathetically to your requirements and cared if the model into which they eased your foot was comfortable or not.

In the chrome and glass temple – where it was a relief to be out of the heat – a ferocious looking matron had demanded her size, with an expression that suggested she had a cheek coming into the shop at all, and after about fifteen minutes, during which Kitty stood wondering whether she hadn't perhaps gone for lunch and forgotten to come back, had thrust a box into her hand and disappeared behind a curtain. When she eventually returned and Kitty had pronounced the shoes too tight, the woman had snatched them away, declaring indignantly that 'shoes stretch', and disappeared once more and Kitty, not sure whether she would ever reappear, had left the shop.

Isolated and dissolving in the *fricassée* of the pavements where designer clothes jostled with singlets and sweat bands and lightweight business suits and cripples in wheelchairs and baby strollers and single roses in cellophane and brown grocery bags and tee-shirts – 'Give Blood' and 'Touche Ross & Co' – and boob tubes and melting ice-cream cones, she traipsed the streets and criss-crossed the avenues trying to get her bearings and welcomed the injunctions, as if of all the passing crowd they addressed Kitty Shelton personally, 'Walk' and 'Don't Walk'.

She was glad to get home. Home. It was hard to believe that in three weeks the studio, in which she had at first felt so awkward, was her refuge, the newfound centre of her world. Each time she turned into 85th, past the doctors' plates by which she measured her approach – David Guttman, Mark Pruzansky, S. K. Fineberg, A. H. Weiss – and saw the familiar canopy and Joe with his uniform hat and his welcoming 'Hi, sweets, how are you?', rushing to relieve her of her packages, she breathed a sigh of relief.

In Maurice's kitchen which he had commissioned Herb to furnish with new pots and pans from Zabar's – a ceramic Apple Baker and Electric Wok! – she had applied herself to cooking nutritious meals for Maurice. With the help of Herb and Joe and Cora she acquired a working knowledge of trans-Atlantic ingredients, from scallions to cornstarch, and forgot her homesickness in the creation of familiar dishes which she set on Maurice's table. It was not like cooking for Sydney who had greeted her every effort with paeons of eloquent praise. Maurice, his mind on the morning's gouache in which he had tried to encapsulate cold and terror, or a passage from Schiller which he would translate for Kitty, seemed uninterested in the good things that she prepared and she was glad when Herb or Ed or Mort turned up (unerringly at mealtimes) to sample appreciatively the stuffed cabbage leaves which had been her nephew Norman's favourite, or her sweet and sour fish.

She had at first resented the trio's attachment to Maurice and their presence in his apartment but as she came to know them better she had been glad of the company while Maurice insulated in the cocoon of his past was at his easel, and enjoyed Ed's dissertations upon literature, Mort's wry humour and Herb's interest in cooking which coincided with her own. From him she learned to bake angel cake and brownies and in return initiated him into the minced mysteries of gefüllte fish, which he had never sampled, and her Eve's Pudding which had won Sydney's heart. Maurice himself seemed not to notice the presence of his friends and it was always Kitty who had to indicate that it was time for them to go.

They left goodnaturedly to reappear with magazines or candies, small gifts over which they'd put their heads together to make her feel at home. They were very kind and she grew used to having them round the place, but home, however hard they tried, would never be anywhere in which Josh and Rachel and Carol and her grandchildren were not nearby. They had all written. Rachel, in an avalanche of green ink, demolishing the claims made by Josh that peaceable Arabs had been forced to flee from 'Palestine' where they had lived from 'time immemorial'. Exiled Jews, she told Kitty, had sat by the waters of Babylon and sung 'If I forget thee, O Jerusalem . . .' a thousand years before Mohamet was born. There seemed, she said, to be one rule for refugees from a Jewish State and another rule for refugees from all other kinds of states. A hundred million people had been displaced since the Second World War – Ethiopians, Ugandans, Kurds, Vietnamese, Czechs, Iraqis, Afghans, Indians. . . . Their resettlement and integration by the host countries had been considered by the world to be the normal and humanitarian course of action. The Arab world alone had refused to take in its homeless, wilfully maintaining them in camps and turning over their support to western countries and the United States.

In a postscript she told Kitty that she and Patrick were to be evicted from their council flat and that as far as her pregnancy was concerned she didn't know what Carol and Sarah made such a fuss about, there was nothing to it.

Carol wrote about Debbie and Lisa who were being taken by friends' parents to discover London (the British Museum and Madame Tussaud's) while she nursed her nausea and Mathew, and missed Alec, whom she had left on his own in Godalming; Josh, that Rachel (perhaps affected by her pregnancy), had taken leave of her senses; Sarah that she had completed her course of instruction with Mrs Halberstadt necessary for her conversion to Judaism and that she would shortly be called to defend her beliefs to the Rabbinical Court of the Beth Din; Debbie and Lisa sent postcards ('Mummies' and the 'Chamber of Horrors'), kisses from Mathew at the bottom. All her children conveyed regards to Maurice in which Kitty detected a distinct half-heartedness.

She'd read the letters aloud to him as he stood at his easel, averting her eyes from a barrack row that stretched blackly into infinity, a hanged man. Sometimes, busy with the selection of a brush, with the daubs of paint, like sombre wormcasts, on his palette, she thought he wasn't listening and was surprised when later in the day he'd come out with 'What did Rachel mean by . . . ?' or 'Why don't they try Carol on some . . . ?'

She'd had to get used to Maurice and his strange silences which had at first made her uncomfortable. Sydney had always answered her chatter with comment of his own, although she realised now after only three weeks of living with (well, next-door to) Maurice, that what she had discussed with her late husband were not so much issues but the fine print of other people's lives. She had been unaware of it at the time but now she could see that the problems of Sydney's sisters, Beatty and Freda and Mirrie, together with the nieces and nephews, their own children and grandchildren and the various members of the synagogue congregation had defined the limits of their *têtes-à-têtes*. She had seemed to spend much of the day on the telephone to her family or friends and when Sydney came home from the office she'd paraphrase Beatty's diatribe, or regale him with secondhand stories gleaned from Carol in Godalming of the children's antics, or of Rachel's intransigence. Much of their conversation, she realised, now, had centred upon where they were going, or where they had been, whether she had sewn the button on to Sydney's suit or remembered to phone the plumber. Maurice had little small talk – he had after all had no one to talk to – and seemed not to hear while Kitty rattled on with the news from England, his expression appeared not to change, but he missed nothing. If the everyday gossip to which Kitty was used did not trip lightly from his tongue – there was a place for silence as well as conversation in every relationship, Maurice said – his eyes were eloquent, even at his easel, following her every move.

In the afternoons, when he'd put away his brushes, they'd go out. Maurice showed her New York as if he had laid every stone with his bare hands and looked into her face for approval. She had never walked so far in her entire life nor, despite the heat, enjoyed herself so much. From the Hudson to the East River, from Battery Park to the Bronx, Maurice, his arm through hers, guided her round the Big Apple. Best of all she loved the art galleries where Maurice pointed out the poetic landscapes of van Ruisdael, Turner's attempt to create luminous atmospheres, his concern with the problem of colours and of light, the abstract Expressionism of Pollock, and Fragonard's hymns of inimitable grace to love. In England she had been neither to the Tate Gallery nor the Courtauld Institute. There had never been any time. In the

Frick and the Guggenheim, and the Metropolitan Museum of Art (with its Tiffany windows and Frank Lloyd Wright room), she'd stand before the paintings, not knowing where to look first until Maurice, with his evaluations of the artist's temperament or an assessment of his approach to the work, opened the door with his key. In her newly acquired sneakers (seeing the state of her feet, Maurice had insisted), Kitty covered more ground in three weeks than she had in her entire life, but it was not the miles that she walked but the new world through which Maurice guided her that made her forget for hours at a time not only Josh and Carol and Sarah and the grandchildren but England itself where her bridge game and the Ladies' Guild were beginning to seem increasingly less important.

Of everything she had seen it was, absurdly, the Statue of Liberty, 'lifting her lamp beside the golden door', which had made the most impression. She would not have believed it. Had not believed Rachel who had cried before the Taj Mahal. Who cried at buildings? They had boarded the launch at Battery Pier and headed out towards Liberty Island in a downstream curve that showed Bartholdi's object of adoration, his hymn to freedom, his New World Symphony in imperishable metal – now soft with verdigris – to its best advantage. Kitty had leaned against the rail, close to Maurice in his flat linen cap, seeing in his profile what a fine young man he must once have been. There were no photos, as if he had not had a past. Watching her watching him Maurice put a hand over hers and, with the boat speeding over the slapping wavelets, they were like young lovers and she had to pinch herself in an effort to believe that on a Wednesday afternoon, when at home she would have been on duty in the Day Centre and thinking what to give Norman for dinner, she was actually sightseeing in the company of her admirer, in New York.

She thought she had been prepared (she'd seen enough postcards) for her first close up of the great lady who had welcomed the 'huddled masses' but she was not. (She tried not to dwell upon the fact that the 'open door' had swung so unequivocally shut in the face of her people during their darkest hour when America had decided, suddenly, that it was full up.) The crowned woman in her bronze gown, raising her torch 305 feet (according to Maurice) above sea level, overwhelmed her with her green and towering majesty, seeming to make the deck disappear from beneath her feet. It was only a statue, never mind what they said about lighting the world, but the 90 tons of metal, the 300 copper plates, the 17 foot high head, the 43 foot long arm with its diameter of 12 feet and its 8 foot finger, brought tears to her eyes. It had been a magic afternoon and she hadn't wanted it to end. Didn't want any of it to end. Despite the moments of homesickness she felt an affinity with Maurice which she could not describe, even to herself, and to her own dismay, for long stretches of time, forgot to think about Sydney.

A new and exciting pattern had imprinted itself on her days. After the morning's chores and a stroll in Central Park (Maurice had cautioned her about avoiding isolated areas) – among the sleeping, burlap-covered winos and the dog-walkers and the sweat-soaked joggers – and the afternoon excursions, if Maurice had not booked for a concert (Kitty's life had suddenly become flooded with music without which Maurice said life would be a mistake) she cooked dinner and they spent the evening at home. She still did not know where the hours went with no television to pass the time, no addictive nine o'clock news. They sat on Maurice's sofa and listened to the Tchaikovsky violin concerto – which made her think of home and the children – or the Haffner symphony, or read (Kitty had finished the Malamud stories and had started on Bellow) or discussed an exhibition they had seen or Kitty's children or the Israeli Government's rift with the Reagan administration over the Lebanon, until Kitty's eyes began closing and to her astonishment she would find that it was almost midnight.

Maurice never went to bed until the small hours, he had difficulty in sleeping he said, but he'd escort Kitty to the door of her apartment with an old world courtesy which touched her, and every night, as he left her at her door, he'd hold her close and tell her how happy he was that she'd come to New York and with what anticipation he looked forward to the next day, she'd so transformed his life. That this was true she learned from Mort who said he'd never heard Maurice laugh before and Kitty herself had noticed that he was looking happier than when they had first met in Eilat. Alone in her studio she was aware of an unaccustomed lightness in her own heart, long forgotten sensations, stirrings within herself which seemed quite at odds with the face she saw in the mirror.

Chapter Eight

Kitty's letter was addressed to Sarah and Josh but it was Sarah who opened it. She missed her mother-in-law. As the only child of a Foreign Office wife whose very definite priorities ranged, in precise order, from her dogs and her gardens to her horses and her offspring, she had found in Kitty a warmth and affection, an *élan vital*, which had immediately entranced her. Before she met Josh she had known few Jews (they were conspicuous by their absence in her father's diplomatic circle) and had distinguished them only by the negative stereotype she had been raised to identify, with its long nose and swarthy appearance. It was not until she had gone with Josh to a concert given by an Israeli orchestra, when she had searched the platform in vain for features that confirmed her mental picture of the 'Jewish face', that she began to question her preconceived notions and wonder whether from a roomful of Italians, of Spaniards, of Asians, of Slavs, she would with any degree of accuracy have been able to nominate the Jews.

When she and Josh had decided to marry, the announcement was received with a decided lack of enthusiasm by both families. Sarah's mother in Leicester, in so far as she was capable of betraying any emotion, had been horrified. She made no secret of the fact – even before she met Josh – that she thought Sarah was throwing away herself and a first-class classics degree on a second-class citizen, an *arriviste* Jewish dentist who would drag her down to an unacceptable level.

Mrs MacNaughton was awkward with Josh on the rare occasions they met, as if he were suffering from some physical disability, and was not in the least pleased that she was to have a Jewish grandchild.

In Josh's family, with Kitty at its pivot round which echelons of aunts and uncles and cousins and nieces and nephews revolved, Sarah found the sense of kinship with others she had missed out on in her peripatetic childhood. She was intrigued by the notion that the birth of a Jewish child was a major event not only for those immediately concerned but for the whole community; that the circumcision of a boy was not merely the antiseptic surgical procedure she had imagined, but a celebration of the entrance of another Jew into the covenant with God; that when the committed Jew travelled anywhere in the world he would find brothers and sisters who would take him in, feed him, show him love; that when the Jew died he was not alone (annual candles of remembrance would be lighted for him) and those who mourned him would be visited and comforted. She countered Josh's argument, that universal brotherhood could only be achieved by assimilation into the majority cultures, with the assertion that any universalism that demanded that smaller groups abandon their identities was totalitarianism rather than brotherhood, and that all people should share their moral values while retaining their ethnic diversity. The fact that Josh was not enamoured of his birthright, that he found his family at times – to say the least of it – an embarrassment, surprised her.

Josh's revolution, unlike Rachel's, had been bloodless. He had not wilfully opposed the orthodoxy in which he had been reared, as Rachel had, but had quietly rejected it – Sarah said he was turning his back on his father – walked away without troubling to glance over his shoulder. Since his broken engagement to the spoiled Paula he had not gone out with Jewish girls. He found them immature and demanding and felt threatened by their families, recognising in them claustrophobic echoes of his own. He was a shy and private man who, measured against his parents' expectation of him, their ever ready judgements, had been found wanting. Sarah compensated for his inadequacies. In her easy going presence Josh found balm for his damaged ego, and his hitherto hidden qualities flourished. Because Sarah expected nothing he was able to give her everything and he amazed them both with the extent of the gift. As far as Josh was concerned, Sarah was the best thing which had happened to him in his entire life. As he unravelled her mysteries more were revealed, perhaps the least explicable of which was his wife's decision to become Jewish. She was certainly not doing it for him. He was discomforted by his faith – to which he had only ever paid lip service – felt it was like a millstone round his neck, and was not the least concerned that, without a Jewish mother, his children would not be Jewish.

At first, as Sarah was able to see now, her actions had been prompted by a desire to belong, a yearning for roots and a place in which to put them down. She did not like it when Josh's aunts and uncles stopped talking when she came into the room, and wanted to be one of them. Amused by her decision, Josh had indulged his wife by going with her to synagogue and fulfilling the obligations of the head of a Jewish household – as he was obliged to do – as she followed her course of instruction. He had thought that Sarah would soon tire of what he held to be the irksome minutiae with which the faith was hedged about, and waited tolerantly for her to discover the whole ethos antiquated and time expired as he himself had done. Had her mentors been other than Rabbi Magnus and Mrs Halberstadt this might well have happened. From the moment, however, that Rabbi Magnus had explained to Sarah that what rendered Abraham (a Mesopotamian) Jewish were his beliefs and not his blood, and that the Jews – unlike any other group in the modern world – were not a race (by any accepted definition of either Jew or race) but a nation, composed of members of every race, defined by its religion, Sarah realised that she had found not only a competent instructor but her intellectual match and knew that there would be no going back.

It was as if she had struck oil, drilled an untapped well. The deeper her involvement became in the legacy – automatic membership of one of the few civilisations that had left its mark on all mankind – to which Josh was indifferent, the richer she found the seam. She steeped herself in Jewish language and philosophy, history and religion. Her sessions with the Rabbi made her realise both that simple acceptance of faith in a deity would not produce a moral society, and that any attempt to be religious, without practising a definite religion, was as impossible as attempting to speak without a specific language.

When she examined the Christianity of her parents – in which the Messiah, for whom the Jews still waited, had already arrived – and contrasted it with Judaism, she discovered that it was neither an ethical code nor a branch of idealism, and had nothing to do with the secular world; that each one of the sentences she had, as a child, repeated in the Lord's Prayer was a Jewish sentence; and that to the Christians a man sinned because he was a sinner while to the Jews he was a sinner because he sinned.

She had, she supposed, regarded herself if anything until meeting Josh, as a humanist, but now she saw her humanism as a set only of personal ideals (restatements, in fact, of Jewish ideals) which had no mode of transmission from one generation to the next and absolutely no system for producing decent people. Her husband's heritage – with its emphasis on right conduct and the sanctity of human life – which she had at first believed to consist of no more than a few arbitrary dietary laws, ritual and defined prayer and a sense of affinity with others, turned out to her amazement to take nothing for granted – there were blessings for all life's experiences – and to possess the most extensive system of legislative good known to mankind. Goodness had both to be defined and formulated (it was as difficult to become a good person as it was to become a good tight-rope walker) and this Judaism had done. Violence and oppression were repugnant to the teaching which embraced the whole domain of life, and paid due regard to the human condition, its difficulties and dilemmas. There were entire texts governing speech alone (speaking evil about someone was a serious sin and one who humiliated his fellow man in public was regarded as if he had shed blood) and the laws of ethics governed not only business relationships, treatment of the elderly, the weak, the poor, but in every area of conduct with titbits from which, at unexpected moments, Sarah would regale Josh.

'Did you know that according to the Talmud a Jew is not allowed to raise the hopes of a shopkeeper by asking the price of an item which he knows he's not going to buy?' or 'Listen to this: it's forbidden to turn back a poor man empty handed, even if one gives as little as a dried fig!'

In reply to Josh's scepticism, that he didn't think such injunctions of earth shattering importance, Sarah informed him that while each particular law might not seem that significant, added together they represented unique consideration for fellow human beings.

After almost eighteen months of application she was able to parry the enquiries of her curious friends in the advertising agency where she worked, of which by far the most frequently recurring were 'Why do they call themselves the Chosen People?' and 'What about "an eye for an eye?"' She learned to explain that the former claim was one of obligation and suffering, rather than superiority or privilege, and that more was expected of the Jews who were obliged to spread ethical monotheism throughout the world and to live as a 'light unto the nations'. Anyone, of any race, could become a Jew and thereby chosen, as she herself would be, by assuming the Jewish task. An 'eye for an eye' and 'a tooth for a tooth', as she found herself frequently explaining, was *not* the doctrine of vicious retaliation it implied, but was based on the concept of the dignity and worth of man and implied *monetary* indemnity. If in the course of a quarrel one person inflicted an injury on another, he was entitled to claim both for the pain suffered and the humiliation sustained, and Biblical law stated clearly the extent of compensation to be paid.

As far as her conversion was concerned Sarah found, paradoxically, that despite the dictum that 'he who befriends a proselyte it is as if he had created him', the matter raised more eyebrows among Jews than non-Jews.

'It doesn't matter what she does, she'll always be a *shiksa*!' Josh's Aunty Beatty had said, in a breath disqualifying both Abraham and Ruth (for whom a book of the Bible was named) from Judaism. Aunty Beatty mistakenly believed, if she thought about it at all, that proselytes should be discouraged when, since it was maintained that the Messiah himself would arise from amongst their number, they must in fact be enthusiastically welcomed.

What puzzled Sarah most was that the Jews themselves, Josh's family at any rate (apart from Sydney whom she had not known), had no real understanding of their culture – its origins, its beliefs, its role in history – no close acquaintance with its classical texts, skimmed only the surface of their vast endowment, carried the burden so lightly that in some cases all that remained of their Judaism was the desire to go on eating and making a noise together. According to Rabbi Magnus, the Jews were messengers who, sadly, in many cases had forgotten their message. Sarah applied herself to the burden of it which she would pass on to her son.

That it would be a son Sarah already knew, although she had not told Kitty. An ultrasound scan had revealed the sex of the child she carried and had spurred her on, aware of future responsibilities, to greater efforts in her studies. What she did not learn from Rabbi Magnus was disseminated by Mrs Halberstadt who had both grown fond of Sarah over the months of instruction and found in her a willing pupil. To Josh's amusement, and occasionally his chagrin (he had liked his prawn cocktails and his lobster), his wife had wholeheartedly embraced the dietary laws – with all their implications – which had to do with holiness, demanding dedication to a purpose rather than health. She had been surprised that such a code as Judaism did not embrace vegetarianism, but learned that while the ideal was not to kill for food, *kashrut* – which placed a strict limit on the number of animal species which were allowed to be eaten – was its compromise. She was intrigued to discover that not only the renowned pig but the lapwing and the vulture among others were forbidden, not because they were considered dirty, a common misapprehension, but because they lacked cloven hooves and did not chew the cud – arbitrary characteristics as random as the selection of colours for the traffic lights; that every permitted animal was a herbivore, and every animal which fed upon others was not permitted.

According to an only partially joking Mrs Halberstadt, food had done more for the cohesion of the Jewish people than all the religious reform movements put together, and from her and from Kitty, Sarah learned the delights of the table. To Josh's amusement she was planning – in Kitty's absence – to entertain his family for dinner on the first night of the forthcoming Jewish New Year. She had mentioned this to her mother-in-law, hoping she would be pleased, and Kitty's letter arrived when she was mentally planning her menu. At her own mother's insistence Sarah had taken a cookery course between school and going up to Oxford, graduating with proficiency in the delights of *Jellied Ham Bourguinonne* and *Scallops Chapon Fin*, but her interests now were in a cuisine that dated from the time that Rebecca had made her casserole of venison, and her son Esau had sold his birthright for what sounded like a bowl of lentil soup. During the two thousand years which followed, the Jews became in turn the subjects of the four civilisations in which the art of the kitchen flourished, but whilst the empires of the Egyptians, the Persians, the Greeks and the Romans had faded into history, their cuisines were preserved to be perpetuated by their one time slaves. Jewish housewives still made the sweetmeat of dried apricots for Passover which their ancestors had learned in Egypt, the baked honey and cheesecake of the Persians, and the strudel stuffed with poppy seeds which had graced the Roman feasts.

While Mrs Halberstadt enlightened Sarah as to the prescribed preparation and serving instructions for the permitted fare (the separation of foods of animal and dairy origin, and the purging of the blood from the meat), it was Kitty who, with her practical demonstrations, had before she went away initiated her daughter-in-law into the Jewish culinary art. At Kitty's elbow (scorned by Rachel who said if you were really into that sort of thing you could buy the whole shooting-match pre-packed and frozen) Sarah learned to make *cholent*, a Sabbath casserole of meat and beans, which in nineteenth-century Russia had simmered all night in the baker's oven (*chaud lent*), and the chopped liver which in certain circles had become the *sine qua non* of Jewish life. Sarah had tried the dish out on her mother on one of her visits to London, with the result that Kitty's special recipe (a little brown sugar added to the frying onions) was now served in Leicester, on triangles of toast, to the members of the local hunt.

Kitty's letter encompassed several pages. To Sarah, reading it, it was as if her mother-in-law was in the room:

'Dear All (please pass this letter round),
'One minute you boil and the next you freeze. I don't think I shall ever get used to the cold indoors or the heat in the streets – it comes right through the soles of your shoes. I used to grumble in London when we had a hot summer but it was never anything like this. Maurice says you get used to it. There's so much to get used to sometimes I wonder if I must have been a little mad, had a brainstorm or something, coming all this way where I don't know a soul, then I look at Maurice and make up my mind to put up with all the annoying little things and being so far away from you all. He makes me so happy.

'I know Rachel can't understand (doesn't want to) but we're like two children, doing things together. I can hardly believe it (having someone I mean) after two years on my own as a widow with people avoiding me as if I had some catching disease. We saw "The Dining Room" (a Sunday matinée) which takes place somewhere in New England with brief scenes about a large assortment of characters over the last fifty years or so, and it reminded me of our dining-room (we've had the same table and chairs ever since we were married) and of the family meals when Sydney was alive and all the changes which have taken place. We go out a lot and it's like being on one long holiday. Sometimes we go to a movie (you have to pay for your seats then join another line for ticket holders)! We saw "Chariots of Fire" – about a Jewish student at Cambridge who runs against snobbery and prejudice – it's a big hit here (that tune and all that slow motion) and I felt very proud of England; and "Body Heat" (as if it isn't hot enough) which isn't up my street; and "On Golden Pond" – Katharine Hepburn still with the cheekbones at seventy-two dancing by herself in the woods, and Henry Fonda, an overbearing and often unpleasant old man squinting into the sun – playing a husband and wife who have been married for forty-eight years. It's about the misunderstandings between the generations (Rachel should see it) and about everyone's parents.

'Generally we go to concerts. The "Mostly Mozart Festival" at the Lincoln Centre – there's a lovely Plaza but the fountains aren't playing right now because of the water shortage – which has an opera stage as large as a football field and holds 13,000 people and 1,000 cars! One afternoon we drove out to Waterloo Village (they're mad on villages) to hear Yitzhak Pearlman play Brahms' Violin Concerto with the tears running down his chin. We parked in a field (meadow) with a million others and had our picnic on a rug (blanket). Some people brought proper (regular) tables and set them up with candelabra and scarlet candles like a wedding or *barmitzvah* – it was something to see.

'When the season starts we're going to the opera: Rosenkavalier, which is on Maurice's list of favourites he wants to take me to, Figaro, Cosi fan Tutte, Don Giovanni, Zauberflote, Fidelio, Falstaff, Fledermaus, Boris Godunov (The Meistersingers and Parsifal, too, but he won't have anything to do with Wagner since the camps), and we listen to his tapes in the evenings when we're home so that I'll have some idea of what it's all about.

'I can't tell you how many miles I've walked. The Statue of Liberty I told you about (did Debbie and Lisa get the postcards? I sent one each so that they don't quarrel) and we've seen, amongst other things, an exhibition of photographs by Henri Cartier-Bresson and Ansel Adams and some seventeenth-century French art, Poussin and Georges de la Tour, in the Metropolitan Museum. I've been to the Guggenheim and the Whitney (Georgia O'Keeffe), and the Jewish Museum on 92nd Street, and we're going to the Museum of Modern Art (Maurice has been saving it) next week. Does it take your breath away? It does mine. A bit different from the Day Centre (Have you heard how they're getting on without me, have they found anyone for the lunches?) and bridge (I can see now it was just to pass the time, wasting it really) in the afternoons.

'President Reagan has upset many people here (Maurice included) by using the word "Holocaust" to describe the Israeli bombing of West Beirut. Maurice didn't say much but his painting seemed to get darker and there was a funny look in his eyes as if he was working against time to say what he had to. About the bombing anyway, an acquaintance of Mort's (Maurice's friend) came back from the Lebanon and said that while he read in the English newspapers that Beirut had been flattened by Israeli bombing into a condition of devastation "worse than Hiroshima, worse than Dresden", the city was standing about him. It *was* badly damaged in parts, some of the streets were in ruins, but they'd been like that since Lebanese began fighting each other in 1973. It just shows you. You hear a chorus (of antisemitism) and everybody wants to join in!

'About *Rosh Hashanah*, Sarah, you're a good girl inviting everyone (don't forget poor Mirrie). I had a letter from Beatty; she's like a button off a coat. You know about the round *challahs* (sometimes they put raisins in the bread to signify the promise of a rich and full year) and that the apple is the symbolic fruit of the season (Josh says your pie is better than mine). You could give them *holishkes* (they taste better if you stuff the cabbage leaves with the meat and leave them in the fridge overnight. You can't get proper cabbage here), or *tsimmes* with dumpling (a slow oven for a long time). I'll put my honey cake recipe, for a sweet year, at the end. It improves with keeping.

'Maurice sends love to all of you and looks forward as much as I do to your letters. I hope you girls are looking after yourselves. Maurice says there's not much Carol can do about her sickness. What does Alec think? We're just off to see "Ghosts" (Ibsen) at the Brooks Atkinson. I've lost nearly ten pounds (and feel better for it) with all the walking. My love and love and love to all of you, Kitty (Mother).'

'P.S. *Lekach* – Honey Cake (It wouldn't hurt Rachel to make one and take it to the Day Centre.)

½lb plain flour, 6oz sugar, 1 level tsp each cinnamon and mixed spice, 10oz clear honey, 4oz oil, 2 eggs, 1 level tsp bicarb. dissolved in 4oz orange juice, a few nuts (I use almonds). Mix together the flour, sugar and spices and add the honey, oil and eggs. Beat well until smooth (a couple of lumps won't hurt). Bake for 1¼ hours until firm to the touch. (Line the tin to stop it sticking.) Wrap in foil and keep for a week if possible. I'm going to make one for Maurice. X K.'

Chapter Nine

'What news from New York?' Hettie Klopman said.

They were having dinner round the mirrored table at the house in Winnington Road, Herbert and Hettie and old Mrs Klopman and Rachel and Patrick and Carol, who was on her own in London and whom Hettie had invited in Kitty's absence.

'Talking of New York,' Herbert said, 'did you hear the story of the Jap who was walking along Fifth Avenue, looking for Tiffany's? He goes up and down the street but can't locate it. Eventually he stops a little old lady. "Excuse me, Madam," he says politely, "but can you direct me to Tiffany's." The little old lady looks him up and down. "How come you got problems finding Tiffany's?" she says. "Pearl Harbour you found!"

'And there's another one about the millionaire who fancies himself as a naval man. He buys himself a ninety-three-foot Browerd and moors it on the Hudson River. He gets a white jacket with Captain's braid on the sleeve, and a peaked Captain's cap, and throws a magnificent party on the yacht. He welcomes his passengers as they come on board, orders the crew around, takes the wheel in his snazzy uniform. When the party's over and the guests have all gone he says to his wife: "How did I do?" She shrugs her shoulders. "Fine," she says. "To me you're a Captain, to the guests you're a Captain, to the crew you're a Captain, to the children you're a Captain. But tell me something, Hymie, to a *Captain* are you a Captain?"'

'She doesn't like the heat,' Rachel said of Kitty, answering her mother-in-law's question.

'She's lucky,' Hettie said. 'We could do with a bit of it here. It's supposed to be summer still but it's freezing outside. You could shut that window a bit, Herbert.'

'Will that make it warmer outside?' Herbert said, getting up from the table.

'The heat wouldn't worry me,' Hettie went on, ignoring the witticism, 'it can't be too hot for me. What I'd be terrified of is getting mugged. Before you know where you are they stick a knife in your back and take everything you possess.'

'That reminds me of the story,' Herbert said, 'about the Jewish couple who had the corner shop. They were locking up one night when Becky says to Abie: "Abie, you know something, all week I'm working and you never take me out anywhere. You never take me to a theatre, you never take me to a restaurant, you never take me to a film. Take me to a film, Abie." "How can we go to a film?" Abie says. "What about the takings?" "I'll look after the takings," Becky says. And she takes the bag with the cash and puts it in her knickers.

'They go to the cinema, sit through the whole programme, and when they come out Becky says: "Abie, I got something to tell you. The takings is gone!" "How come the takings is gone?" Abie says. "Well I'll tell you. There was this man sitting next to me in the pictures and the whole time he had his hand up my skirt. When the film finished and the lights went up I realised the takings had gone."

'"Becky," Abie says, "how can you let him do such a thing?" "I'm sorry Abie," Becky says, "but how was I to know he was a thief?"'

Rachel had to laugh. It was not so much Herbert's jokes as the way that he told them. He was much sought after as an entertainer at charity events or as an after dinner speaker.

She had ambivalent feelings about Patrick's parents. There was no denying their affection for her but sometimes Rachel felt strangled by it, wishing that they would leave her and Patrick alone. Not a day went by when Hettie did not ring up, on one excuse or another, to speak to her son, and sometimes Rachel wondered if he had ever, other than physically, left home. Take tonight. Two of Rachel's college friends, Sue and Duncan, had invited them to drive out to the river and have dinner in a pub. Because it was Tuesday they were expected at Winnington Road. It had become a ritual as had Friday nights.

'I don't want to go there every Tuesday,' Rachel told Patrick.

'Grandma gets upset.'

'Duncan only sees his grandmother once a year at Christmas.'

'She lives in Perth.'

'Sometimes I wish we lived in Perth. Ring up your mother.'

'We can't let her down at the last minute. You should have said before. . . .'

'How could I? Sue only just phoned.'

'Anyway you can't let Carol go on her own,' Patrick said. Rachel said nothing.

'And what about my shirts?'

Patrick's shirts were a bone of contention and had been the subject of their first married row. Ever since leaving home Patrick had taken his dirty shirts home to Winnington Road where they were washed and ironed by the maid. Rachel had protested.

'Are *you* going to iron them?'

She looked at Patrick as if he had gone mad.

'Who irons shirts?'

'I happen to like them ironed.'

'I'll buy you an iron.'

'When have I got time?' Patrick was working for his membership of the Royal College of Psychiatrists.

'I didn't say you had. I just said . . .'

'She likes me to bring them.'

'I dare say she does.'

'I can't see the objection.'

'Can't you really?'

And he couldn't. Any more than he could see that they should have gone out with Sue and Duncan. Patrick, Rachel had discovered, had a blind spot as far as his mother was concerned. It was as if she were fine china – when she was tough as old boots – which must be handled with care; a vintage wine which must neither be shaken nor upset. Rachel did not dislike Hettie but resented her hold upon Patrick. Lately her mother-in-law had been putting her oar in about where they should live. Although when they had to leave the council flat they had decided upon rented accommodation before their planned world trip, Hettie had made it clear that she thought they should 'settle' and that their child should not be born in what she referred to as a 'make-shift' home. Apart from offering to buy them a house (their wedding present), Hettie fed Patrick with details of three-bedroomed properties which happened, by chance, to be just round the corner from Winnington Road, or sent estate agent's details through the post of 'suitable' residences and 'convenient' semi-detacheds. Rachel, whose plans did not include three-bedroomed domesticity, threw the missives into the waste-paper basket without glancing at them, but sometimes she caught Patrick looking at her as if he were torn.

They had decided before they had married – theirs was to be a way of life which eschewed the bourgeois values in which they had both been reared. Watching Patrick engaged in conversation with old Mrs Klopman, Rachel knew that she was ensconced in the camp of the enemy and that it was going to be an uphill task. It was strange how she had been duped. Struggling to release herself from her own parental stranglehold, she thought she had found in Patrick a like-minded spirit whose thirst for independence matched her own, but it had been all talk. She wondered if she was going to succeed in prising him from his mother when she had not even managed to extricate his shirts.

Her sister Carol (who was deep in conversation with Herbert, Rachel would not have been surprised if he were telling her another joke) married to Alec, who had a country practice, represented the epitome of the lifestyle to which Rachel had been determined she would not subscribe. With lives circumscribed by the constraints of their religion, horizons bounded by the next festival or communal activity, what margin was there for growth?

'Found anything yet?' Hettie asked Patrick. She meant a house.

'I haven't had time.' Patrick addressed his plate.

'We haven't been looking,' Rachel said.

'You haven't got long.' Hettie meant before the baby. 'How are your renovations going?' she said pointedly to Carol.

'It's still at the demolition stage,' Carol said of the Queen Anne house. 'Another few weeks and it should be taking shape.'

'Six bedrooms, isn't it?' Hettie said pointedly. 'A guest suite on the top floor for your mother when she wants to stay, a nursery for the new baby, and a great big garden for the children.'

'Children need a garden,' old Mrs Klopman said. 'I remember Patrick . . .'

'Did anyone hear the news?' Rachel said, changing the subject.

'The Israelis have bulldozed Arab houses,' Hettie said, successfully deflected from the topic of Carol's new home, 'I saw it on the six o'clock news.'

'To punish terrorists and their collaborators,' Rachel said, 'which is exactly what the British did during the Mandate.'

'What annoys me,' Herbert said, 'is that the whole *meshugasse* is described in Arab terms.'

'Herbert's very touchy,' old Mrs Klopman said.

'They will talk about PLO "guerillas" . . .'

'For the love of God, Herbert, what are they then?'

'Terrorists. Murderers. Take Judea and Samaria,' Herbert warmed to his theme, 'inaccurately referred to as the "West Bank" . . .'

'The Arabs don't want a state on the West Bank,' Rachel said, 'they want to eat us up alive!'

'If your friend Begin had his way,' Patrick said, 'Israel will subject the Arabs on the West Bank . . .' he looked at his father '. . . all right, Judea and Samaria, to discrimination, as aliens, in a territory where many of them have lived for generations.'

'If a state created by newcomers on land where there's already a long settled population is illegitimate,' Rachel said, 'then most nation states are illegitimate. Look at America, look at. . . .'

'The land was promised,' Herbert said, interrupting. 'And the settlers are there as proof of that promise.'

'The Bible also says that we must treat the alien and the stranger with kindness and sympathy,' Carol ventured. She was not well versed in the political argument but felt somehow that the activities of Menachem Begin, approved of by her sister Rachel, were not in accordance with the spirit of Judaism which she had learned from her late father.

'You can't be obsessed with a Holy Land,' Patrick said, 'to the extent of annexing great chunks of it and then expect to be respected as a Holy People. Rachel would like me to believe that the refugees simply don't exist.'

'Not at all, merely that they have not been "displaced".'

'If the Arabs *feel* themselves to be displaced, Rache, then they're displaced. You can't tell an Arab you don't really feel what you feel and I will define your feelings for you.'

Old Mrs Klopman nodded.

'To say that they're not a group, with a separate national identity, is no different from Arafat saying that the Jews are nothing more than a religious sect with no rights to national self-determination.'

'Telephone!' Herbert said, looking to the women at the table as he heard the bell.

Rachel stood up and made for the hall.

'You shouldn't have let *her* go, Patrick,' Hettie said in deference to her daughter-in-law's pregnancy.

'It might be for me,' Carol said, 'I left this number with the baby-sitter.'

'God forbid!' Hettie said.

'At least it's a diversion,' old Mrs Klopman said.

'It's Alec!' Rachel called to Carol.' 'I think he's in a disco.'

'Will you excuse me?'

Carol picked up the receiver in the hall. The telephone was mottled to look like marble and was trimmed with ormolu.

'Where are you?' she had to shout against the pop music that emanated from the instrument.

'In the bar.' Alec was staying at the King's Arms and Royal Hotel in Godalming. 'How are the children?'

'Fine. A bit cooped up in the flat. They keep squabbling. They miss the garden.'

'Wait till they have the new one.'

'How's it going?'

'They've found some wet rot which is holding things up a bit, and one of the steels we'd waited two weeks for was the wrong size. Are you getting the curtains organised your end?'

'I can't walk very far.' Carol said. 'I get this pain . . .'

'Don't overdo it. We'll manage without curtains.'

'. . . and I'm still feeling sick.'

'When are you seeing Morris Goldapple?'

'On Friday.'

'Don't forget to tell him everything.'

'I miss you.'

'I miss you, too.'

'We're in the middle of dinner. And the West Bank. Rachel is doing her number. . . .'

'Give my love to everyone.'

'What was that?' Carol said.
'What?'
'I thought I heard someone say something.'
'There are people waiting for the phone.'
'Love you.' Carol said.
'Love you, too.'

In Hettie's dining-room the plates had been cleared away and a pavlova the size of a cartwheel, groaning with raspberries and kiwi fruit, had been set on the table.

'Pavlova was Jewish,' Herbert said to no one in particular.
'Alec sends his love,' Carol reported.
'Sounded as if he was having a rave up.'
'He was in the bar.'
'When the cat's away . . .'
'Shut up Rachel,' Patrick said.

'Did you hear the one about the two acquaintances who run into each other in a bar after an absence of many years?' Herbert said. 'They have a few drinks together then one of them gets up and says to his friend: "I don't like you, I can't stand you, and what's more I don't want anything to do with you." "What's the matter?" the other one says. "What have I done?" "I think you're unpleasant, you're overbearing, I don't like your political views, and above all I think you're pretentious." The second man looks at his friend in amazement. "Who on earth are you talking about".' he says. "*Moi?*"'

Chapter Ten

Kitty was not sure exactly when it was she realised that the shawl she was knitting for Rachel, the first stitches of which had been cast on over the Atlantic, had stopped growing. At home in the evenings, since Sydney had died, there had been little to do – while she watched the television – but knit. In the past year alone she had made cardigans for Debbie and Lisa, a sweater for Mathew (with little flaps which lifted up beneath which she had sewn buttons in the shape of elephants and giraffes), a pullover for Josh, an Arran for Alec, a stole for her sister-in-law Mirrie who was always cold, and half-a-dozen matinée jackets which she had started on (getting out her favourite patterns) when she had heard that she was to have three new grandchildren.

She blamed her dilatoriness, the fact that the shawl had hardly been out of the drawer, on New York, the dynamism of which, even in the enervating heat of summer had galvanised her; its sheer exuberance had liberated pent up reserves in herself. She had not been aware that since Sydney's death she had been stagnating. She had thought, often congratulating herself, that she had been coping rather well. What had been missing in her life was a positive approach, the deficiency of which became illuminated only now by the enthusiasm with which she greeted each day. Whereas at home it had been a case of stretching what she had to do to fill the hours – with the Centre and her bridge afternoons as the highspots – it was now almost a question of there not being sufficient time in the day. Had anyone told her before she came to New York, she would not have credited it, would not have believed that an unfinished letter to the family (this time addressed to Carol) would have lain for so long on her table.

Had anyone told her that since Sydney's death she had not been herself she would not have believed them, it was not in her nature, after the initial shock had worn off (and she had had long enough to prepare for it), to mope, to let things get her down. It was only now, when in the mornings she listened to her heart singing, when at night she could hardly sleep, her mind racing with the events of the day, that she realised that for the past two years she had been going through the motions, had been only half alive. It was like the sun breaking through an overcast sky, a breach in a dyke, an eruption of light, of bubbling energy, which transformed her view of the world.

To begin with she was needed, not only by Maurice, of whose growing attachment to her she had become increasingly aware, but by Herb and Ed and Mort, the 'poker-game', to whom she had become both confidante and friend. In the early days of her visit there had been no cards played but as the weeks progressed Kitty had been aware that on Tuesdays and Thursdays after dinner the door bell would be rung, first by Ed, then by Herb, then by Mort, and the three of them would dispose themselves around the apartment, sitting down and jumping up uneasily as if they were on hot bricks. The conversation – unlike the other occasions when they called, singly or together, when the argument (more often than not over the events in the Middle East) became heated – had been desultory and Kitty had been aware that something was amiss but had not been able to put her finger on it until the evening when Ed, looking out of the window and jingling the loose change in his pocket had said: 'Remember that night you declined to see my two pairs when you had threes, Mo? When Herb and me walked away with two hundred dollars?' and the penny had suddenly dropped. Kitty had cleared away the dinner things, taken the cards from the kitchen drawer and laid them unequivocally upon the table where they were devoured with disbelief by four pairs of hungry eyes.

Maurice had been the first to speak. 'What's that for, Kit?'

'Why don't you have a game of poker?' she said. They advanced on the table as if mesmerised.

'Poker?' Ed said, as if he had no idea what she was talking about.

'A nice game of cards.'

'What about you?' Maurice said.

'What about me?' Kitty arranged the plates in Maurice's dishwasher which offered a choice of six programmes each with further permutations.

'What will you do?'

'Don't worry about me,' Kitty said. 'I'm going out.'

And she was, for in this fast moving, hard living city where everyone seemed always to be running and, though she spoke the language, she had felt peculiarly alien, she had found a friend. On one of her downtown shopping expeditions she had spent the morning in Bloomingdale's, taking the elevator to acquaint herself with the floors. In London lifts nobody spoke; a self-conscious silence isolated the retracted bodies as everyone, blankly expressionless, faced the doors. New York elevators were an entertainment in themselves as between the storeys love lives were laid bare (leaving you with a cliff-hanger as the passengers disembarked), secrets revealed, friendships renewed, rendezvous made, shopping exhibited, garments tried on, shoes changed, fast food consumed, cosmetics applied and the political situation discussed. Having tired herself out tramping through the various departments (although she had not bought a thing) Kitty took one of these moving microcosms of life to the ground (first, she would have to remember) floor.

A southern belle, in a black bathing suit, yellow sash and high-heeled pumps, stepped into the aisle and drenched her in a gratuitous cloud of something that smelled for all the world like over-ripe pineapples, and thrust a leaflet into her hand as she made her way over the black and white floor to the glitz of the Estée Lauder counter to replenish her make-up. A sour matron with a bright blonde perm and irridescent eye-shadow, who came on strong with her sales pitch urging Kitty to further extravagance for her skin's sake, lost interest immediately when Kitty tried to pay for her purchases with a traveller's cheque, which her bank had assured her was just like currency, and, removing an imaginary mote from her eye, demanded identification.

Opening her wallet, with its display of English credit cards, Kitty found that nothing would satisfy the gorgon short of her passport. Flustered and embarrassed she was regretting she had embarked upon the whole transaction when the Bloomingdale's personal shopper (an American institution which saved the pampered customer time and energy), in scouring the departments), a pencil-slim, elegant lady dressed in ice-pink, even to her shoes, had come to her rescue. Assessing the situation she sanctioned the sale with a flick of her pencil and, taking Kitty by the elbow, whisked her up to the coffee shop where over the *espressos* she revealed herself as one Bette Birnstingl – to Kitty's amazement a contemporary – grandmother of three.

Over snapshots of their respective families: Kitty's in Godalming (Debbie and Lisa and Mathew outside Peartree Cottage which had now been sold), and Bette's in New Jersey and Palm Springs, they found an immediate rapport. Addresses were exchanged across the laminated table top, and from that moment Bette took Kitty under her wing. Like Kitty she was a widow, having buried two husbands. She lived in a duplex high above Manhattan and her talents embraced not only the ability to select suitable outfits for Bloomingdale clients (which occupied her two days a week), but interior decoration. Apart from transforming herself (lifted face, capped teeth, silicone-filled bosom, tucked 'tush' and the punishing regime of the Beverly Hills diet) she had converted what was once a few dark rooms connected by a narrow hallway into an area of unlimited space and light and had oriented her living-room, she told Kitty on her first visit, towards the sky.

Kitty followed her new friend round her apartment while she explained enthusiastically how she had opened up the entire first floor, expanding the area both vertically and horizontally, eliminated interior walls (leaving only the kitchen and the powder room) and raised the ceiling to expose beams and add visual interest. The staircase was 'floated' by tearing down the walls surrounding it and the closet underneath was made to 'disappear' by covering it with mirrors. A large solarium window, which enclosed the terrace, had not only made the shape of the room more interesting (reclaiming, Bette enthused, valuable living space and light) but was a creative *tour de force*.

'I wanted to break down barriers to the outside and draw the city's best aspects into the room,' Bette said. 'There's nothing more exciting than that view!'

The cityscape, dramatic by day and magical by night, grew familiar to Kitty as Bette's apartment (each area with its own 'discreet identity') became her second home. Sitting on Bette's peach and green print sofa, or on her bed (walls upholstered with floral fabric — sunshine and flowers — to give a special feeling of warmth and coziness), Kitty would reminisce about her family in England, sometimes reading aloud their letters, and talk affectionately of Maurice while Bette practised her yoga on the off-white carpet or made up her face (she had almost as many brushes as Maurice) at the lady's writing desk, positioned strategically to catch the natural light, before the bedroom window.

As far as the city was concerned Kitty could not have had a better guide. While Maurice introduced her to its cultural delights, Bette, who had been born and bred in New York where her father had been in the rag trade, showed her where to bargain hunt in Chinatown and Little Italy, and how to find designer labels (with last year's skirt length) on the Lower East Side. On Bette's free days, while Maurice painted, they took the F train to Delancey or the Second Avenue bus downtown, exchanged gossip over midday salads at One/Fifth, or sat on the sidewalk with coffee and cannoli (Kitty) on Bleeker Street. In less adventurous mood they'd lunch at the Russian Tea Room where the Cossack waiter, who had known Bette for years, served them *Blinchiki*, discreetly pointing out the whereabouts, on the red leather chairs among the pink tablecloths, of Garson Kanin with Ruth Gordon, or Peter Shaffer or Lauren Bacall.

Kitty had always enjoyed good health and considered herself no slouch but, trying to keep up with the lithe form of Bette Birnstingl as she tapped swiftly on her impossibly high heels along Fifth or sasheyed down the stairs at Bergdorf's (scorning the elevator), she became uncomfortably aware of her years. According to Bette this was due to her negative childhood encounters with sports (common in women over thirty) and she suggested that Kitty come with her to aerobic dancing — conditioning of the heart and muscles without going into oxygen debt. Egged on by Bette, Kitty bought a shimmering leotard like a green second skin (Kitty had opted for black but Bette had said she must think more positive), and now got out of bed twice a week at the crack of dawn to accompany her new friend to the bare church hall where she kept her special shoes in a plastic carrier amongst the rows of others — 'Fast Feet' and 'A Bagel Store & More' — on the hooks.

She had at first been apprehensive, it was so long since she had taken any exercise, had thought she was too old. The eager class of leotarded ladies (in all shapes and sizes) dispelled her fears with the warmth of their welcome. In exchange for a dollar she was given her own street door key for security reasons (once class had started the bell could not be heard), and was instructed not to leave any valuables in the dressing room, to take her furs down to the hall in winter, and to keep her pocket book (handbag) with her at all times.

Doubting she would ever get the hang of the rapid dance routine demonstrated by what looked like a filleted Miss America in time to a hit tape, Kitty, after the initial warm-up, had stepped and stumbled, struggling to keep up. She could scarcely believe (as she had written to Rachel) that now she moved to the music – "Clap, clap! Turn it! Shimmy! Pony-trap! Disco! Do it again! Break! Two! Inside! Outside! Heel-toe! Heel-toe! Snap! Lunge it! Break two! One more!' – counting her carotid pulse at the end of each routine as to the manner born. There was no doubt that she felt better for the classes and as she crowded round the water-cooler at the end of each session, her body damp, her hair plastered to her forehead, she felt a glow of achievement, an aura of well-being, and wished that her children could see her.

Kitty had not introduced Bette to Maurice. Although he said nothing, Kitty sensed that he was jealous of her friend. She knew that he fought shy of strangers, had difficulties in trusting people, and thought it politic to keep the two of them apart. Bette, however, who despite her natural gregariousness was lonely (Kitty could detect beneath the frenzied activity the little girl), loved to hear about Maurice and thought it romantic that Kitty had crossed the Atlantic to be by his side. With her customary forthrightness she asked Kitty whether she was going to marry him and was not satisfied with the reply that the subject had not, as yet, been broached.

'You must have thought about it, honey,' Bette said over lunch at the dairy restaurant on the corner of Grand and Ludlow, but the truth was that Kitty had ignored the issue whenever it had insinuated itself into her mind. She was fond of Maurice, she would not otherwise have come to New York, but he was not Sydney with his devotion to his faith for which Maurice seemed not to have the slightest feel. She had tried to keep up her standards, to perpetuate the ritual she had followed for so many years with Sydney. It had not been easy. She had bought a white, easy-care tablecloth in Macy's, and stainless-steel candlesticks, and set them on Maurice's kitchen table on Friday nights, inviting Ed and Herb and Mort to inaugurate the Sabbath.

She had blessed the candles (Ed watching with amazement) and pronounced the benediction over the wine (Maurice could not bring himself to, although once he had quoted his beloved Heine: '*Komme, Freund, der Braut entgegen, lass uns den Sabbat begrüssen*') from the *siddur*, the mini-encyclopedia of Jewish life she had brought with her from England. Over the traditional meal she had cooked she had tried, haltingly (Sydney would have done it so much better), to explain to Ed how the Sabbath with its many laws constituted Judaism's attempt to create, on one day each week, a taste of the Messianic age, and that one purpose of it was to produce a state of inner peace by relying for twenty-four hours on the resources of mind and body rather than external sources of technology. It was a day for family and friends, of communication between human beings, for returning to oneself.

Ed said it sounded like the super-Sunday Norman Mailer had suggested when he was campaigning for Mayor of New York, minimizing traffic in the city and limiting transportation. Kitty said that the Jews had been observing super-Sabbaths for three thousand years and that Mailer's idea was not so original.

She did her best to reproduce in Manhattan the Friday nights she had known, even to the recitation, in its shortened form, of the Grace after Meals (insisting that the men covered their heads) but the spirit of the evening was marred by Herb and Mort who glanced constantly at their watches afraid they would be late for the ball game.

When they'd gone Maurice cleared the dishes and started to fold the tablecloth but she explained that it had to stay in place until the following sunset and Maurice had put his arms round her and said: 'You're a good woman, Kit, I'm sorry I can't go along with all that praying'. And she'd thought that if *her* youth had been spent in Dachau and Bergen Belsen instead of north-west London she might have had a few questions to ask too. They had spent the evening listening to Bach's B Minor Mass which Kitty thought went oddly with the Sabbath candles which guttered from the kitchen but she did not say anything and sat companionably close to Maurice in the knowledge that, without Sydney, as far as sanctifying the day of rest was concerned, she had done her best.

For Herb and Ed and Mort her Friday night meals became an institution and she was touched when Ed turned up for one of them with four embroidered velvet skull caps which he distributed proudly to her new family before she blessed the wine.

This evening she had spent with Bette who had entertained her with a blow by blow account of her day bedizening her clients with Calvin Klein and Albert Nipon and Bill Blass, and they had watched 'Annie Hall' on video over plates of gravad lax on pumpernickel, leaving her 'boys' to their poker game with a plate of butter cake she had made. Now, in the privacy of her studio which with its pots of trailing *Alo'* and *Dracino Marginata* – which later would have star-shaped blossoms – selected by Bette, and her photographs of the family in their frames, already had the comfortable feel of home, she followed her mind across the Atlantic and opened her pad of airmail paper on the unfinished letter, her diary of the New World, and cast her mind back over the past frenetic week.

'Last Monday, or was it Tuesday, we saw "Ghosts" at the Brooks Atkinson, with Liv Ullman (she's lovely) as Mrs Alving. She has a real tomboy laugh. I thought it extraordinary and could see it again, especially after Ed explained about how Ibsen was able to find the universal in the commonplace and that Ibsen's characters were later stolen and used by Bernard Shaw. Did you know that Engstrad was the inspiration for Alfred Doolittle in "Pygmalion" (remember when we all went to My Fair Lady on poor Daddy's birthday?), and Oswald is the model for Dubedat in "The Doctor's Dilemma"? According to Ed, Ibsen saw plainly that the past is a beast in chains, and that out of the unchaining of the beast comes art. We live willingly among ghosts (don't we all?) and draw nourishment from them as well as pain. The first production of the play in English was given here in New York in 1894 and it wasn't shown in London until 1914.

'Ed is a mine of information. I told him about your writing Carol and he said why don't you send him one or two of your poems? Why don't you? He wants me to go along to his literature class. He's given me the most fascinating book to read, Alice Walker's *The Color Purple*, a story which is set in Georgia between the wars, written in the form of an ignorant girl's letters (of hope and hopelessness) to God, and is about incest and brutality and the will to survive. Celie's letters are full of misery – "I'm poor, I'm black, I may be ugly and can't cook" – but they burst with a terrible poetry which despite everything is sometimes very funny as well as sad and moving.

'What other news? Israel is getting a bad press here, I suppose it's the same in England. Herb says the Jews are divided from the Israelis. The Jews want to live in accordance with the Bible but the Israelis only pay lip service to it (the "land of Israel" is only a biographical accident) and want to be a completely new people, a satellite of western culture. If they were offered better jobs elsewhere, they'd pack up and run. *Eretz Yisrael* means nothing to them!

'What do you mean Rachel refuses to go to Sarah's for *Rosh Hashanah*? Surely she can be adult enough to have a difference of opinion with Josh without going to those lengths (we have long arguments here round the kitchen table and still talk to each other)? In any case I don't think it's very nice when Sarah is taking so much trouble to entertain the family. I've given her my honey cake recipe but forgot about the *tsimmes* with dumpling which Grandma always used to make for a sweet New Year. She used prunes or dried pears but I prefer the carrots cooked with sugar or golden syrup. I am making it for Maurice and the "boys" (they're looking forward to it). I'm inviting Bette, she's really lonely poor soul (she doesn't get on too well with her children), not that she keeps any of the holy days but she wants to see Maurice's paintings (she has an entire wall of Kandinsky prints and wants to talk to Maurice about his Russian years) and the apartment. I'm not too sure how everyone will take to her (she's a bit brash) but it will be nice to have another woman at the table.

'I shall be going to the Congregation *Kehilath Jeshurun* on Lexington, where I have been for the last few Saturdays, but I shan't know a soul. They have a very touching notice outside – commemorating the number of Sabbaths the Soviet "refusenik" Anatole Scharansky has spent in prison and how many more he must spend there before his sentence is complete – and a guard on duty. Inside, the red velvet benches in the gallery are not divided into seats like at home, the ladies wear little lace mats instead of hats on their heads according to the colours of their dresses – the tunes are all unfamiliar, the rabbi drags out the service and the heat is like a Turkish bath. I shall be thinking of you girls at home and probably shed a little tear.

'New York has its funny side too (apart from me doing aerobic dancing at which you'd all have a good laugh). You know me and my feet – I have to put my shoes by the air-conditioner before I put them on in order to get a little relief – it seems to be a common problem here judging by the shops, "Accent on Feet", "Ambulatory Foot Rehabilitation Services", "The Foot Doctor". Anyway I was having such trouble I went into one of these places and a very nice young man in a white coat, who seemed most sympathetic, attended to my callouses and massaged my swollen legs, then said would I like to come into his private office where he had some special equipment? Like a fool I said yes, and we went into a back room and he started this playing around which had nothing to do with my feet at all! I got out of there post haste and when I told Bette she laughed till the tears were rolling down her face. The "foot parlour", with its handsome practitioners, is apparently well known for its services to lonely middle-aged women such as myself. I didn't tell Maurice!

'I'm glad to hear that all the pregnancies are going well now, I really must get on with Rachel's shawl (I just can't imagine her with a baby). I hope Alec manages to get up from Godalming for Rosh Hashanah and that the locum doesn't let him down. Look after yourselves. Maurice sends his love. Mine as always. Mummie.

'Tsimmes with Dumpling (You'll need to double everything up for all of you.)
2lb carrots cubed, 1½lb potatoes peeled and cubed 2lb brisket cubed, 4 tbsp golden syrup, 1 tbsp cornflour (they call it cornstarch here)
Dumpling: 6oz self-raising flour, 3oz fat, 3–4 tbsp water to mix.
Put the carrots and meat into a pan, barely cover with hot water, 2 tablespoons of the syrup, pepper and ½ teaspoon of salt, bring to boil and simmer for 2 hours (I do mine in the oven). Chill and skim off fat. Four hours before you want the *tsimmes*, make the dumpling by rubbing the margarine into the flour and salt. Mix to a soft dough with the water. Put the dumpling into the middle of a large casserole, with the meat and carrots round it. Slake the cornflour with water and stir it into the stock from the carrots and meat. Bring to boil and pour over. Arrange potatoes on the top (with more water if necessary so that they are submerged).

Sprinkle with salt and two tablespoons of syrup. Cover and bring to boil (Gas No 2) for 3½ hours. Uncover to brown for 30 minutes then serve. (The potatoes and the dumplings should be turning brown and the sauce slightly thickened.) Serves 6. God bless.'

Chapter Eleven

On the day that the electronically triggered bomb shattered the headquarters of the Christian Phalangist Party in Beirut, killing President-elect Bashir Gemayel, Alec sat in the bar of the King's Arms and Royal Hotel in Godalming, with its red patterned carpet, its imitation gas lamp and arrangement of artificial flowers on the brick mantelpiece, and read the letter from Kitty which Carol had passed on to him. He had in a way felt a sense of relief when Kitty had elected to join Maurice in America. It was not that he did not get on with his mother-in-law – he was in fact quite fond of Kitty – but he had always resented her influence upon Carol, the fact that he had had to do constant battle with her for the affections of his wife.

The path of their marriage had not been smooth. Its early years had been dogged by Carol's lack of physical response and Alec's attempt to free her from the dependence upon her parents (Sydney in particular), on which he laid the blame for her condition. For years, until the time that Mathew was born, although Carol's nights had been spent ostensibly with Alec, her days had been passed with Kitty near whom they lived and from whom she was inseparable. In an effort to sever the cord which still attached Carol, inappropriately, to her mother, Alec had taken the draconian step of moving to Godalming, leaving Carol to make up her mind whether or not she would follow him. That more than the thirty odd miles which separated the town house in north-west London from Peartree Cottage was involved, they both knew.

When, after her father's death and the birth of their third child, Carol had joined her husband, she had experienced an unexpected sensation of freedom which followed the period of mourning for Sydney. Her loss had been Alec's gain. It was for a time as if life, having let Carol out on parole from her punishing conscience, had waved its magic wand. While Debbie and Lisa, released from the concrete constraints of the patio whose size had dictated their choices of pastime (sevenses against the wall or hopscotch), explored the delights of the garden and the pleasures of the countryside, their parents had enjoyed a second honeymoon, superior to the first, and for a long while their happiness had vindicated Alec's summary decision to move.

The elation had not lasted. Alec could not put his finger on the moment of its demise. For a long while after his father-in-law's death he had felt that Carol had belonged exclusively to him, and that his marriage was going to be alright. But even before Carol's move back to London with the children to her mother's flat, all had not been well. The decline had been gradual, the erosion of their relationship so imperceptible that neither of them had been really aware that they were – with the enthusiasm over the Queen Anne house, the new baby, and their disparate interests – papering over the cracks. Alec's general practice, with its surgery in the High Street – his name in white on the darkened glass of the window – kept him busy. The demands and the *douleurs* of the local residents filled his days, and both eroded and prevented him from dwelling too long upon his unsatisfactory nights which he attributed to the fact that although Carol's father was dead, he had not died within her. He loved his wife but with her recent withdrawal into her herself, her insistence on keeping him at arm's length, he felt increasingly excluded. Her small success as a poet had not helped.

From the time her first verses had been published she had gone through the day with a faraway look in her eyes and often reprimanded him when he spoke for interrupting her train of thought. He had done everything to please her. Appreciating how much the religion, in which she had been so successfully indoctrinated by her father, meant to her, he had held Sabbath services at Peartree Cottage on every first Saturday and did his best to support her in bringing up their children in the ways of their faith.

As far as he himself was concerned, he was a backslider. His upbringing had been similar to Carol's, but the years had brought a weakening of what had been carried out by force of habit rather than conviction. He no longer had any strong feelings about religion, and left to himself would have let any observances (which he privately felt had been postulated by the rabbis to suit the times and guard against assimilation) fall into desuetude. As far as the Middle East was concerned he was surprised to find that he felt personally responsible for Israel's every move and in the past weeks, often against his better judgement, had leaped to her defence. With the assassination of the moderate Bashir Gemayel he feared an escalation of hostilities, realising that Israel had lost a friend.

He put away Kitty's letter which, in a loving postscript, sent hugs and kisses to Debbie and Lisa and Mathew whom she missed. Alec missed his children too. He spoke to them every night on the telephone as he did to Carol, and on Friday would be seeing them at his sister-in-law Sarah's New Year dinner. Alone in the saloon bar, separated from his family, the new house far from completion, he felt at a low ebb.

'This chair taken?'

'Sorry?' Alec, in his reverie, had not heard the words against the lunchtime laughter, the cacophony from the juke-box.

'Anyone sitting here?'

An extraordinarily tall girl wearing pale skintight jodhpurs, a white shirt and black tie, her hair – in a chignon secured by a net – auburn against an ivory skin, holding a slopping shandy, had her hand on the only vacant chair in the room.

'Go ahead.' Alec moved his lager on its *Oranjeboom* mat fractionally nearer to him on the circular black oak table on to which the girl put her hard hat.

'I'm dry as a bone.'

Alec could feel her skin glowing and wasn't sure if he imagined the slight, animal smell.

'I've not seen you before,' the girl said. 'Do you live round here?'

'I'm a local GP.'

'No kidding?'

'The High Street practice.'

'I wouldn't know. We've had a doctor in Eashing for years. I come to Godalming for fabrics. I run my own interior decorating business. Take patterns and whatnot in the back of the Land-Rover. Personal service. Hotels, houses, offices, you name it. That's better!' She put her empty glass, froth sliding lazily down its side, on the table and fixed Alec with eyes which were neither grey nor green.

'Will you have the other half?' Alec, surprising himself, said.

He fetched it from the bar and one for himself. The girl looked at the gold band on his left hand as he set down the glasses.

'Are you married?'

Alec nodded.

'So am I,' she said.

Sarah, in anticipation of Josh's family, his Aunts Beatty (newly widowed) and Mirrie, and Frieda with her husband Harry who had with alacrity accepted her invitation – was putting the finishing touches to her dinner at which she was determined to excel.

Her will and her staying power had paid off and she was shortly to take the final steps which would acknowledge her conversion, the criterion for which was love of Judaism rather than love of her marriage partner – an important distinction insisted upon by the rabbis as valid. Having completed the requisite period of intensive study with Rabbi Magnus, steeped herself in environmental experience both with Kitty and with Mrs Halberstadt, run her home in the prescribed way, attended synagogue services regularly and presented herself to the Rabbinical Court at six monthly intervals, she was now ready to satisfy them that she was genuinely willing and able to accept the religious discipline – which would endure for a lifetime, and through children beyond – without reservation. This would be followed by the formal act of conversion, a visit to the ritual bath.

Rachel had said she was mad. Although she had herself (out of curiosity) visited the *mikveh* before her marriage to Patrick, she considered the hidebound laws concerning family purity both archaic and repugnant, and teased Sarah about her determination to live by them after her first immersion. The detailed code of behaviour – the direct result, according to Rachel, of the fear and distaste with which rabbinic Judaism had regarded the primary functions of a woman's body – designed to impose a suspension of all bodily contact during a woman's menstruation and for seven days afterwards (during which time she could not even pass her husband the salt), implied a negative animus hardly calculated to enhance a woman's self-esteem. She was unimpressed by the notion, subscribed to by Sarah who thought it both practical and romantic, that by denying a husband access to his wife for part of every month (at the end of which she would purify herself in the *mikveh*) their physical relationship would be raised to a spiritual level, she would remain as attractive to him as when she stood beneath the marriage canopy and the relationship would never grow stale.

Sarah was not bothered by Rachel's ridicule. The institution of the Sabbath, she told her sister-in-law, had also been mocked until it came to be universally accepted. Their only meeting ground, as far as the religion was concerned, was their mutual condemnation of the fact that in Judaism while the men were well catered for ceremonially, from circumcision and redemption of the first-born to coming of age, there was no 'hallelujah of childbirth,' no 'barmitzvah of the menopause' to celebrate a woman's rites of passage.

Now that she had come to the end of her course of instruction Sarah had, Josh said, an answer for everything. Often she kept him awake into the night with bizarre queries such as whether the blessing for vegetables was as pertinent to a bag of crisps as to potatoes, or an exposition of illegitimacy, which in Jewish law referred not to a child born out of wedlock but to the offspring of a proscribed marriage, who was thereafter referred to as a *mamzer*, and could never be relieved of his condition.

She was a mine of information and was determined, starting with the New Year dinner, that the door of her house, like that of Josh's mother and those of the Abrahamic tent, would always be open, and that she would be for Josh like 'a fruitful vine in the innermost parts of his house'.

Coming into the kitchen Josh watched her at the stove, her hair casting shadows over her face, her tee shirt tight over his child in her belly, and wondered how all his life both disappointed and a disappointment, he had got to be so lucky.

Being married to Sarah was, he thought, like being on perpetual holiday. He had not, as when he had lived at home beneath the aegis of his father, constantly to be minding his 'p's' and 'q's' for fear of giving offence; he was not required, as when he had been engaged to the demanding Paula, constantly to be dancing attendance on Sarah. There was in their relationship at the same time a closeness and a distance, which he had never found in the confines of his own family where there had never it seemed been sufficient room to breathe.

Busy with tasting and with wooden spoons, Sarah had not heard him come in. He crossed the quiet vinyl of the floor and put his arms around his wife.

'Take care!' she said. 'According to the school of Hillel you can divorce me if I spoil your cooking!'

Chapter Twelve

By the time Maurice in New York bought flowers for Kitty for the New Year, and Sarah in London put the finishing touches to the table she had put up in her living-room to accommodate Josh's family, the PLO had left Beirut, the remains of Bashir Gemayel had been laid to rest in a hill-top church, and to the disgust of Jews throughout the world Pope John Paul the Second had received their avowed enemy, Yasser Arafat, at the Vatican. Following the PLO's withdrawal, it was the received opinion of Israelis that an assault upon the Palestinians in the camps – which still sheltered some two to three thousand terrorists – might be expected in revenge for the President's murder. The names of the camps, as yet unknown to Kitty, and her family, who sat down to celebrate New Year 5743, on either side of the Atlantic, were Sabra and Chatila.

At Sarah and Josh's with the company crammed round the trestle on the random collection of borrowed chairs, the subject of the Lebanon had been avoided until Beatty, who had a reputation for it, had opened her mouth and put her foot in it.

Looking round the table – with Josh at its head, to whom she had said no more than to wish him a tight-lipped Happy New Year – at the remnants of her father's family, Rachel was aware of an altering of perspective, of shifting sands. It seemed so very little time ago that these gatherings, these holy day get-togethers, had been at her parents' table, when her father had been very much alive and his sisters and their respective spouses had been forces to be reckoned with. She remembered that once she had been terrified by her Aunty

Beatty with her opinions on everything; now, as she looked at her aunt, she seemed not only to have lost her husband, the long suffering Leon, by whose death she had been silenced, but to have an air of defeat about her, as if she had given up. Beatty had mesmerised with her tongue. Now that it no longer wagged so incessantly, she seemed like an old woman, her clothes slightly shabby as if she no longer cared, capable of no more than passing the time of day, the wind completely gone out of her sails.

Next to her, Mirrie, who had for as long as Rachel could remember fulfilled the traditional role of the spinster aunt – filling breaches in the exigences of the family – sat with her pale eyes vacant, and although she smiled when you spoke to her you felt that she was not really there. She had never been all that bright but Rachel had always been fond of her Aunt Mirrie and was distressed that there were fears now for her safety in the flat where she lived on her own, and talk of putting her away in a home.

Frieda, too, seemed not the same. It was not exactly that she had become smaller, but she appeared (and it was not just the fact that the chairs were packed close together) to take up less room. Even her husband Harry, who spent his life on the golf course, looked less ebullient, less fit.

'The leaf falls that the bud may grow,' Rachel thought – and she was not pleased with her conclusion – the decay of autumn is necessary for the coming of the spring, and sooner or later the non-viable material round the table would be removed from the gene pool to make way for the young. As Debbie and Lisa and Mathew, in their ignorance of the place they occupied in the inescapable order of things, fidgeted and giggled, Rachel, recalling her own youthful inability to sit still at her father's table, understood how they felt and realised with a shock that now she too had become one of the 'aunts'. She wondered if she were terrifying, as once she had found Beatty terrifying, and whether her nieces and nephew found her as formidable as at their age she had found Aunty Beatty.

Tucking into Sarah's *tsimmes* with dumpling, which although prepared to the same recipe bore only a pale resemblance to her mother's, Rachel wondered if the remnants of her parents' generation gave any thought to their mortality or to the three new lives which would eventually replace them. In her womb – as in

Sarah's and Carol's – her unborn child, presaging her own demise, awaited the moment of his birth and she realised with surprise, and for the first time, that with her perception altered by the small miracle which was taking place within her, she was seeing her aunts as people, as individuals who might too have feelings such as her own.

Alec, who to Carol's distress had arrived late at Sarah's from Godalming, was helping the two-year-old Mathew with the dinner which Sarah had so painstakingly cooked but which patently lacked the love which was the main ingredient with which her mother had seasoned it, when Beatty said: 'I see the Pope's been entertaining that Arafat!' and sparked by her unconsidered remark the dry tinder of the assembled company was not slow to ignite.

Frieda's husband, Harry, who was in the antique silver business, said: 'All at once he's everyone's darling while nobody's got a good word to say for the Israelis.'

'Scratch a *yok* you'll find an antisemite,' Beatty, who had a poor opinion of non-Jews said. 'They're having a field day over this Lebanon business.'

'"Peace Now" want to negotiate with the Palestinians, no matter who represents them,' Josh said.

'"Peace Now",' Rachel said scathingly. 'They're sick in the head. When everyone was fighting the Germans did they have "Peace Now"? When the French were fighting did they have "Peace Now"? Begin is "Peace Now". He's clobbered the Syrians, hit the Iraqis in their reactor, made peace with Egypt, is in the process of wiping out the PLO, and when he puts a few more settlements on the West Bank there'll be peace and quiet there, too.'

'Begin should not be allowed to pursue his fanatical aims unfettered,' Josh said.

'Sometimes I wonder whose side you're on.'

'It's deeply hurtful, Rachel, to be accused of being anti-Jewish every time I happen to disagree with you.'

'What about the Warsaw Ghetto? They wanted "Peace Now", but they left it too late. If they'd had the uprising when there were still half a million Jews left – instead of a few thousand – it might have been a different story. We can't *afford* to sit and wait until they come and wipe us out.'

'We're always the scapegoats,' Beatty said, warming to her theme. 'As soon as there's trouble anywhere . . .'

'Frieda and I have been thinking of buying a little place in Netanya,' Harry said. 'Perhaps we should all go.'

'Rubbish,' Rachel said. 'If every Jew in the world moved to Israel tomorrow there is no reason to suppose that antisemitism would disappear.'

'There's been antisemitism ever since they accused us of murdering little children and drinking the blood,' Harry said.

'Uncle Harry!' Carol glanced at Debbie and Lisa who were sticking forks into the holes of the white lace tablecloth which Carol had lent Sarah from her mother's collection for the occasion.

'The strange thing about the blood libel,' Sarah said, speaking from authority, 'is that it was directed against the first people in history to outlaw human sacrifice, and the only nation in the Near East to prohibit the consumption of *any* blood. It's all there in Genesis and Leviticus and Deuteronomy.'

'No Jewish mother ever so much as killed a chicken with her own hand,' Beatty said with satisfaction.

'Beatty's right,' Harry said. 'The blood libel's the one thing we *can't* be guilty of. Every Jew in the world who's been brought up amongst Jews knows that it's an indisputable fact . . .'

'You're implying that we *are* guilty of all the other crimes we've been accused of,' Rachel said, 'from the Crucifixion of Christ to the Plague – which killed hundreds of Jews as well as Christians – to the absurdity of Stalin's doctors' plot.'

'It's the moral demands made on us,' Harry said. 'The vocation of Israel which the world hates.'

'Does that embrace the murdering of innocent children in the Lebanon?' Josh said.

'What about the Jewish children,' Rachel said, 'who died as the result of PLO attacks in Galilee, in Kiriat Shmona, Ma'alot, Misgav Am. . . .'

'Since when have two wrongs made a right?'

'You know perfectly well Begin never gave orders to kill children.'

'Nevertheless more children have been killed already in Beirut than in thirty years of terrorism in Israel.'

'I am not sitting here,' Rachel said, standing up.

'We'll change the subject,' Patrick said, pulling at her skirt.

'The Israel Defence Force,' Rachel laid down her napkin and stared at Josh, 'a civilian army, does not, as you know perfectly well, aspire to kill children.'

'Look what you're doing!' Carol said, pointing to Debbie and Lisa who were watching Rachel and Josh wide-eyed.

'Unless he apologises, I'm going home.'

'I haven't the slightest intention,' Josh said. 'You know I'm right.'

'I'm sorry Sarah,' Rachel addressed her sister-in-law, and went to the door followed by Patrick.

'Sit down and have your dinner,' Aunty Mirrie said, waking up for the first time. 'He doesn't mean it.'

'No more than Begin's army, firing at the children,' Josh said. 'Like the Nazis they were following "orders from above".'

'Trust you, Beatty,' Harry said when the front door shut after Rachel and Patrick, leaving two empty chairs and an uncomfortable silence at the table.

'What did I do?'

'Started the conversation. You know Rachel gets all worked up.'

'How should I know? I never see her. I never see anybody since Kitty left. Nobody comes to see me. I don't see a soul except Mirrie and she's not much use to anyone. I'm like a pariah as far as this family's concerned.'

'We took you to the cinema,' Harry said.

'A lot of language,' Beatty said. 'Disgusting. I'd rather stay home and watch television. You'd think he'd shave now and again.'

'Who?' Frieda said.

'Arafat.'

'There you go again,' Harry said.

In bed Josh said: 'I suppose you think I'm to blame.'

Sarah put her head on his shoulder. 'You're entitled to your opinion.'

'Which you don't go along with?'

'I suppose that if somebody continually throws stones at you while you're sitting in your garden, it's not unreasonable to go after them in the hope of a bit of peace and quiet.'

'Except that there have been no stones thrown for over a year. You can't say a word to Rachel.'

'You do goad her.'

'I'm sorry she walked out. You cooked a splendid dinner.'

'Aunty Beatty didn't think much of my *tsimmes*.'

'Aunty Beatty doesn't think much of anything.'

'Do you think they'll accept me at the *Beth Din*?'

'On the basis of tonight's dinner they'll probably make you Chief Rabbi. Come closer.'

'In eight things excess is harmful and moderation beneficial: travel, sexual intercourse, wealth, work, wine, sleep, hot water (for drinking and washing) and bloodletting.'

'Bloodletting was not what I had in mind.'

'According to the Oral Tradition – presented to Moses on Mount Sinai along with the written law – the sexual act was recognised as serving functions other than procreation. Cohabitation is not only permitted but required, as a mutual obligation of husband and wife during pregnancy.'

'Point taken.'

'The Talmud also provides a list of the times when a wife could expect her husband to be with her for the purposes of what you have in mind. Twice a week for labourers; once a week for ass-drivers; once every thirty days for camel-drivers; once every six months for sailors. . . .'

'What about dentists?'

'It doesn't mention dentists. Not in so many words. I love it when you do that.'

'And this?'

'A wife can demand that the sex act be performed while they are both naked,' Sarah said, removing the pyjama trousers in which Josh slept, 'and if the husband insists on being clothed . . .'

'Not another excuse for divorce?'

'Why did Auntie Rachel go home?' Debbie said, as Alec sat on her bed to say goodnight to her.

'She didn't feel too well.'

'She was fighting with Uncle Josh.'

'You fight sometimes with Lisa.'

'You told a lie.'

Alec said nothing. The girl in the saloon bar's name was Jessica and she lived in Lower Eashing next to the riding stables. They had got into the habit of meeting, for lunch in the King's Arms or in the car park behind the supermarket where he waited for the Land-Rover with its chrome horse mascot to turn into the space beside his. They were never at a loss for words. Alec told her about Carol and his children. Jessica's husband, who was in oil, was away; Hong Kong, Singapore, Malaysia.

Yesterday Alec had driven out to their cottage with its bowed windows, its old slate roof, its climbing roses and wistaria, and parked his car behind the Land-Rover. He saw Jessica in a faded blue shift, strong back, stomach, arms, legs – 'the legs are vital', she had said, 'they must be like steel' – through the wrought-iron gate, against the summertumbled urns, for the first time without riding habit. Even in her bare feet she was taller than he.

There was food on a rickety table in front of the swinging hammock. Alec couldn't remember eating it, nor drinking the wine, although the bottle was empty. The late bees investigating the antirrhinums, the nicotiana, the overgrown tubs, intercepted the stillness with their droning. He put his hand to Jessica's ivory neck and released her chignon.

'Let's go inside.'

He had been late for his clinic, had not paid much attention to his patients.

After the love Jessica had been the first to speak.

'How superbly we go together,' she said into the spent afternoon.

'You sound as if you're talking to your horse.'

'Alec . . . how long did you say your wife had been away?'

In the light of the past hour it seemed that Carol had never been there. He had watched Jessica dress – breeches, white shirt, tall black boots – tie back the lustrous hair, secure it in its net.

'You'll come tomorrow?' She took her hat from the valet stand.

He had to touch her. Could not stop.

'I'm going to London tomorrow.'

He didn't explain about the New Year.

'You'll have to come early then.'

She said it for both of them.

It was the reason he had been late. He had come straight from Jessica's arms in the cottage bedroom with its sloping ceiling, its view from the pillow of cornfields with their poppies, to Sarah's. He had told Carol they had been busy at the clinic and that he had been late finishing his house-calls. She had no reason to disbelieve him.

He said good night to Debbie and Lisa, and kissed Mathew who was already asleep, and went into the bedroom where Carol was getting into the bed which had been her mother's. The room depressed him with its thirties furniture – he dismissed an image of the cottage – and he didn't much like sleeping in his late father-in-law's bed.

'I've missed you,' Carol said, but he could tell by the way that she had secured her short hair with silver clips that she intended going straight to sleep. He undressed and put out the light.

'By the way,' he said into the darkness, 'I've found an interior decorator. She can take over all the furnishing if you like so that you won't have to worry.'

'They're terribly expensive,' Carol said.

'Not this one.'

'It would be a big help,' Carol said. 'It's very difficult choosing everything from here and I still feel too sick to get about much. I'd have to discuss my ideas with her.'

'She wants to meet you.'

'Fix it up then. Rachel's offered to look after the children.'

It was too easy. He had expected there to be some opposition, for his sins to be found out.

'Will you take Debbie and Lisa to *shul* in the morning? I'm not too good first thing.'

To stand in synagogue would be to accentuate his flouting of the fourth commandment for which he felt not the slightest remorse. He said goodnight to Carol and dreamed of Jessica. It was midsummer madness although it was the end of summer.

Chapter Thirteen

While Kitty presided over her New Year dinner in Maurice's kitchen, a massacre was taking place on the other side of the world for which the Israelis were not responsible but for which the blame, both by direct accusation and by subtle innuendo, would be laid at their door.

At the very moment that Kitty served her *tsimmes* (the genuine article) and thought wistfully of her family at home round Sarah's table, Lebanese Christian militiamen were murdering scores of Palestinians, including women and children, in the Chatila and Sabra 'refugee' camps in the Lebanon. The Israeli cabinet denied responsibility for the incident. They knew that the Phalangists were planning to enter the camps but never imagined that a blood bath would occur. Their protests were not believed and in the eyes of the world the people of the Book were as guilty as if they had perpetrated the atrocities with their own hands.

Unaware of what was taking place in Sabra and Chatila (names henceforth to add fuel to the undousable flames of anti-semitism), Kitty dispensed apples dipped in honey to her guests in Maurice's kitchen in anticipation of a 'sweet' year.

It had not started badly. Watching her make the preparations for her dinner – flitting from her pots on the stove to the salads she was preparing – Maurice followed her every move.

'What's so interesting?' Kitty said, sculpting radishes expertly and dropping them into iced water where they would open like flowers.

'I was thinking how in tune women are with the harmonies of living.'

Kitty smiled at the tribute.

'We're not much of a family for you,' Maurice went on, meaning Ed and Herb and Mort who were sharing the celebration with them, and Bette who had also been invited. Kitty said nothing. That it was company was undeniable but it was not the same. The motley crew was no substitute for Rachel and Josh and Carol, and for the unmitigated pleasure of the grandchildren who would be growing up without her. It was at times like this that she really dwelled upon how much, in coming so precipitately to New York, she had given up.

'If it's any consolation,' Maurice said, 'I've never been so happy. I used to think that if you're in good health, have enough money, and nothing is bothering you in the foreseeable future, that's as much as you can hope for. Now I wake up in the mornings and look forward to the day. I might not say much, Kit, I find it hard to express myself in words – I could paint it for you – but from the moment you walked out of customs at Kennedy my life has been transformed. You're not going to believe this, but since they took my parents away, I haven't felt, had feelings. I imagined they were dead. That my heart was ice. It's been melting at the edges, Kit.'

It was the nicest, the most romantic speech anyone had ever made to her and Kitty cried into the *tsimmes*. Maurice had looked at her, then out of the window. 'I'm not much good with women, Kit. I don't know what to do when they cry.'

'You don't have to do anything.'

'"Never make a woman cry, God counts her tears."'

'I thought you were an atheist.'

'So did I. I'm beginning to wonder. If he sent you to New York I may be willing to reconsider.'

Kitty arranged the flowers Maurice had given her in the vase she had had to rush out and buy – he had never had occasion for one – and placed it in the centre of her table, smiling her thanks.

'A small token of my appreciation for sticking it out for so long,' Maurice said. 'I don't know how you put up with me.' He meant his dark moods and his silences.

'I don't take any notice,' Kitty said, and she didn't. On the days when Maurice found it impossible to speak, when she was aware that he was totally engaged in his struggle with the dark forces which occupied him at his easel, she'd leave him alone and go shopping or sit in her own apartment writing her letters or go out with Bette until he had rid himself of his abstraction with the past which tortured him, which would not let him rest, and he would see her in the evening – although she had been in and out all day – as if for the first time.

He was not like Sydney, for whom she had been the traditional helpmeet occupying but never testing the boundaries of her clearly defined role. Here, nothing was expected of her and although she supervised Maurice's flat and cooked his meals because so to do had been the pattern of her life for so many years, her life was assuming novel and interesting dimensions about which she wrote, covering pages of air-mail paper, to her family back home. Apart from the cinema, the opera, the theatres and the concerts she went to with Maurice, the sessions with Bette and the aerobic dancing classes (which already were making her feel fitter) and Ed's literature classes at NYU which she had started to attend, the most exciting change which had come about was that which she noticed within herself.

She was reluctant, almost, to admit it, it seemed somehow disloyal, but Sydney's death had presented her with a newfound freedom, a sense that she was no longer accountable, with its rider that anything was now possible. Sydney had restricted her neither practically nor financially but she could see now from her transatlantic distance that beneath the weight of his opinions her own had been stifled; against the demands of his uncompromising lifestyle her private wishes were both denied and suppressed. Although the words had never been spoken, Sydney had always given her the impression that she would die the second that he left her, but paradoxically since his death her life had turned out to be unbelievably exciting.

To be mistress of her own time, her own thoughts, gave her a sense of power and at times she became quite drunk with it. She was still lonely (as she recognised each night when, having said goodnight to Maurice, she went into her studio and double-locked the door), still aching from the wound, now cicatrixed, that Sydney's death had left, but a joyous sense of self-awareness, of freedom, had forced its way through what she had once considered to be permanent despair. As, in her skin-tight leotard, she lunged and snapped and shimmied to the music in the church hall, or sat, an entranced tyro, in Ed's class listening to him talk, and making notes, about literary genre, she felt with the tiniest sensation of regret that perhaps she had been too wrapped up in the raising of her family, in the meticulous running – according to Sydney's guidelines – of her home. Where had it got her? To aerobic dancing and an Adult Education Class when properly trained she might have been a physician, or a lawyer, or a senior executive.

As she activated muscles she had forgotten she possessed or discussed Faulkner's use of allegory, she considered such thoughts out of place and ungrateful, blasphemous almost, but was convinced (although she missed the children dearly) that in spiriting her away to New York, Maurice had given her, in her late middle age, a new lease on life. Her feelings towards what Bette referred to as her 'young man' were hard to define, perhaps because she did not look at them too closely. That he was not Sydney she had established – God forbid anyone should take her late husband's place, preserved for all time in her heart – but there was about him, despite his often patent despair and his melancholy, a sweet and lovable caring quality which, although Maurice was not demonstrative, shone through his quiet demeanour. As she moved about his apartment, picking her way among the books and the canvases, she would look up to find him watching her, and his expression said more than any torrent of words. If she was not clear as to her own thoughts on their relationship it was because she had not taken them out and examined them, possibly because she was afraid of what she might find.

The 'boys', Ed and Herb and Mort, wearing suits in honour of the occasion, were the first to arrive. They had bought a giant pot of chrysanthemums (she still hadn't got used to the size of everything in New York) and kissed her, each in turn, Herb awash with aftershave, wishing her a happy New Year. She had a momentary sensation of guilt – of wondering what she was doing so many miles away from home, surrounded by these strange men, when she should have been with her family – which she sent summarily packing, then settled down to enjoy her evening. As they helped themselves to Maurice's Southern Comfort and juice from the refrigerator, as if it were their own home, she noticed that Ed had had his hair cut and Mort was wearing a new bow-tie, or at any rate one she hadn't seen before, and guessed that both were in honour of

Bette whom none of them had met. When Kitty had broached the subject of inviting her to Maurice, he had said 'sure', not wanting to upset her, but from the look on his face she could see that he wasn't at all keen.

Bette herself had been ecstatic and had talked of nothing else but Kitty's invitation for the past few days. When Maurice opened the door to her, Kitty could see that in preparing herself for the occasion Bette had tried too hard. Herb swallowed, Ed and Mort stared wide-eyed at the apparition in the doorway, and Kitty could hardly recognise her friend.

'Hi!' Bette breathed, in a passable imitation of Marilyn Monroe, raising one hand in greeting, and it was obvious to Kitty that in her apprehension, before she set out, Bette had made inroads into the gin bottle.

She was dressed in a silver lamé sheath – the daring decolté of which revealed glimpses of her bra with its wired undercups – with silver shoes and, inappositely, had twined a camellia into her newly dressed and heavily lacquered blonde hair. As Bette kissed Maurice, leaving a double arc of vermilion on his cheek, Kitty could see him recoil.

Determined to put everyone at their ease, although it was clearly she who needed reassurance, Bette, having shed the long gloves beloved of New Yorkers which Kitty privately considered a solecism, went straight to Maurice's easel and said: 'Isn't that just darling?' when the haunted face of a hungry child cried out from the canvas on which Maurice had been savagely working all day.

Nervous and overdressed as she was, Ed and Mort took to Kitty's friend immediately and as they fought to pull out a chair for her at the white-clothed kitchen table, Kitty exchanged an amused and knowing glance with Maurice. This brittle and painted lady was not the Bette she knew and, watching her flash her capped teeth at Ed or flutter the synthetic eyelashes, with their overkill of mascara, at Mort, Kitty's heart went out to her. Maurice did not address her directly and as he pointed out to Kitty that Bette's plate was empty, or enquired of her, 'Does Bette want some more wine?' Kitty realised that he was as ill at ease as her friend.

The conversation was lively. Sharpened by the sauce of Bette's presence, Ed and Mort vied with each other in a mordant display of wit. Flattered by the dinner companions on either side of her Bette did not forget Herb and leaned across the table, with a plentiful display of cleavage, to draw him into the conversation although he was impervious to her charms. Bette was one of those people who said everything, verbalised it, as soon as it came into her head. There was no clutch – as Sydney used to say – between her brain and her mouth, no secrets. Between the *tsimmes* and the honey cake with its spiking of slivered almonds, Bette had treated the table, as she had Kitty when first they met, to a resumé of her life. Despite the sophistication of her dress and the artifice of the face she had applied, there was, Kitty thought, a refreshing innocence to Bette. Ed and Mort were captivated. She fluttered between them like an attentive moth, making Kitty feel quite superfluous.

Bette's conversation, her monologue really, which erupted from her painted mouth like a silver stream, was animated, but it was when the time came for the prayers, for thanking God for the New Year meal and enabling his people to reach that particular season, that she surprised them all. She not only joined in with Kitty's recital of the Grace but she sang the hundred and twenty-fourth psalm which preceded it with a voice so pure and a Hebrew so fluent that the kitchen was filled with melody and the company reduced to silence. Afterwards Bette told them that she had not only studied Hebrew into her late teens but had sung in the temple choir, and, although she no longer practised them, had not forgotten her accomplishments. With her virtuoso performance Bette seemed to relax. Kitty would not – *pace* the silver lamé – let her help with the dishes, and while she loaded the dishwasher with Maurice, Bette sat quietly on the sofa between Ed and Mort, and showed them pictures of her grandchildren. When Maurice came in with the coffee, a ritual in which he took pride and with which he would never allow Kitty to interfere, Bette asked if she could see his paintings, and reluctantly – he did not much care for the public baring of his soul – with a glance for help from Kitty, he agreed.

Bette didn't say they were 'darling'. She didn't speak. As he turned over his catalogue of wretchedness, his sombre chronicle of his people's descent into the inferno, so that the skull-like heads, the bodies in their tattered rags, were caught for a moment in the lamplight, Bette watched in silence and could not have uttered if she had wanted to because in the face of such human degradation, there were not, even for her, any words.

Afterwards, she did not ask Maurice about Kandinsky, it would have been like talking of birdsong to a man who had dwelled in hell. She sat on a chair by the window and told him about her former husbands and the illnesses from which each had died. It was after midnight when the telephone rang and Kitty rushed to take it.

'Rachel,' she said excitedly into the receiver, and to the assembled company: 'It's Rachel! And a Happy New Year to *you*. Where are you?' She put a hand over the mouthpiece: 'She's in bed.'

'They're five hours ahead,' Bette said.

'How was Sarah's dinner?' Kitty said. 'What do you mean you walked out? . . . Who brought the subject up? . . . Trust Beatty! He didn't mean it, Rachel. Maybe Josh did say it but he didn't mean it . . . Yes, we've had a lovely evening . . . Herb and Ed and Mort and my friend Bette. Bette used to sing in the temple choir. She's got a wonderful voice. How are the children? Give my love to Patrick, and Carol and Alec, and Sarah. And Rachel . . . give your brother a ring in the morning and apologise, it's not fair to Sarah in her condition . . . I know you're in the same condition. I think of nothing else but the three of you . . . Don't say you've no intention. Sleep on it . . . All right . . . And a happy New Year to everyone. Thank you for phoning, darling. God bless.'

'She wishes you a happy New Year,' she said to Maurice.

'Wonderful children,' Bette said.

'Josh said Begin was behaving like a Nazi and Rachel walked out.'

'He doesn't know what he's talking about,' Maurice said.

'I feel sorry for Sarah,' Kitty said. 'After she'd gone to all that trouble.'

'Sweet of her to call,' Bette said, trying to pour oil upon the troubled waters. 'My kids don't even know it's New Year.'

'5743,' Maurice said. 'To find the Jewish year quickly you subtract 239 from the last three figures of the Gregorian year and add 5000: (1)982 − 239 = 743 + 5000 = 5743.'

'The world is more than 6,000 years old,' Ed said.

'Sure. The date is poetic really.'

'She's always been like that,' Kitty said.

'Who?' Bette said.

'Rachel. Takes after her father.'

'She'll get over it. Stop thinking about it.'

'How can I stop thinking about it. If I wasn't so far away . . .'

'I'd better go,' Bette said, seeing that Kitty was upset and that it was best to leave her on her own.

Ed and Mort sprang up like jack-in-the-boxes.

'I'll come down with you,' Ed offered.

'It's time I was off,' Mort said.

Kitty found Bette's gloves.

'It's been a divine evening.' Bette kissed Kitty. 'Real homey.'

'I'm glad you came.'

'I'll see you at class. My car will be in the shop for service.' She usually gave Kitty a lift to aerobics.

'She'll take a cab,' Maurice said.

'May you have a real sweet year.' Bette embraced Maurice and winked at Kitty over his shoulder. 'Take away 239 and add 5000. You learn something new every day.'

Against a chorus of 'Happy New Years', flanked by Ed and Mort and with Herb bringing up the rear, she hobbled in her tight skirt across the hallway.

'See you Tuesday, honey.' She put two scarlet tipped fingers to her lips and blew a kiss to Kitty. 'Don't be late.'

She exited into the elevator.

It had been her evening.

Chapter Fourteen

The day began much as any other. Maurice was already at his easel, putting the finishing touches of lamp black to the painting he called appositely 'Agony' when Kitty had crept out of the apartment and taken the elevator downstairs to ask Joe to get her a cab.

She was nervous now about cabs. Once she had flagged down a yellow car in the street, thinking it was a taxi, and a disreputable looking driver with glazed eyes had appraised her insolently before asking if she wanted a ride. She had given him the address of Bette's building, not five blocks away, and had barely sat down on the naked springs when she began to have her doubts. Outside Bette's the man had held out a lazy hand.

'Ten dollars.'

'What are you talking about?' Kitty said. She had done the journey many times and had never paid more than two. 'Where's the meter?'

His lip curled. 'In the trunk, lady!'

Suddenly realising her mistake, and that it was not a regular taxi, she had handed over the money and made her escape, putting the price of it down to experience.

'Morning, Mrs Shelton,' Joe said, coming from behind his desk where he was sorting mail. 'Not very nice out there today. Look like it gonna' rain.'

Kitty waited beneath the canopy while Joe, with his magic fingers, went to whistle up a cab. Unusually, it took him almost fifteen minutes. Apologising for the delay, and blaming it on the lowering skies, he opened the door for her. 'Take care!'

Kitty gave the address of the church hall where she was to meet Bette and, engrossed in the shocking revelations from the Middle East which she had seen on breakfast TV in her studio, had paid off the cab before she realised, looking in her handbag where she usually kept it, that she had forgotten her key to the hall.

As she leaned on the bell, realising that it was unlikely anyone would hear against the music – the class must already have started – the first drops of rain began to fall. The passing pedestrians produced umbrellas as if from nowhere, not slowing their pace as they put them up. Kitty had not brought hers. She tried knocking. A passerby glanced at her curiously as she hammered at the door. She was getting wet. It would be quicker, she decided, to take a cab back and pick up her key which she remembered had got left behind when she changed her handbag.

She stood on the corner, her hand raised. A cab stopped but a man in front of her, whom she hadn't noticed, jumped in. The traffic, swishing by, made her dizzy as she watched it. Her light dress was getting soaked. To find an empty taxi in New York, as in any other city, when it was raining was like prospecting for gold. With the sound of Maurice's voice in her ears cautioning her, Kitty decided to walk. As she negotiated the avenues, stepping delicately to avoid the puddles, 'walking' and 'not walking' in accordance with the signals, her mind wandered from the forgotten key to the universal vilification of her people by the world press as they rushed to condemn Israel for a massacre they had no part in, while those who had perpetrated the crimes in the camps of Sabra and Chatila seemed to have been forgotten in an outburst of anti-Jewish hysteria.

While Kitty knew the allegations and exaggerations not to be true, she found herself half believing the barrage of criticism and although the sins were the sins of others she was unable to stop herself feeling guilty. There was no doubt that the invasion of the Lebanon had brought death and destruction, and that it was a cruel business in need of a lot of justifying. Any Jew knew in his heart, however, that Israel would not kill for the sake of killing. Foreign analysts did not share the same sentiments. They blew up the horrors (accepting stories of Israel's ferocity at face value without checking the sources) and did not even consider what western countries had done in similar circumstances without a quarter of the brouhaha.

Take the last war alone. If Adolf Hitler had taken shelter in some apartment building alongside innocent victims, would anybody have had any compunction about shelling the apartment? There had been no reporters describing the victims, cross-examining the maimed or recording on television the sobs of surviving relatives when the British and Americans – without military necessity – had destroyed the city of Dresden on carnival night, killing more than a quarter of a million people including children still in their fancy dress, or when the Allies had sent five hundred planes to bomb an open city – houses, schools, hospitals, shops, the lot – to save the lives of its own soldiers. At the time it had seemed normal. True it had been a war and in times of peace values altered, but what was going on in Lebanon was also a war despite the fact that the media persisted in treating it as an outburst of gang violence. Its partiality was following ancient and well trodden paths in using Israel's errors and shortcomings as a stick to beat her with. The Jews of Europe had been familiar with such policies and little, it seemed, had changed.

Ruminating on such thoughts, Kitty, her head down, keeping close to the buildings to avoid the worst of the downpour, decided to take a chance and a short cut down a street which she knew was not particularly salubrious. After two months New York no longer seemed frightening and she forgot for long moments at a time the gentler world of London built to a more human scale. If it had not been for her loneliness she might almost have begun to love the city where Maurice felt so much at home. As it was, not an hour went by – no matter how involved she might be in a morning's shopping with Bette or an afternoon's exploration of its cultural delights with Maurice – that she did not think of her family. She was concentrating on Rachel, trying to picture her in her advanced pregnancy, she had always been so skinny, and thinking how the recent news was sure to set her wayward daughter even further apart from Josh, when having turned into the cross street she stopped – attracted by the photograph of a young girl who might have been Rachel – to read a flyer on a lampost and realised that there was no chance she was going to make even the tail end of her class if she didn't hurry, and that Bette would be wondering what had happened to her.

Reading the message: 'Missing. Joanna Katz-Rosenbaum . . .

graduate student at Long Island University . . . last seen in the vicinity of the Metropolitan Museum in Central Park . . .' Kitty became aware not through observation, she was too engrossed in her thoughts, but by a kind of tingling at the back of her neck that she had left the bustle of the avenues and the shop windows with their early winter displays behind her, and had entered a kind of no-man's land of the underbellies of buildings and bursting garbage cans. She couldn't understand where everyone had suddenly disappeared to. It seemed she was alone among the dank shabby brownstones and conscious suddenly of feeling, apart from very wet, very isolated, very small. The street was not long and at the far end she could see the criss-crossing movement of the traffic. She tucked her handbag into the bend of her elbow and hurried on.

She wasn't sure when she first saw them. At one moment there seemed to be no one about and the next she was advancing towards a corrugated, graffiti-covered hoarding, against which lolled three youths, one in a white suit with matching cap and two in sweatshirts, who were watching her approach. In a moment of *déjà-vu* she knew exactly what was going to happen, although she told herself that it was not. She had faced the situation before in her nightmares, waking cold with terror to find that there had been no nocturnal prowler, no loaded gun pointed in her direction, and that she was safe. She tried to concentrate upon her thoughts of Rachel and the new grandchildren she was expecting – the three new grandchildren – but they would not come in any recognisable pattern and she took a step, Rachel, a step, Carol, a step, Sarah. She wished Josh were here, or Bette, or Maurice whom she had promised that she would always take a cab. Perhaps one would come along – a car, anything, even a person, an everyday pedestrian, a human being going about his business.

The youths, heads protected from the rain by baseball caps, were about twenty yards away and although they watched her timorous progress towards them, only their mouths moved, rotating rhythmically. She told herself that she was being foolish, but her imagination had never been fertile and she knew what she knew. She glanced to one side. In England there were always welcoming houses with their garden paths, small shops run by friendly Asians. The backs of the moist buildings stared blankly. Her legs moved, one after the other, but she did not move them. She was aware of the proximity of the young men but kept her gaze on the decreasing distance to the end of the street and did not look at them. She remembered, as a child, closing her eyes and thinking herself invisible because she had them shut! Perhaps they couldn't see her. Perhaps she was too small. Against the towering buildings, between their peeling pillars, she felt like Alice in Wonderland when she'd drunk the potion, minute.

She was almost level with the hoarding against which the three youths lounged, staring at her; she could hear the beat of her heart but not the fall of her feet. She wondered if she had forgotten about God, who must be here amongst the rusty railings, the uneven paving stones, and found herself *in extremis* addressing him. She apologised for not waiting for a cab as she had promised Maurice, for being so foolish, for not listening to Josh who had told her a hundred times to take care in New York (a city renowned for its violence), and for thinking that the criminal acts which took place were directed towards other people, towards satisfying the requirements of the statisticians, and that they couldn't possibly have anything to do with her. She tried to remember the words of the *shema*, the universal prayer of Jews used thrice daily and in distress, but could get no further than the first words although she had known it by heart since she had been a child, had learned to pronounce it before she had memorised her nursery rhymes, to lisp its syllables before she could even read.

'Hear, O Israel; the Lord our God, the Lord is One. Blessed be his name, whose glorious kingdom is for ever and ever. And thou shalt love the lord thy God with all thine heart and with all thy soul, and with all thy might . . .' She had certainly done her best although since Sydney's death she had been slipping a bit. '. . . And these words which I command thee this day shall be upon thine heart: and thou shall teach them diligently to thy children. . . .' She had done that all right, or rather Sydney had. He'd been as strict with Rachel and Carol as he had with Josh – not that it had done any good in Rachel's case, she had no time for the religion. Maybe when she had a child of her own, she'd change her views. . . .

From the corner of her eye she could see the sweatshirts and the white suit, all of which looked as if they could do with a wash. If she survived the next few seconds she would survive. Maurice would have known what to do. He had survived the concentration camps. He was a survivor. Kitty had never been put to the test.

Until it came to the crunch you never knew how you were going to react in a given situation. Often you surprised yourself. Some years ago she had been having pains in her stomach and Lennie Silver, who was their family doctor and had looked after them all for years, had sent her to have an X-ray. They'd taken a couple of pictures then the radiographer had frowned and told her to get up off the table. 'We've seen enough, Mrs Shelton, we don't need to keep you any longer', and she'd gone home and pruned the roses (they were still in Hendon then) with the tears pouring down her face wondering whether Sydney would marry again and how Josh and Carol and Rachel were going to manage without her. She had thought herself philosophical when it came to her own mortality but she had been scared out of her wits at what she thought was the prognosis, desperately lonely and afraid. As it turned out she had been eating too many peaches (she never could digest stoned fruit) and a course of anti-spasmodics had seen her right as rain.

The young men were strung out in front of the graffiti (she could just make out a few of the words which were not very polite), standing quite still as if they had been pinned like butterflies against the corrugated iron. Kitty tried not to look, neither to the right nor the left, but straight ahead as she drew level with the trio. 'Keep going,' she told herself, 'just keep going.' As she passed the watchers she felt a pull, as of a current, drawing her towards them (although it was ridiculous), and that as the only human beings within sight they must, were destined to, make contact. She kept her eyes on their sneakers, each pair more disreputable than the last. The six laced feet, at bizarre angles at the ends of nonchalantly crossed legs, did not move. She counted them silently. One . . . two . . . She was level with them now. Three . . . four . . . She had been stupid after all, how Bette would laugh when she told her of her fears.

There was a movement beside her, towards her, she tried to hurry but seemed to be suspended between the buildings, reviewing her life although she knew that it was over.

'Pardon me, Ma'am.' The white suit confronted her, blocking her path, but she knew that the others were behind her.

'Do you have any idea of the time?'

Time.

Time.

She had been silly.

They only wanted to know the time.

She looked at the watch with its gold bracelet which Sydney had given her for their last wedding anniversary. She squinted at its tiger's eye face.

'Five past nine.'

The aerobics class started sharp at eight-thirty to accommodate the working pupils – in this town women such as herself, without careers, were almost invisible – she was certainly going to be late.

'Five *parst* nine!' The youth who towered over her imitated her accent. Perhaps she wasn't going to get away so quickly after all. She felt something cold against her throat and recognised, weak with fear now, the blade of a knife.

'I don't want to have to use this,' a menacing voice drawled. He wasn't kidding. The man in front of her reached for her watch, pulling at it and hurting her wrist. If he'd waited a moment she would have given it to him. A watch was a watch, it was not so important. He tugged, his black fingers with their ragged nails against her pale skin. She opened her mouth to scream with the pain of the twisting, burning flesh but an unpleasant hand covered her mouth from behind, and the sound subsided into a stifled sob as, surprising herself, she fought to hold on to her handbag with her passport, her little bit of England, and for breath.

Someone was kicking, someone was struggling as she clung for dear life on to the navy pochette with its navy strap in which were photographs of her grandchildren. A palm slapped her face and she felt the blood trickle from her nose. She tried to scream as they took her watch and the gold chain from her neck, showering her with obscene epithets, hurting her head, but she clung to her possessions until she felt the steel of the knife bite into her flesh and realised that this was New York and there would be no compunction about using it.

She let go her pocketbook at the same moment as a great weight came crashing down on her skull and the pain was so exquisite it was almost beautiful and she didn't feel the ground as it rose up, no hesitation at all as in her summer dress, now moulded wetly to her skin, she collapsed like a rag-doll beneath the blind eyes of the tall buildings.

'OKAYMOVEOKAYMOVEOKAYMOVEmovemovemove . . .'

The words ran off with the squelching feet and an incandescent light which she strove to meet through the taste of her own vomit came like a meteor towards her and gathered her up in the welcome arms of its silence.

Chapter Fifteen

The news that Kitty was in hospital was passed on by a telephone call from Maurice to Carol in London, from where it was relayed to the more remote members of the family and was responsible, indirectly, for setting the final seal on the quarrel between Rachel and her brother Josh. Carol, as had her mother, had thought that mugging, like rape or kidnapping, was something that happened to other people and was stunned when Maurice told her, breaking the news as gently as possible, that Kitty had been concussed and as a result of the *coup de grace* now had twenty stitches in her head.

Never having had any first-hand experience of brutality, Carol had not really come to terms with a world in which no daily news bulletin was complete without its story of innocent victims – security guards or postwomen – who had been maimed or annihilated by some gratuitous act of violence. The world of her three children was different. She remembered breaking the news to Debbie, then aged three, that her grandmother, Alec's mother, had died. Quick as a flash the child had replied: 'Who shot her?'

She had tried to get hold of Alec at the hotel in Godalming but he seemed never to be in his room. She had passed the news on to Rachel and Josh and had called a family conclave. Rachel had said that if Josh was going to be present she wasn't interested in coming, having no desire to be in the same room as her brother, and Carol had to persuade her that there were more immediate things at stake than their unresolved quarrel and that it had to be decided if one of them was to go over to the bedside of their mother in New York.

'If he says one word,' Rachel told Patrick. 'If he so much as mentions Begin. . . .'

'We were talking about your mother.'

'I don't wish to discuss it with Josh.'

'It's probably mutual.'

'Whose side are you on?'

Patrick put his arms around her. 'My wife's. And son's.'

'It could be a girl.'

'There'll be others.'

'Women are people.'

'Did I say they weren't?'

'You've been brought up to believe it. You've only got to listen to your father belittling your mother's work at the Children's Home. When he mentions it – if he talks about it at all – he refers to the fact that she drives almost a hundred miles twice a week and cheerfully does the most soul-destroying, unrewarding tasks for those pathetic outcasts as "keeping busy". He unconsciously denigrates her efforts in order to conserve his own dignity as breadwinner. Her voluntary work is only "keeping busy" because it's unpaid and part-time and because her "proper" job – also unpaid – is keeping that great big house and your father in the manner to which he has grown accustomed, a full-time job in itself. In actual fact your mother does one and a half jobs although your father would rather die than admit it!'

'I'm not like that.'

'I heard you the other day. "Rache is filling in time," you said, "in her uncle's gallery."'

'You are, aren't you?'

'I'm on the go for eight hours a day – not to mention the travelling – dealing with Joe Public, God help me, who doesn't know his art from his elbow, and has most probably only come in from the rain, and if he hasn't he doesn't want to see me but to go into the back room and play telephone numbers with Uncle Juda who has me keeping the books and humping the paintings and looking up the catalogues and running out for his sandwiches and finding non-existent taxis and acting as errand boy for a miserable pittance most of which goes at the supermarket checkout on a Saturday morning from where I emerge with at least four heavy carrier bags weighed down as women have been throughout the ages with water on their heads or firewood on their backs for the benefit of . . .'

'Can I help it if I've been on duty for the last few Saturdays?'

'"Filling in time", as I'm sure you would realise if you really thought about it, is hardly an accurate assessment of the way I spend my day, which although it maybe less charismatic than yours is equally valid.'

'OK, OK.'

'The exploitation of women at work is simply an extension of their exploitation at home where they work not for *low* pay but for *no* pay. We both live here yet *I* am supposed to be responsible for getting the vacuum mended and remembering to buy the loo paper.'

'I'd get it if you asked me.'

'Exactly. I have to ask you.'

'Well, you can hardly expect me to think about loo paper while I'm at the hospital.'

'What about me at the art gallery? Don't answer. I'm only "filling in time" – which is what I said in the first place!'

'Are you sorry you married me?'

'Patrick, we were talking about loo paper.'

'You're always fighting. Rachel Klopman versus the world.'

'What about you?'

'What about me?'

'Are you sorry you married me?'

'On the contrary. You'll be a magnificent mother for our . . .'

'Yes?'

'For our child, Rachel. God, I love you.'

'I can't help it if I've got a lot to say. I take after my Aunty Beatty.'

'You care passionately.'

'Too passionately?'

'Never too passionately.'

'Cut it out. We have to go to Carol's. . . .'

'Did you know,' Lisa said, 'that there are more eight-year-olds in China than there are people in Great Britain?'

'I can't say I'd thought about it,' Carol said, handing her youngest daughter a tin. 'Put these biscuits on a plate.'

'Is Auntie Rachel coming?'
'Yes.'
'And Uncle Josh?'
'Yes.'
'Why are they always fighting?'
'You fight with Debbie.'
'They're grown up.'
'Sometimes people don't feel very grown up inside.'

Carol didn't feel very grown up herself. In her mother's kitchen talking to Lisa who, biting her tongue, was arranging the biscuits Carol had made from her mother's recipe in concentric circles on a plate, she had the strange sensation that she was Lisa, enacting the scene she had played so many times with *her* mother, whom physically at least she so resembled. She remembered how, as an adolescent, a well-meaning friend of her parents' had commented on their similarity, adding: 'Not as good-looking as your mother was at your age!' It hadn't helped. Carol was painfully aware of her limitations. She wasn't clever like Rachel, nor sure of herself like Josh. Encouraged by Sydney she had married straight from school, going from one family to another without having learned independence.

Her poetry had turned out to be a lifeline. In it she was able to express feelings for which elsewhere she could find no words, hopes, fears and dreams which troubled her. That these days she lived largely in her head seemed to irritate Alec as did the fact that her uncomfortable pregnancy, in addition to looking after the other three children, consumed so much of her energy and time. It was not that she did not care for Alec – she hated every moment of her separation from him and Godalming – simply that she was incapable of demonstrating her love (except for a short while following the death of her father) in ways he would have liked. Here in this flat the shades of her parents made her feel once more uncomfortably like a small girl, and the news of Kitty's accident had filled her with terror. If it hadn't been for the children she would have taken the first plane to New York. It was as if *she* had been mugged, and yet she was also Lisa putting out the biscuits. It was painful and confusing to have no clear idea of exactly who she was.

Rachel and Josh sat on opposite sides of the room.

'Biscuit?' Carol handed the plate to Rachel.

'Sugar and white flour,' Rachel said, recoiling from the cherry-topped hearts as if they were about to strike her.

'Mummie made them,' Lisa said.

'She should know better. Sugar is the . . .'

'It's like the antenatal clinic in here,' Patrick remarked, changing the subject before Rachel got on her wholefood hobby horse.

'You still going to give birth swinging from a tree?' Josh addressed Rachel.

'When Morris Goldapple delivered me . . .' Carol began.

'He didn't *deliver* you,' Rachel said. 'You delivered yourself. Morris Goldapple was there.'

'You're always arguing,' Josh said, 'even if there's nothing to argue about.'

'Carol thinks that Morris Goldapple gave her a gift! A present at the end of her pregnancy for being a good girl. In actual fact he is just protecting himself from the undesirable connotations of the birth situation by shrouding himself in ritualistic procedures; shaving, enemas . . .'

'The children!' Carol said.

'. . . confining women to bed in an inferior position, sedating them if they make a fuss, withholding food – I'm taking sandwiches – reducing them to a state of childlike dependence which denies their sexuality by emphasising their "plumbing".'

'There's no need to be offensive,' Carol said.

'It's better than being passive and docile, relinquishing all control and allowing other people to make decisions for you, to run your life. Morris Goldapple, if I am not mistaken – '

'You don't know anything about him,' Carol said.

' – if you'd let me finish: Morris Goldapple, together with others of his kind, looks upon birth simply as another manifestation of human pathology, on a par with fibroids or carcinoma of the cervix.'

'God forbid,' Carol said.

'He becomes so detached that he can no longer function at the required instinctual level. Birth is most probably as painful for the child as it is for the mother but obstetricians like Morris Goldapple . . .'

'Take it easy, Rache,' Patrick said, 'you're upsetting Carol.'

'She upsets everyone,' Josh said. 'I thought we were here to talk about Mother.'

'Poor Kitty,' Sarah said, putting an arm round Carol. 'She must have been terrified. Mugging is the sort of thing one reads about.'

'She should never have gone to New York,' Rachel said. 'Running after that old man!'

'I wish I was with her,' Carol said, 'If it wasn't for the children . . .'

'I'd go,' Sarah said, 'but it wouldn't be the same.'

'That leaves me,' Rachel said. 'I'll go.'

'I'll come with you,' Josh said.

'You must be joking.'

'I promise not to say a word about the "Butcher of Lebanon".'

'Watch it,' Patrick warned.

'I'll make some more tea,' Carol said.

'It's not the first time General Sharon has overstepped the mark,' Josh continued. 'In 1956 he was accused by four of his own battalion commanders of exceeding his orders. He only escaped a court martial by the skin of his teeth.'

'The Israelis did not enter Sabra and Chatila!' Rachel said.

'They were in charge.'

'The British were in charge in Jerusalem in the 1920s when for two days the Jews were slaughtered by the Arabs under al-Husseini. They arranged to have the army sent out of the city.'

'You can't cite past misdeeds to justify new ones.'

'In June 1941 they allowed a mob in Baghdad to murder four hundred members of the Jewish community.'

'That doesn't give Israel the right . . .'

'You have to look at the facts in historical perspective and not believe every emotional picture you see of the "conquering Israeli soldier" and the "weeping Palestinian refugee". Television has let itself be carried away by the anti-Israel atmosphere it helped to create.'

'Sabra and Chatila are not a figment of the imagination Rachel. The massacre has happened.'

'All of a sudden five hundred Arabs becomes a massacre! Harry Trueman wiped out half a million Japanese with two bombs.'

'That doesn't make it any better!'

'It was a *Christian* atrocity. They were driven to it because of the reign of terror and murder and torture imposed on them by Yasser

Arafat and his madmen. If this is what the Arabs are capable of doing to their own brethren, God help us if we ever fall into their hands.'

'We could have prevented it.'

'Perhaps we could, perhaps we couldn't. The civilians in those "camps" – which incidentally are urban neighbourhoods consisting of concrete buildings – *could* have left West Beirut but the PLO needed them as hostages.'

'Massacre or no, people have been killed.'

'By the Phalangists! The Christians! The Lebanese! Call them what you will. They were grown up human beings who pulled the triggers, plunged the daggers, bulldozed the corpses, not puppets manipulated by Ariel Sharon. Like all Jews, because people say you're guilty you think you have to feel guilty. Not just guilty like other human beings but peculiarly and especially guilty in an exemplary way. The next thing you'll be doing when you've finished apologising for our conduct in the Middle East is to make us feel guilty for the Holocaust!'

'There must be no criticism of Israel,' Josh said. 'There must be absolute silence.'

'And that's what there will be from now on,' Rachel said, 'Don't ask me to join in your festival of self-hatred.'

'The phone's ringing, Lisa,' Carol said, and when the child had left the room: 'Josh is only expressing an opinion. . . .'

'Well, I don't want to hear it.'

'It's a Bette Birnstingl,' Lisa, returning, said to her mother.

'No one I know.'

'Isn't that Kitty's friend in New York?' Sarah offered.

Carol left the room. Lisa looked wide-eyed as the grown ups sat in silence.

'A message from Mummy,' Carol said, coming back. 'She's as well as can be expected and she's quite adamant that she doesn't want any of us to come.'

Chapter Sixteen

'Cream of rice, Cheerios or cornflakes?' Bette said, her pencil poised to circle Kitty's choice of breakfast cereal on the hospital menu.

'I'm not hungry.'

'You must eat. I brought you some cookies. Maurice will be along later. He says to call him if there's anything you want. You want I should call him?'

Kitty shook her bandaged head wishing that Bette, with her bright smile, her tinkling laughter, would go away. She was not ungrateful. Bette had been her lifeline, taking and fetching nightdresses, which she washed and ironed herself, and telephoning and bringing messages from her children. There was a pile of envelopes with their English stamps on her bedside table; they had all written, shocked into unaccustomed confession by what had happened. It was sad that one had to be mugged to appreciate the extent of the regard of one's nearest and dearest. Rachel's letter had filled five pages in which she had expressed concern and affection for her mother that Kitty, until this moment, had had no idea that she felt. It was one of life's ironies. Until death, when it was too late, or at best catastrophe, one remained in ignorance of sentiments one would have liked to hear but which were in the normal course of events never expressed.

She had often discussed the phenomenon with Sydney in the old days when on Friday nights in the *shalom bayit* of their living-room, the Sabbath peace towards which she worked all week, she had perused the 'deaths' in the Jewish Chronicle for familiar names, and had never ceased to be surprised at the generous sentiments publicly aired.

Had the 'wonderful mother, mother-in-law and grandma', 'the incomparable and beloved wife' who would be sorely missed by her heartbroken family and friends in an announcement which filled two columns and ran to twenty-three separate insertions, been aware in the smallest measure of her profound effect upon them? Did the widow of the lifelong companion who 'slipped peacefully away after a long illness patiently born' ever convey to her husband, while he was alive, her appreciation of his 'selfless devotion' or give him the smallest inkling that his humour and courage were an inspiration to her? How ironical, Kitty thought, that she had not only to put the Atlantic ocean between herself and her youngest daughter, but to be set upon in broad daylight for Rachel to give voice to the regard in which she held her mother. That there was always a degree of hostility, a certain sense of rivalry between mothers and their daughters, Kitty recognised (she noticed its absence in her relationship with Josh), but underlying this, apparently – she had not known for Rachel had never told her – was an admiration and affection, a yearning and a need, which coming from Rachel, whose pronouncements had always verged on the flippant, had brought tears to Kitty's eyes.

So moved had she been by the final paragraphs in Rachel's letter that she had shown them to Bette. Rachel had been reading the riot act to Kitty about the hazards of the New York streets: '. . . I don't want to hear that you've been walking alone, no matter what time of day, down deserted alleys. If you do anything so foolish again I shall be on the next plane to fetch you. I don't want my child to be deprived of a maternal grandmother (as well as a grandfather), especially one as patient, sympathetic, loving, caring, long-suffering, kind, generous, sensible, understanding, tolerant, accessible, charitable, honest, accepting, considerate and thoughtful as yourself. So don't go getting yourself coshed again.

'And don't worry about your appearance. To return your epithet (it's been ringing in my ears since my childhood!) "Handsome is as handsome does", and judged by this standard you are the most beautiful mother in the world. Your hair will grow again, and the bruising (Bette says it's all colours of the rainbow) will fade. The contusions to your psyche will take longer to heal but you mustn't be like those women who have been beaten up in their homes and will never again answer the doorbell. When they discharge you, you must force yourself to go about as usual but you must be *sensible* (I never thought that I'd be saying that to you) and TAKE CARE. If your experience results in nothing more useful, it will be a story to tell your grandson/granddaughter, to dine out on when you come back to England (when you've stopped this nonsense), a cautionary tale. Meanwhile hurry and get better soon. We love you and miss you and think of you constantly. Sorry that this had to happen to such a special mother to her devoted daughter, Rachel (Sadie) Klopman.'

Josh's letter had been more pragmatic and had to do with her insurance claim for personal injury (the wheels of which Maurice had already put in motion) and how she must be sure, if required to identify the criminals, not to point the finger if she was in any doubt. A police detective had already been to see her and she had done her best to describe her assailants although she would rather have forgotten the whole episode, eradicated it from her mind. She was glad he had not been in uniform. The police in New York – unlike the English constables she was used to, who now appeared to be no older than schoolboys – seemed so frightening, and carried guns and a menace in their demeanour of which you couldn't by any stretch of the imagination accuse the British Bobby. Josh wrote that he felt responsible for having let her go to New York (as if she were a child not capable of deciding for herself) and offered, despite Bette's relayed protestations, to come and take her home. Neither he nor Rachel as much as mentioned Maurice; it was as if for them he did not exist.

Sarah had added a paragraph hoping that Kitty would be cheered by the fact that she had presented herself before the three *dayanim* at the Beth Din who had questioned her at length about her knowledge of Judaism and observance of the *mitzvot* after which, to her great joy and relief, they had congratulated her and accepted her as a fully fledged Jew. All that remained now was the final step of the ritual bath (Mrs Halberstadt was to accompany her to the *mikveh*) after which she would be presented with the *te'udah*, the formal document of conversion.

Carol had composed a poem. There was no doubt that she was neither a Sylvia Plath nor an Emily Dickinson but the feelings which shone through the verse had compensated for its inadequacies. In addition to their letters, Rachel and Carol and Josh had sent a huge bouquet of flowers – carnations, alstroemeria lilies and sweetheart roses – and Bette had arranged them, saying 'It's almost worth getting mugged', but Kitty knew that what she meant was how lucky Kitty was in her family because it had become evident as their friendship had developed that Bette's children seemed to want to have little to do with their mother.

Debbie and Lisa had sent letters and drawings. Lisa's was quite talented (artistically she took after Carol), depicting a hospital ward with her grandmother in it with a bandaged head. Mathew had covered a piece of brown paper with multi-coloured crayoned scribbles (no worse than some of the so-called modern art Kitty had seen with Maurice) and had signed his name, helped by Carol, in wandering letters of irregular height. Alec had sent a note from Godalming in his small precise writing on his practice stationery, telling her how sorry he was about the incident and describing in detail the metamorphosis of the Queen Anne house which was now taking shape, and telling her that the top floor, as well as belonging to the children, would have a guest room which he hoped that Kitty would feel free to use whenever she wished.

There were a few words from Patrick, wishing her well. He was not a letter writer but the sincerity of the sentiments compensated for the paucity of the text. Mirrie had sent a card: 'I hear you've had an operation' – which was slightly off the mark – and Beatty had covered three pages of pink notepaper with violet ink mainly about the trouble she was having with her bunions. There was a cable from the Ladies' Guild and notes from her bridge friends. Word had certainly got around.

'Buttered linguine or asparagus spears?' Bette said.

'What?'

'Lunch.' Bette held the stiff card at arm's length. 'Or corn *soufflay?*'

The menu read very nicely. Americans were so imaginative about describing the food, but it was so traumatised and treated, so choc-a-bloc with chemicals and preservatives, so frozen and microwaved that it tasted of precisely nothing and sometimes Kitty thought that the food tasted no more delicious than the carton in which it was presented. The hospital tried. It offered diets that were salt free, sugar free, vegetarian, kosher, as well as six varieties of coffee and as many choices of bread. With its Klingenstein Clinical Center and its Guggenheim Pavilion it was one of the oldest and largest voluntary, non-profit, acute care hospitals in the country.

According to the Bill of Rights which her clinical nurse, a Miss Bronstein, had given her to read as soon as she was able, the hospital was committed to providing its patients with excellent care 'given in a considerate and courteous manner, with respect for the patient's individual dignity and privacy'. Like the food, the 'quality care', the 'best medically indicated treatment and access to programs without regard to race, colour, sex, age, religion, natural origin, handicap, veteran status or source of payment' was better on paper than in actuality. Not that Kitty had any complaints – if she had, a 'patients representative', who could be reached by dialling the Hot Line, was there to assist. But despite her 'rights' – to complete current information concerning her medical problems, the planned course of treatment, the probable length of hospitalisation and the prognosis or medical outlook for the future in terms she could be reasonably expected to understand – there was a conveyor belt quality to the place, a soulless efficiency (her Clinical Nurse looked as if she had stepped straight out of a soap opera) that made her long for England where, in her limited experience, the wards were haphazard but the nurses indubitably human. She shared her room with a grandmother from Alabama who had so many children and was so fat that it was hard to believe her massive body had ever had a shape, a schoolteacher from the Lower East side who wanted to know all about Princess Diana and Prince Charles (she was amazed that Kitty hadn't been invited to the wedding), and a walking surgical disaster from the Bronx who had been hospitalised countless times and never wearied of talking about it.

They had not been unkind. As soon as she was in a fit state Miss Bronstein had introduced both herself and Kitty's roommates and had explained – in much the same monotone as the New York waitresses enquired 'Soup or salad?' then went into detailed and memorised descriptions of the dishes of the day – the safety precautions and meal schedule, the call bell and bed operating systems, the visiting and smoking regulations, the location of bathroom, showers, and lounge, the denture cup precautions and the routine particular to the floor. The visitor limit (two at a time and no smoking) had not been hard to obey. Apart from Maurice and Bette there had only been Herb and Ed and Mort – for whom Miss Bronstein had stretched a point, Kitty being a foreigner – who had arrived together, Ed with books, Mort with cologne and Herb with a jar of chicken soup he had made from Kitty's recipe in which were suspended *kreplach*, the small pockets of meat-filled dough, which he assured her he had bought from the kosher counter.

'Lime Jello with vanilla wafer,' Bette said. 'You have to circle something. Maybe tomorrow you'll have more appetite.' She put on the apple-green gloves which matched her apple-green Bloomingdale suit. 'I'm going to be late for work. Maurice will be along soon.'

'Not in the morning,' Kitty said. 'He paints.'

Bette stared at her, smoothing the kid over her fingers. 'I don't think you know, Kitty, how much that man loves you.'

When her friend had gone Kitty closed her eyes, partly to avoid talking about the Royal Family and hearing the ongoing saga of the anaesthesiology and surgical pavilions, the Atran-Berg Laboratories and the Emergency Room, in which her other roommate seemed to have spent half her life. As soon as her eyelids blotted out the four walls with which in the past two weeks she had become familiar, she began to relive the nightmare. She tried to be brave when Bette was there, or Maurice, to shrug the incident off, put it down to bad experience, but she didn't think she would ever rid her mind of the terror, the sheer horror – which, recalled, now paralysed her legs and caused her arms to twitch involuntarily – of that seemingly endless progression along the wet sidewalk between the brownstone houses. In her dreams and waking moments the street with its corrugated wall, its graffiti, went on forever, the safe and moving traffic of the avenue at its end seeming, as seen through the wrong end of a telescope, to get further and further away.

The images of the three youths grew disproportionately large, disproportionately threatening. She could not purge herself of the mental picture, reliving the events over and over, her heart pounding, its beat increasing in speed and intensity until it seemed it must burst her chest wall. It was no effort to remember the blows – her body was still sore, her head aching. The strange part was that when the deed was done, no one had come to her aid. She remembered, through a cloud darkly, the police sirens, the whine of the ambulance, yet according to Maurice she had lain in the wet street for almost an hour before she had been noticed.

What happened then she scarcely remembered. Voices: 'Stand back' and 'No identification', glimpses of hospital green through her pain and reassuring hands and relief-giving needles. Because of the concussion they had kept her for days in special care, scanning her skull for signs of permanent damage. By the time she opened her eyes to find herself in the four-bedded room, the flowers from the children at the end of the bed and Maurice sitting beside her, her hand in his, willing her to get better, she had been in hospital for a week. To her amazement Maurice was crying. There were definite tears in his eyes.

'I'm all right,' she said.
'I told you: take a cab.'
'I forgot my key. It was raining. It didn't seem far to walk.'
'You got to know where to walk.'
'I can see that now.'
'You could have been killed.'
'I was lucky.'
'I've been so worried. We've all been worried.'
'All?'
'Herb and Ed and Mort. They've called every day.'
'Who's been taking care of you?'
'Never mind about me.'
'But I do.'
And she did. Maurice looked as if he hadn't slept for a week. He was unshaven and dishevelled.

Kitty put a hand to her head and felt the bandages. 'What do I look like?'
'Beautiful.'
'I can imagine. Can I have a drink?'
Maurice picked up the feeding cup with its spout and as he put it to her lips Kitty remembered the ice-cream he had spooned from his plate to hers, so solicitously, in Eilat when they had first had dinner

together. He held the cup tenderly, compassionately, as if its contents would heal her wounds.

'I'm so tired,' she remembered saying. 'I could sleep for a week.'

'You already did.'

She had managed a smile which hurt her bruised face. 'Thank you for the flowers.'

'They're from your children. I didn't bring anything.' He didn't need to. His feelings for her were in his gaze, in the touch of his hand on hers.

When he'd gone the woman in the opposite bed had said: 'That sure is some husband!'

'He's not my husband.'

'Some fella! I been through half a dozen, ain't any one of them looked at me like that!'

It was Bette who had raised the alarm when Kitty had not turned up at the church hall. She had called Maurice who had alerted the police, the hospitals.

Sometimes the aerobic dancing came into Kitty's dream. She was struggling, fighting for her life and her handbag in the alley in her green leotard, bending and stretching as she had been taught. Blows rained on her head, on her shins, about her body. She was gasping for breath, sweating. 'Sydney,' she screamed. 'Sydney!'

She opened her eyes to find Maurice, with a two foot long salami, standing at the end of the bed.

Chapter Seventeen

'We're going on a trip . . .' Maurice said.

Kitty stared at him, dear and familiar, holding the carrier bag from the 2nd Avenue Deli – 'The Best Chopped Liver in Town'. '. . . to Florida. As soon as you're better. I've just come from the travel agent. I've put our names down for a cruise out from Miami, the sea air will do you good, then we'll take a drive down to Key West.'

'I haven't the strength,' Kitty said.

Maurice's suggestion touched her but did not fill her with enthusiasm. The euphoria on the wave of which she had crossed the Atlantic had – helped by the obscenity of the blow to her skull – finally worn off. Apart from the aching and soreness of her head and the cuts and bruises which had transformed her body into a painful and uncomfortable mass, she wondered with a sinking sensation of alienation how she had come to be in this strange bed, surrounded by these strange women, in this strange place, in this foreign country, so many miles from home.

'You were calling for Sydney,' Maurice said, not moving from the end of the bed.

Kitty said nothing. There was nothing to say. Sydney had understood her. After almost forty years they had been as one. It was the first time she had heard Maurice mention her late husband's name.

He put the carrier bag down on her feet. His visit to the kosher delicatessen had been a kind gesture but it wasn't salami that she needed but to be in England, in her flat, with Sydney. To put the clock back.

Maurice drew up a chair, took her hand in his. With the other he smoothed her hair from the side of her face which wasn't covered with the bandages.

'I keep blaming myself.'

'It was my own fault. I wasn't thinking what I was doing, I was upset about Sabra and Chatila. I keep going over it in my head.'

'Don't think about it, Kit. It won't do you any good. Another week you can come home. . . . I've done nothing. I can't work without you. You've breathed life into my life. I miss you.'

It wasn't until he had gone that Kitty realised that, despite the fact that in her weakness she had yearned for the easy familiarity and the comfort of Sydney, when Maurice wasn't there by her bedside she missed him too. Although her first reaction to the suggested trip had been unenthusiastic, now that he'd painted a word picture for her of what they would do, places they would visit, she began to look forward to getting well. Sydney had not cared for the sea and she had neither been on a cruise (Bette would have to help her select appropriate clothes) nor to the Caribbean with its white sands and blue skies which Maurice had described. Their ports of call on the 'Song of Norway' were to be Georgetown, Montego Bay, and Cozumel. The unfamiliar names – Sydney had liked Herzlia or the Grand Hotel at Rimini – had taken her mind off both the war in the Lebanon and her own confrontation with violence and she was unable to avoid, when her roommates returned from their lunch, announcing with pride that when her wounds had healed she was being taken on a convalescent sea voyage.

She told Bette on her next visit and watched her eyes cloud, just for a moment, at Kitty's good fortune. There was no substitute, Bette was fond of saying, for the love of a good man, and Kitty knew that for all Bette's frenetic lifestyle she was only filling the days – as Kitty not so long ago had done – and companionship such as Kitty shared with Maurice was what she missed.

'Put me in your pocket,' was what her new friend had actually said facetiously, but by the expression on her face Kitty knew that although she herself had been assaulted and robbed, Bette was jealous of the ensuing trip Maurice had proposed, the Caribbean dream.

Kitty wrote to Rachel, her first letter, excitement at the voyage ahead of her propelling her shaking pen.

Sinai Hospital

'Dear Rachel, all of you,

'I'm sorry to have given you such a shock. It gave me a shock, too, you just don't think about it, getting mugged I mean, if you did you wouldn't go anywhere although I don't suppose it will be exactly at the back of my mind from now on. I jump at the slightest thing, somebody dropping a tray or the elevator doors (elevator!), sometimes I start if someone just speaks to me when I've drifted off into a daydream, which I'm apt to do, although as you can imagine it's more in the nature of a nightmare. I can't describe what happened so I won't try, only say that it's quite the most unpleasant experience of my entire life (you feel so helpless and convinced you're going to die) and one that I wouldn't wish on anybody or want to repeat. The odd thing was that although I thought I was screaming for help, I don't think that any sounds actually came. It was like one of those dreams, I'm sure you know what I mean, when you want to move but can't.

'I was very touched by all your letters and the drawings from the children (I'll write to them as soon as I feel a bit stronger) and your offers to come over. Honestly, there's not a thing you can do. I've had most of the stitches out and it's just a question of waiting for the bruises to heal – the ribs are the worst, excruciating every time I breathe, and as for coughing! – and to try to regain some strength after being in bed for so long. I have physiotherapy every day but progress is very slow. The worst thing is the headache and the difficulty I have in remembering things, but there's no permanent damage, according to the reports, so soon this too should improve. I spend a great deal of the time sleeping, they have to wake me up for visitors. I can't concentrate on reading except for the newspapers, but I watch the television a bit – you see Ronald Reagan in "Brother Rat" on Channel 4 with Jane Wyman then you switch channels and in the same voice he's berating Israel, which brings me to you and Josh.

'I do wish you wouldn't quarrel. How do you think it feels lying here and knowing that the two of you (four including Patrick and Sarah) aren't speaking to each other?

'Maurice is like a lost lamb. He doesn't know what to do with himself. He told me that he sat through Bruno Bettelheim's lecture "The Metaphor of the Soul" at the Cooper Union on 3rd Avenue and didn't take in one word. He's really worried about me although there is absolutely no need, thank God. Bette comes in every day (sometimes twice) and is wonderful at doing all the fetching and carrying. She wanted to look after Maurice in my absence, but when I suggested it he said, "keep that woman away from me" (he's not too keen on Bette), so I had to tell her tactfully that he prefers to be on his own (which he does).

'The boys (Herb and Ed and Mort) also visit, much to the amusement of my roommates (they call them my "beaux") and we had an interesting discussion on aggression (they'd just been to see "A Clockwork Orange" which is showing here and is about a future in which men lose their capacity for moral choice). There must be some way in our society for the unemployed (and unemployable) to release their energies other than in vandalism and crime. I don't feel in any way vengeful towards my attackers (I doubt if they'll be able to trace them), only sorry that the society we live in seems to have left them no alternatives. Don't worry about me (it's not good for the babies), it could have been much more serious.

'When I've pulled myself together a bit Maurice is going to take me on a cruise (Grand Cayman, Jamaica and Mexico) then to Key West. Ed is jealous because we'll be able to visit Hemingway's house although despite *The Old Man and the Sea*, which I liked, I can't say it means anything much to me. I just look forward to seeing a bit more of America and the Keys are said to be beautiful. First I have to get on my feet. Thank you all for the wonderful flowers – I almost forgot – they were the first things I saw when I opened my eyes. Love and love and love to everyone and please don't worry about your rapidly recovering Mother.

'PS. How was your Yom Kippur? For the first time in my life I missed it. I was going to send Sarah the recipe for carp with which we usually break the fast. Josh likes it so here it is anyway.

'You just put the fish into a pan with sliced onion and carrot and seasoning. Cover with boiling water and simmer for about 45 minutes. Arrange it on a plate and strain the liquid over it. It will set into a jelly and looks very attractive. Mind the bones!'

*   *   *

Sarah's anticipation of her first visit to the *mikveh* had turned out to be worse than the event.

'Be thankful you're not a man,' Josh had said, referring to the traumatic circumcision statutory for all male converts. Accompanied by Mrs Halberstadt, like a criminal after nightfall, Sarah had made the journey to the running waters of the ritual bath where she would immerse herself naked as an infant, to re-emerge, having confronted her own death and resurrection, as a Jew.

The 'running waters' of the original purification had been ponds, lakes, rivers and seas. Now it was a purpose-built bath in a north London suburb, presided over by a motherly *mittel* European wearing a *sheitel* (in accordance with the precept that married women must cover their heads, except in the presence of their husbands). Before the ritual bath had come the preparation. Availing herself of the up-to-date facilities, Sarah had in the prescribed manner removed her jewellery and bathed meticulously, paying particular attention to the nails of her fingers and toes, washed her hair (combing it free of tangles) and proceeded to the next room where the attendant waited to supervise her immersion.

Her fears had been groundless. As instructed by Mrs Halberstadt, who had been over and over the procedure, Sarah had descended into the pool and had stood for a private moment – strangely moved by the experience which had spiritually cleansed so many Jewish women before her – with her feet slightly apart, her arms outstretched before her, fingers spread, lips and eyes loosely closed. Slowly, deliberately, aware that this was the culmination of her two years of study, the final affirmation of her intentions, she had bent her knees until her entire body including her hair (confirmed by the attendant) was covered by the water. Surfacing, she had recited the blessing: 'Blessed are You, Lord our God, King of the Universe, who had made us holy with Your commandments and commanded us concerning immersion.'

Her words had been recorded by a representative of the Rabbinical Court, present for the specific purpose in an adjoining room who would vouch for the fact that Sarah was now eligible for the official document of conversion. A second immersion reiterated the rebirth of a gentile as Jew. The end of days is the beginning of days. It had not been so bad after all.

Josh, more nervous than she, had been waiting when she got home. In his silent embrace was his gratitude for the thing she had done for him although he had neither asked nor expected her to do it.

He held her at arm's length, looking at her with pride.

'I wish your mother was here,' Sarah said.

'Why?'

'I like talking to her. My friends think I'm mad, Rachel won't speak to me because of your political views, Carol has her hands full with the children . . .'

'And you miss your "Jewish mother"!'

'Jewish mothering is a holdover from the ghetto where it was she who kept the family together.'

'We no longer live in the ghetto, Sarah.'

'The Jewish mother, I grant you, is inclined to encourage her children to be emotionally dependent . . .'

'You can say that again!'

'. . . but at least she's proud of them, and interested in fostering their talents. I miss Kitty. Do you think she'll come back?'

'She seemed to be having a good time until she got mugged.'

'I'd like her to be here when our child is born.'

'Your mother's coming down, isn't she?'

'She's probably expecting me to give birth to a foal.'

Chapter Eighteen

Kitty sat in the fading light of Maurice's living-room, her thoughts dancing in time to the Diabelli Variations, watching Maurice paint. He rarely worked either in the evenings or when he was not alone. While she had been in the hospital there had been a perceptible change. She had noticed it soon after coming home. Maurice had come to fetch her – he refused Bette's offer of company – and had fussed around her not allowing her to carry even her cardigan. Her roommates had been sorry to see her go, they had enjoyed hearing the stories about Rachel and Carol and Josh and life in England which seemed so quaintly remote from their own. She gave the Teuscher's Handmade Candies, given to her by her 'beaux', to the grandmother from Alabama, a postcard of Princess Diana and Prince Charles – sent by Hettie Klopman – to the schoolteacher from the Lower East Side, and an Estée Lauder atomiser to the lady from the Bronx.

'We're gonna miss you, honey,' her fellow grandmother said.

'Good luck with the babies.' The schoolteacher was tickled pink by the prospect of Kitty's forthcoming grandchildren.

'Let's hope you don't have to come back,' the fourth room occupant said lugubriously, dousing herself with 'Youth Dew'.

Kitty had said goodbye to Miss Bronstein, who while no Florence Nightingale had done her job, and leaving the room with its picture windows overlooking Central Park, leaning heavily on Maurice, had gone down in the silent elevator through the Klingenstein Pavilion with its naked bronze statue of 'Mother and Child', its spotlit decorative tiles, 'Horse Racing' and 'Children going to School', and its piped music – none of which she had seen when she had arrived, unconscious – to the unfamiliar street where a garbage man picked up the trash from around the wheels of Maurice's waiting car.

She had not been prepared for the reception committee. Maurice opened the door of the apartment revealing a banner which stretched across the hallway, reading: 'Welcome Home Kitty', underneath which stood a beaming Herb and Ed and Mort. She wished Rachel could have seen them, or Carol. As it was, tears of weakness and appreciation came into her eyes and, although she assured them she was feeling fine, they would not let her lift a finger. She sat like royalty on the sofa while Maurice went into her own apartment which he had filled with flowers and unpacked for her, and Herb, in his element in the kitchen, put the finishing touches to the lunch which Mort let on had taken him three days to prepare and had entailed multifarious changes of menu. Exhausted from her journey Kitty wanted nothing more than to sleep, but when Herb declared himself ready and opened the kitchen door on to a table set with lace mats, not wanting to offend him she sat down to artichokes gribiches, eggplant rollatini with three cheeses and rugola salad, followed by ginger poached pears. She was unaccustomed either to being cooked for and waited on or to the pleasurable feelings these attentions gave her, the sensation that she was being cared for instead of caring for others. After the meal and the coffee, made with extra attention by Maurice, Ed got to his feet.

'This isn't a speech – ' he looked at Herb and Mort for support – 'I just want you to know how much we've all missed you and how pleased we are to have you back. We'd like to drink a toast to your very good health.' They raised their wine glasses – California Rioja – to Kitty and she'd thought it was the end of the proceedings but Herb and Ed and Mort had a further expression of their regard for her which they manifested in a spirited rendering of 'God Save The Queen' at which Kitty tried hard not to smile.

'What can I say?' she asked when they'd sat down again, somewhat discomforted by their own exhibition. 'Except thank you.' She got up from her chair and kissed them each in turn before Maurice took her off to her own apartment to the bed which he had personally prepared. He closed the curtains and stood by the door.

'It's good to have you back,' he said. 'Sleep well.'

It was the following morning that Kitty noticed the changes. She had slept the clock round and risen feeling refreshed and well except for the slight throbbing in her temple which seemed now to be a permanent feature of her life. Maurice had told her to call him when she woke, not to dream of getting up, and that he would come across and make her breakfast. She dressed, conscious of her happiness at not being in the confines of the hospital ward with the three other women who, although pleasant enough, she could have done without at times, and taking her key entered Maurice's flat.

He did not hear her come in. He was painting, which was not unusual, and he was whistling, which was. Kitty stopped in her tracks. Generally he worked in silence. She recognised the staccato tremolandoes of Mendelssohn's Octet for Strings, which Maurice had so often played for her, and marvelled at the sound. But that was not all. As she approached the canvas she saw, over Maurice's shoulder, that on the easel there was no sombre verisimilitude of 'Smoke', 'Agony', 'Bodies in a Pit', but a landscape in blues and yellow of fields that rolled into some European distance illuminated by the sun.

She did not move but Maurice sensed her presence. He put down his palette and brushes and came to her. Neither of them commented on the canvas because there was no need; neither of them spoke. Maurice put his arm around her, holding her to him, then led her into the kitchen where he squeezed oranges for juice and put the muffins – which Herb had made and left in the freezer – in the oven to warm up, and made coffee and looked at Kitty, watching her every move as if she might disappear at any moment from before his eyes.

She had been home for almost a week now of which they had spent almost every waking moment together. Maurice had painted, and whistled or hummed arias from Mozart and Rossini while Kitty worked at the bargello stitch tapestry Bette had given her for her convalescence – which she would make into a cushion for Carol – or wrote thank you letters to all the people who had written to her after her misfortune telling them she was now well. They did not talk a great deal. Sometimes in the evenings Maurice read to her, Heine's poems, one of them 'To Kitty', from a thumbed and tattered volume; *'Den Tag, den hab ich so himmlisch verbracht* . . . The day I spent was a heavenly day, The evening with godliness flowering; The wine was good and Kitty was fair, And the heart was all devouring . . .'

Kitty had grown used to Maurice's habit of expressing his sentiments, which she knew did not trip lightly from his tongue, through the words of others. In Auschwitz, he had told her, they had organised evenings of song and poetry in order to retain some vestige of humanity. Once, before her accident, she had been in the kitchen making pastry when Maurice, from his customary position by the window from where he seemed never to grow tired of watching her as she went about her chores, had recited: 'I don't believe in the heaven, Of which the preachers drone: I believe in your eyes only – There is my heaven alone', and she had almost wept into the lemon curd tarts.

Watching him now, totally absorbed in the application of colour upon canvas, Kitty recognised in their non-verbal communication – her aloneness with Maurice was different from her aloneness with Sydney – an understanding, a mutual caring and respect.

The music came to an end and Maurice removed the Beethoven from the turntable, returning the record meticulously to its sleeve. He put on another but did not go back to his easel. He came to sit on the sofa beside Kitty. The music, a song, was unfamiliar. Kitty, looking up from the wool she was selecting, raised questioning eyebrows.

'"*An die Geliebte*'," Maurice said. 'Beethoven wrote it for his sweetheart.'

She put down her needlework.

'I know I said six months,' Maurice said, 'but I'd like for us to be married before we go on the cruise. I've never loved anyone else, Kitty. There doesn't seem to be anything to wait for.'

A feeling of panic overtook her. Although she had not been unaware of the meaning of the growing intimacy between them in the past few days, and the strength of Maurice's feelings for her, she had been unprepared, before the agreed time, for his proposal. How could she take such a step without consulting her family? What was she doing contemplating sharing her life with another man only two years after Sydney had died? She knew that had they been there, Josh, always practical, would have asked her if she knew what she was doing, putting doubts into her mind. Carol would have unnerved her, and Rachel, treasuring the memory of her late father, would have been angry. She had to make the decision, away from everyone she held dear, on her own.

Whilst Maurice waited for her reply and Beethoven serenaded his 'Immortal Beloved', Kitty tried to impose some semblance of order upon her thoughts. The most pressing question she must address was, Did she love Maurice? She did not 'not love him'. Because of his history he had more than his share of idiosyncrasies, more dark and inward thoughts which she must not try to probe. What man, what person, did not carry with him his private hell which he had both to overcome and live with? That Maurice was kind there was no doubt; that his generosity was directed exclusively to herself was flattering. That he worshipped her was manifest; Herb and Ed and Mort referred to him jokingly as a lovesick adolescent.

Kitty considered her own feelings *vis-à-vis* Maurice. She was happy when she was with him. Extremely happy. Of course she was homesick in New York, separated from her nearest and dearest, but that was hardly Maurice's fault. It was no fun being alone. She had had quite enough of widowhood since Sydney had died. Did she want to share the rest of her life, more intimately than she had in the past few months, with the man, a good many years older than she, who was waiting, as if he had all the time in the world, for her answer?

She was fond of Maurice. Love? Love was something else. She had loved Sydney from their first meeting. It had never waned. She did not know Maurice. To marry him would be like diving from a high board into waters of whose depth she was unsure.

And yet the thought of plighting her troth to him certainly did not alarm her. That there was a possibility of it she had, after all, acknowledged when she had agreed to come to New York. Inside she felt, she realised with amazement, as if she were eighteen and receiving her first proposal. The psyche, as well as having no colour, was ageless. She looked round Maurice's apartment at the books extending from floor to ceiling with which Maurice had replaced his murdered family and with which he inured himself from the world. It was not London, her ordered sitting-room with its formal bird's-eye maple furniture most of it from when she had first married

Sydney, but it was certainly no punishment. Could she live in New York where, other than Bette Birnstingl, she had no friends? Could she, most importantly, live so far away from her children and grandchildren, her memories of Sydney and everything she held dear?

'I'm not much of a catch,' Maurice said, misinterpreting her silence. 'I don't have any family. There's only me. Maybe you'd be lonely.'

Kitty was silent.

'I'm expecting too much,' Maurice said.

Still Kitty said nothing.

'There's only one thing I have to offer you and it's of no great value.'

She looked at him.

'My love. But it's a big love. An overwhelming love. A painful love. It's been in cold storage since they took my parents away, and my brothers and sisters. Since I lost my aunts and my uncles and my grandparents. Since I discovered, when I was no more than a child, what human beings were capable of. It's the love of an adolescent, the love of a young man, the love of my middle-age, mature love. It's the love of the family I never had, the love of the life I have never lived. It's yours, Kit. All of it.'

The music came to an end, the arm lifted from the record and the player switched off, leaving the room soundless. Maurice was waiting for her answer.

Tempted to call upon Sydney for guidance as she was in the habit of doing when she was in a quandary, Kitty checked herself. This time she was on her own. She looked round the room at Maurice's possessions, redolent of the man, inhaled the smell of paint and turpentine to which she had become accustomed, felt the presence of Maurice next to her and knew she must not walk away, that she did not want to. She thought of Rachel and Carol and Josh and that they had their own lives, were busy establishing their own dynasties, and that she must not make them the excuse for jeopardising her future.

'I don't expect you to love me,' Maurice said. 'Perhaps in time . . .'

'But I do,' Kitty said, surprised that she had spoken. And looking at him, the face with its furrows of suffering, the eyes that had witnessed what no man should be obliged to witness, the ardour in his regard that would kindle a fire in any woman, the current that passed through his skin to hers, she realised that she did. Afterwards she could not recall the exact sequence of events. There had been a lot of laughing and crying – 'Where is it written that you can't laugh and cry in the same day?' Maurice had said – and he had opened a bottle of champagne.

'"She loves me! She loves me, the beautiful maiden."' And Kitty's sun, which she had thought had gone down with the death of Sydney, had risen over the horizon and started to fill her world with a warm and golden light. They had talked into the small hours. Having made her decision Kitty found herself opening out to Maurice, releasing her hopes, fears, expectations and dreams, bombarding him with emotions she had for so long been unable to share.

'You have made my life joyous,' Maurice said. 'For many years I have only pretended to myself I was a happy human being.'

Perhaps it was the dim light of the lamp in which they sat, perhaps some trick, some delusion that deceives lovers, Kitty wasn't sure, but when she looked at Maurice in his open-necked shirt, at his wayward shock of white hair, he appeared suddenly youthful as if he had shed the snakeskin of his past life and, rejuvenated, come to claim her. Later, alone in her apartment in front of the mirror, she had had to smile, wondering how anyone in his right mind could have proposed marriage to a woman with the scars of stitches on her forehead, whose face was black and blue, whose untended hair with its grey roots made a bizarre frame for her face, and thought that Maurice – a 'beautiful maiden' was what he had called her – must indeed love her.

They decided to get married at once, as soon as the ceremony could be arranged. They would call the rabbi of the *Kehillath Jeshurun*, which Maurice knew was what Kitty wanted. There was nothing to wait for.

It was two in the morning when Kitty said: 'What time is it in England?'

'Nine p.m. You want to call your children?'

Excited as a young girl Kitty hadn't thought what she would say, had not anticipated their reaction.

'Married!' Rachel said. 'You can't!'

'Why not?'

'You just can't.'

'It's what I'm going to do. You want to speak to Maurice?'

'No I don't. What about us?'

'What about you?'

'Don't you want us to be there?'

Kitty didn't. She just wanted to get married quietly as they had decided. Not to make a big thing of it. They were too old.

'We're going to Florida on honeymoon.'

Rachel was speechless.

'I've got to answer the doorbell,' she said stiffly. 'It's Patrick.'

Carol was incredulous.

'I don't believe it,' she said when Kitty announced her intentions.

'People get married all the time,' Kitty said. 'What is there not to believe?'

There was silence on the line while Carol digested the news.

'Mummy?'

'I'm still here.'

'I hope you'll be happy.' Her daughter's grudging tone belied the words.

Josh, surprised in the midst of a dinner party, said: 'What's wrong?'

'Nothing's wrong. We're getting married – Maurice and I.'

Against a hubbub of animated voices Kitty heard Sarah call: 'Who is it, darling?' Then Josh said: 'I suppose you know what you're doing', when it was perfectly obvious that he didn't think that she did. He congratulated his mother then spoke to Maurice in a civilised manner, but the coolness with which he had greeted her announcement was patent across the Atlantic. It was Sarah, who insisted on speaking, who had wished her *mazeltov*.

'It was a mistake to phone,' Kitty said, her enthusiasm dampened as she sat cradling the telephone.

'They'll come round,' Maurice said.

Kitty knew her children. None of them, when Maurice had come to Rachel's wedding, had made any attempt to hide how they felt about him. The joy of the evening was dispelled.

'I'd better go to bed,' she said.

Maurice looked at her, touching the bruised forehead. 'I shouldn't have kept you up so long.'

He kissed her mouth and it was more than compensation for Rachel's rudeness, Josh's coolness and Carol's disbelief. They were at the door to his flat when the telephone rang.

Maurice went back to answer it. He held the receiver out to Kitty who had followed him.

'It's Rachel.'

'Mummy?' Rachel said.

Kitty waited.

'I'm sorry. I was upset for a moment.'

'It was my fault,' Kitty said. 'I should have broken the news gently.'

'Congratulations, anyway.'

'Thank you.'

'I really mean it. Do you believe me?'

'Of course.'

'You deserve a break. I'd like to speak to Maurice.'

It was typical of Rachel to have called back when she'd got over her tantrum, not to have let her mother lose sleep over her daughter's churlish reception of the news.

The conversation with Maurice seemed to go on for a long time. When it was finished and he had hung up, Kitty said: 'What was all that about?'

Maurice chuckled. It was the first time Kitty had seen him so carefree.

'Instructions about how I was to take care of you, you are the only mother she has . . . and something else.'

Kitty looked at him.

'She's going straight to the travel agent to book her flight. She says we're not to dare to get married without her.'

Chapter Nineteen

Kitty leaned over the polished rail of the 'M/S Song of Norway', trying to convince herself that she was actually here, on board ship, one day out from Florida (a thousand miles long and one inch high), a bride for the second time in her life. The passenger list, left by the steward that morning in her stateroom together with the daily news bulletin and a printout of the day's shipboard activities, had brought the fact home to her. Her name, Kitty Morgenthau, beside Maurice's, sandwiched alphabetically between Buck and Serita Matheson of Tom's River, and Gerald and Monica Thomas of Albuquerque, had given some substance to the dream in which she had been living for the past three weeks when her life, seemingly set on a dull and uneventful course after Sydney's death, had miraculously changed tack.

The morning after Maurice's proposal, exhausted by the unaccustomed late night and the excitement generated by her decision, Kitty had slept until noon. As she opened her eyes, her head was throbbing but she found that she was smiling although there was no one to see and she couldn't remember why. Then she did, and stopped smiling because she was thinking of Sydney. She could see him as clearly as if he was in New York in her studio. He was not reproaching her.

'I'm sorry,' she said aloud.

Sydney put his arms round her and she could feel them as surely as if he were there in the flesh. 'Be happy,' he said, and then he was gone.

She lay there for a long while, treasuring the moment, before she got up to dress in the cream-coloured two piece she had been saving for a special occasion and crossed the landing to Maurice's flat.

Herb and Ed and Mort were there, as she had thought they might be, and to her surprise Bette Birnstingl, too. In front of them all Maurice had taken her in his arms and held her for a long, long time, almost lifting her off her feet, then he had opened another bottle of champagne and, amidst the congratulations, announced he was taking everyone out for lunch. She had hardly recognised Maurice. He had not been working for the first morning since she had been in New York, and was not wearing his paint-spattered slacks and his cotton sweater but a black, pin-striped suit from the days when he had practised as a physician, and a formal white shirt with a silver tie which echoed the hair which had been freshly cut and brushed back smartly, and she saw what a handsome suitor she had agreed to marry.

Bette, flushed with the excitement of the occasion (as if she were to be the bride), had brought her camera and she posed Kitty with Maurice, their arms around each other happily, then Kitty and Maurice with the 'boys', then Herb took the camera so that Bette could be in a picture, and they finished two more bottles before they left for the Windows on the World where Maurice had reserved a table. Kitty didn't remember much about the lunch except that there was a great deal of hilarity and Bette flirted outrageously with Ed and Mort, and Maurice, although he ate little and said less, let go her hand only to pick up his fork and had never looked so happy. Afterwards, back in the apartment, having left Herb and Ed and Mort and Bette to sober up in Central Park, Kitty had been clearing the glasses away to the music Maurice had put on when he said: 'Come and sit down, Kit.'

She felt suddenly shy, as if she had to face him, her future husband, for the first time alone, and had fussed with the glasses and the empty bottles until he had taken her by the hand and led her to the sofa.

Maurice had taken a small box from his pocket and laid it in her lap. Kitty, a middle-aged woman, had forgotten about rings – it was only afterwards that she realised Maurice was playing 'take this ring' from La Sonnambula – the traditional trappings of engagement which she associated with youth. She opened the velvet-lined box and saw an emerald in an antique setting of pearls which made her heart miss a bit.

'Nothing fancy,' Maurice said, and removing the ring from its box, put it on her finger over Sydney's worn wedding band. Kitty was suddenly afraid. That she might get ill and die. That Maurice might get ill and die as Sydney had, leaving her alone again. That their future together might be short lived. The moment passed. She must not be greedy. She embraced Maurice and forgot her throbbing head, and her doubts, and the fact that she was in New York, and had the curious sensation that for the first time since her widowhood she had come home.

Later Maurice said: 'There's something been bothering me, Kit'. He circled the room, his hands in his pockets, and Kitty waited for him to speak.

'The past is over,' he said, and Kitty knew that he meant the concentration camps in which he had lost so much. 'But it doesn't go away . . .'

He was looking out of the window, at the rooftops of New York, seeing things which she could not.

'. . . a door banging. Smoke from a chimney. A train moving off . . .'

He turned to face her. 'I have nightmares. I'm sitting naked in a tree with the snow on the ground while they hose me with icy water. Being buried alive. Sometimes I scream.'

'It will be all right,' Kitty said. She had slept for months beside Sydney while his frontal lobe tumour made its remorseless inroads on his brain. She was no stranger to suffering.

'I just wanted you to know,' Maurice said.

Afterwards everything seemed to have happened so fast. The rabbi from the *Kehillath Jeshurun* agreed to marry them and Maurice finalised the arrangements for the cruise. While Kitty wrote letters to her family – including Beatty and Mirrie and her nephew Norman who was getting married himself at Christmas time – in England, Bette, in her element, insisting that Kitty was nowhere near well enough to go shopping herself, indulged her role as 'image maker' and brought home boxes of clothes from Bloomingdale's for the bride's approval.

'I don't need anything,' Kitty said. She was not extravagant and had a wardrobe full of clothes at home suitable for Florida which she would ask Carol to send her but she allowed Bette to bring her some appropriate outfits from which she would choose one to wear at her wedding. Bette tried to get her into *eau de nil* or old rose but Kitty, being practical, insisted on something she would get some wear out of afterwards and settled for a classic grey suit, letting Bette have her head over the accessories and her own outfit as Kitty's attendant.

There was one disappointment. Rachel was not coming. In a graphic letter to Kitty, in which she explained how she had been packing up her belongings so that Patrick could make the move to Putney, where they had found a flat, while she was in New York, she described that suddenly moving her legs had felt like dragging around two lumps of wood, and that her normally tiny face had become puffy. She had made an appointment at the clinic where it was found that her blood pressure was raised and they had said that she must on no account travel, and that it was unwise to move house and that she must either come into hospital where she could rest or go where she could be looked after. At Patrick's insistence – and against her will – Rachel had gone to stay with his parents in Winnington Road where his mother could wait on her. She was devastated not to be coming to New York for Kitty's wedding.

It had cast a blight on Kitty's happiness.

'What do you think is the matter with her?' she asked Maurice.

'Sounds like toxaemia.'

'Is there a cure?'

'Birth.'

'She's got another six weeks,' Kitty said.

While Maurice was out picking up the travel documents for the honeymoon trip she had taken his medical encyclopaedia from the shelf and found 'toxaemia' in the index. When he returned with the tickets – 'The Royal Caribbean Cruise Line welcomes *Dr and Mrs Morgenthau* to the "Song of Norway" and wishes them *Bon Voyage*' – Kitty was sitting with the appropriate volume on her lap.

'"One in ten women suffer from toxaemia in their first pregnancy",' she quoted, '"and are considered at risk".' Maurice took away the book, but Kitty could see from his expression that Rachel's symptoms must be considered seriously. That she would hate it at the Klopmans' Kitty had no doubt. While Hettie was kind enough – there was not a selfish bone in her body – her lifestyle was anathema to Rachel who would not take kindly to the enforced proximity with Herbert and his jokes.

So it was that at her wedding Kitty, like Maurice, had had no one of her own. Rachel's discovery of the complication of her pregnancy had come too late for Josh to cancel his dental patients and Carol was in no condition to travel had she wanted to.

Two days before the wedding Kitty had attended an identification parade at the 19th Precinct. A row of youths with numbered placards round their necks were lined up before a two way mirror and she was asked to point out her assailants. She thought one of them looked vaguely familiar and he was asked to step closer, then she was by no means sure and shook her head. The men were marched away and Kitty was not sorry for she did not want to be responsible for putting any mother's son in prison, but she was glad that she would have the respite of Florida before she must once more face the New York streets.

The wedding had been dignified and simple: the most moving moment when Maurice unequivocally stepped on the glass. Bette had insisted on providing the wedding breakfast and the little party had gone back to her flat for a sumptuous buffet catered by Fraser-Morris, after which, in an embarrassing shower of confetti, they had left for the airport.

The days following the wedding had not yet resolved themselves in Kitty's mind which was awhirl still with new and unusual sensations. By the time they had left Palm Beach for Miami and boarded the 'Song of Norway', on which they would spend the next seven days, Kitty's last doubts about the wisdom of her decision had been resolved, and when she looked at her reflection, if she half closed her eyes she could convince herself that the face which regarded her, alight with happiness, was that of a girl. She did not think about Sydney. He was laid to rest peacefully, for all time, in her past. As the ship, cutting its way through the grey, uncompromising water, steamed in the direction of Cuba, Kitty, her face buffeted by the wind, looked forward with relief and contentment, to her new life.

That it would not be without problems she did not delude herself. They had already run into difficulties. Maurice, an inexperienced cruiser, was not gregarious, and the knowledge that he and Kitty must sit at a table with others in the 'King and I' dining-room had filled him with alarm.

The only activity in which he had so far joined (in accordance with International Law which required that all passengers be mustered at their lifeboat stations to be instructed in emergency procedure no more than twenty-four hours after leaving port) had been the boat drill.

Their table companions proved to be pleasant enough. Chuck ('What you all doin' today?) and Marlene (whose fourteen stones were not minimised by stretch pants by day and gossamer layers of pastel chiffon by night) from South Carolina, and Wayne and Susan, an ingenuous couple from Milwaukee with anti-seasick patches behind their ears, who had won the trip playing 'Guess the Price'. Kitty, all the way from England, with her funny accent and her hesitation the first night over the broiled fillet of Caribbean grouper about whose *kashrut* she had doubts, was the centre of attention. When the curiosity of their table companions – 'Are you retired?' and 'What line were you in?' – was directed towards Maurice, it was Kitty who answered. After the dessert he excused himself, telling Kitty to take her time over coffee and that he would see her on deck.

'My husband's not very sociable,' Kitty said when he'd gone – it was the first time she had used the nomenclature in reference to Maurice. 'He likes his own company.'

'My father's the same,' Marlene said. 'They get like that when you've been married a long time.'

'We're on our honeymoon,' Kitty said without thinking, and realised her mistake the moment the words were out. She didn't tell Maurice of her slip but the next evening, after the Cherries Jubilee, the white-jacketed *maitre d'* from Manila, flanked by a posse of waiters, entered the dining-room bearing a miniature wedding cake which to Kitty's mortification he put on the table in front of them, with 'the Captain's compliments'.

The band struck up with a chorus of 'Second Time Around' and the entire second-sitting rose to its feet and applauded.

Kitty, wishing the decks would open up, consigning her to the deep, looked at Maurice. He took it like a man. Afterwards, in the cabin, she apologised.

'I'll get over it,' he said, but she could see that it was not easy.

He did not avail himself of the ship's diversions. While Kitty went to the Welcome Aboard talk ('Turn to the person on your left and say, hi!'), the Grandmothers' Bragging Session (where she circulated photographs of Debbie and Lisa and Mathew and announced proudly that her quota of grandchildren was shortly to be doubled), and the daily Walk-a-Thon, where she strode round the deck determined to win her yellow ship's sun visor and tee shirt, Maurice sat with a book in the lee of the Promenade Deck or in a sheltered niche, protected from the sun by his white hat. She went alone to the South Pacific Lounge where the moustached cruise director (together with his 'lovely wife and singing partner, Sheree'), masterminded the Bon Voyage Get Together, to the Friday night service for the Jewish passengers in the Carousel Lounge where they served *matzoh* ball soup beneath a star of David sculpted in ice, to the Bridge Tournament in the Lounge of the Midnight Sun, and the afternoon screening (curtains closed over the portholes) of Barbra Streisand in 'Yentl'.

Maurice's withdrawal did not perturb her. She appreciated his tolerance of her own foibles and did not expect him to alter the habits of a lifetime. While he was happy for her to enjoy to the full the life on board ship, Kitty was content in the certainty that when she went in search of her new husband she would know instinctively in which secluded corner of the vessel she would find him.

There was one distraction on offer of which Maurice availed himself. Each evening after dinner would find him at the blackjack tables or watching the roulette wheel in the Casino Royale. Kitty was not a gambler. She stood behind the silent Maurice as he threw his chips on to the baize cloth, and it was only when they had been at sea for three nights that she realised that he always bet on the same numbers. The familiar sequence of them bothered her until with a shock she realised that the 2 and the 9 and 5 and the 3 and 1, monotonously repeated, were the numerals of the concentration camp number she saw nightly engraved on his arm. When she realised what he was doing she no longer cared to watch him play. She'd wait for him on deck and, to the faint sounds of 'My Way' or the 'Tritch Tratch Polka' coming from the dance floor, they'd stroll arm in arm beneath the stars, and Maurice's tongue, for Kitty alone, would become unleashed and in the mutual shorthand of small talk and ideas they would pass the time until bed.

Kitty, in her reverie, leaning on the ship's rail, wondered sometimes if she deserved such happiness, two bites at life's cherry when there were so many unfortunate people – her sister-in-law Mirrie, for instance – who had not even managed one. She did not hear Maurice come up behind her but was aware that he was there. When he put his arms round her she turned to him and, as the 'Song of Norway' scythed rhythmically through the awe-inspiring deeps towards Grand Cayman and Jamaica, laid her head on his accommodating shoulder.

Chapter Twenty

While Kitty enjoyed the Caribbean sun, Rachel railed against her enforced inactivity in Patrick's parents' house in Winnington Road. She was not used to being idle. She was never ill and had always felt superior to her sister Carol, made of what Rachel had considered less stern stuff and prey throughout her life to a succession of minor illnesses either real or imagined. That her own pregnancy, in which Rachel had been revelling in her image of earth mother, might turn out to be complicated had not entered her head. She who had been convinced of her influence on events – from conception to the therapeutic rendering of 'Ten Green Bottles' – and that any deviation from the norm, or weakness, was in the mind, had received a blow to her pride. It was mortifying to be reminded that the workings of one's body were not, as she had previously considered, entirely under one's own control.

As she lay in bed in Hettie's guest room with its William Morris curtains, its matching bedspreads, and its toning carpet which unsubtly picked up the dominant yellow of the print, Rachel had more than enough time to think. She had already entered the lists with her mother-in-law who, now that she had Rachel physically in her clutches, had increased her efforts to influence the life of her first grandchild even before it was born. As she brought up bowls of home-made broth or bunches of grapes (as if she were really ill) for Rachel's delectation, she would sit on the bed and, her eyes sparkling with enthusiasm, tell her daughter-in-law of the crib bedecked with a million layers of peach tulle – such as had graced the royal nursery – or a streamlined pram (which converted with a 'hey-presto' into a carrycot) which she had seen. Rachel, having bought a Moses basket at Camden Lock, and a sling in which she would transport her child for the first four months of its life – after which it would be the folding buggy – was unmoved.

She did not dislike Hettie who, glad to have some purpose to her life, was killing her with daily doses of kindness, but there seemed to be no meeting point between them. She fed her patient tit-bits from the delicatessen when Rachel yearned for her familiar casseroles of mung beans and tofu, and came, seeking to please her, into the bedroom with armfuls of glossy magazines (women as object) and copies of Maisie Mosco.

Their only mutual interest was Kitty, and already, each reading the other her postcards with the news of the wedding and the forthcoming honeymoon in Florida, the subject had been done to death. Despite herself, when Kitty in juxtaposition to Maurice was discussed, Rachel, irrationally, still felt her hackles rise. While her good wishes to her mother on the telephone and by letter had been genuine enough – she dearly wanted her to be happy – something within her still screamed 'Judas' and she dreamed many a night of her dead father. No matter how hard she tried to sort the matter out in her head, to make Kitty's welfare her prime concern, her mother, in committing herself to Maurice Morgenthau, had gone down several notches in Rachel's estimation. To hear Hettie discuss the romance as if her mother's elderly suitor was Prince Charming and Kitty herself Cinderella, sickened Rachel and she preferred to direct the conversation to Hettie's main concern, what she was going to put on her daughter-in-law's tray, with its drawn-thread traycloth, for her next meal.

Herbert, surprisingly, was more congenial. Rachel had even grown used to the jokes. Delighted to have a captive audience he would come up to her bedroom as soon as he got home at night and sit on her bed, trying to make her laugh: 'A Jewish doctor gave a patient six months to live but when the man didn't pay he gave him another six months!

'How's your mother enjoying Florida? 'Mr Cohen comes home one night and starts to pack his bags.

'So where are you going?' asks his wife.

'To Tahiti.'

'Tahiti? Why Tahiti?'
'Simple. Every time you make love there they give you $5.'
Then Mrs Cohen starts packing her bags.
'And where are *you* going?' asks Mr Cohen.
'I'm also going to Tahiti.'
'Why?'
'I want to see how you make out on $10 a year!'

'Did you hear the one about a group of Jewish women who wanted to improve their intellectual level? No more talk of maids or children – but only politics and social questions: Poland, El Salvador, Afghanistan, the Bomb. Then one said 'And what about Red China?' 'I love it! I love it!' says another member of the group. 'Especially on a nice white tablecloth!'

Once she had reconciled herself to her father-in-law's stories – some of which were not unamusing – his commitment to find the Jew in everything, and his appraisal of people according to the degree of their support for Israel, Rachel found him straightforward, informative and entertaining, and loved to hear stories of the famous old-time Jewish coach 'Yussel the muscle', who had managed Max Schmeling, and the boxers, Ted 'Kid' Lewis and Jack 'Kid' Berg, who had come out of the East End after the First World War.

'Houdini was a Jew,' Herbert said one night as he gave Rachel the evening paper. 'His name was Ehrich Weiss and he was born in Budapest. His father was a rabbi. They called him Ehrie for short, which when they went to America became "Harry". He took "Houdin" from Jean Eugène Robert-Houdin, "The Father of Modern Magic", and later, as a stage musician, added the "i", Harry Houdini.'

Through Herbert, whose eyes lit up at the mere recitation of their names, Rachel learned to know the Jewish footballers, Abe Rosenthal – his hero – Bela Guttman from Hungary, Miles Spector, the Chelsea left winger, Avi Cohen and Mordecai Spiegler from present day Israel over which country, Rachel discovered, she and her father-in-law were on the same side. Herbert Klopman, of everyone she knew, endorsed her political views.

Sometimes Herbert's mother, old Mrs Klopman, coming into Rachel's room without knocking whenever the mood took her, interrupted the discussions, picking up the fag ends of the conversation and adding her own two penn'orth.

'A lot of stuff and nonsense,' she'd say when the subject came round to the military actions of the Palestinian refugees. 'My grandmother, God rest her soul, was a refugee, but I ask you, did that make her a terrorist? Sure it did not.'

When her son talked about 'the Jews', she'd say: 'For heaven's sake, Herbert, it's as bad as talking about "the Irish", you dehumanise people, put them in a lomp, isolate them from the human race.'

Rachel got on well with Patrick's grandmother. When Herbert was at business and Hettie out shopping, at which she seemed to spend an inordinate amount of time, or at the Children's Home, she'd have long discussions with old Mrs Klopman whose views on childbirth seemed to have skipped a generation. From the choice of cradle on which she sided with Rachel against Hettie ('Sure, as long as you've got a drawer to lay them in') to the management of the newborn, their views coincided. According to old Mrs Klopman (who didn't hold with hospital maternity wards where the babe was put behind glass in a cot to cry itself to sleep because nobody came nigh nor by), he should rest in enfolding arms near to his mother's heart, hearing the sound of her voice, close to the warmth of her breast.

'Carol's having a nanny,' Rachel said. 'She's decorating the nursery in the new house with yellow ducklings.'

'Yellow ducklings or no, it'll not be different from the maternity ward,' old Mrs Klopman said. 'He'll be wanting and waiting from one feed to the next. Will I tell you a secret, Rachel? I had Herbert at the breast until he was two years old.'

Carol had been to see her, and Sarah, each commiserating with the unfortunate turn Rachel's pregnancy had taken. Josh had made enquiries but she refused to allow him to visit.

Carol looked out of the window of the train as it trundled towards Godalming and hugged to herself the surprise that she was going to give Alec. Because of the persistent nausea and discomfort which had prevented her both from choosing her own decorations for the new house (apart from the yellow ducklings) and getting down as often as she would like to Godalming, Morris Goldapple had insisted on another ultrasound scan, although strangely enough in the last few days the malaise which had dogged her for the past nine months had lifted, and despite her bulk she felt an unaccustomed energy, a lightness of mind and body.

Before the other children were born she had thrown herself into an excess of house cleaning, 'feathering her nest', Alec had called it. In her temporary accommodation in her mother's flat there was little point. She had prepared her nursery – temporary until such time as the move could be made to the yellow ducklings – packed her case and the baby's vests and matinée jackets (opening it a dozen times a day to see if there was anything she had forgotten), prepared small gifts for Debbie and Lisa and Mathew to compensate for each day of her absence, and installed the nanny – a pleasant enough girl whose presence would give her more time for her writing – in her smart brown uniform.

There was nothing to do now but wait for the onset of her labour to which she was not in the least looking forward. She was, she admitted, a coward. While her sister Rachel had, for the last six months, lain on the floor with dozens of other women in rows like beached whales, huffing and puffing in an attempt to simulate natural childbirth, Carol had put her faith in Morris Goldapple with his epidural – which according to Rachel came into the same category as surgical inductions, unnecessary episiotomies, the use of forceps and caesarean sections which were purely for his own convenience and that of the hospital staff – to ensure a painless delivery. Rachel, for all her didactic approach to parturition, her lofty assertion that 'a healthy woman is not designed to suffer in childbearing: she is wonderfully constructed and equipped for this her most desirable attainment', had no idea what it was about. No matter how much you huffed and puffed, no matter how many times you sang 'Ten Green Bottles' in an effort to relax, there was no getting away from the fact that giving birth was like no other thing on earth, and that the pain of it was both indescribable and unbearable. It was not simply a question of physical exertion. Pushing a baby out was a sheer wrench of undiluted agony. What Rachel, in her determination to imitate childbirth in the bush or the harem, failed to consider were the prolapses, the puerperal fever and all manner of other equally 'natural' but undesirable consequences that her proposed behaviour might precipitate. Rachel had accused Carol of compliance, of being turned into a mere receptacle by Morris Goldapple who insisted that the foetal heartrate could only be monitored satisfactorily (ensuring that the baby was not suffering undue stress or being deprived of oxygen) if the mother were lying down, and who would have no truck with his patients crawling around a darkened room on all fours. Rachel would have to find out for herself.

Morris Goldapple had broken the news gently. In his elegant rooms – which had become familiar to Carol through the births of Debbie and Lisa and Mathew – where she had gone for her consultation, he had settled her in the comfortable armchair and, being an old friend of the family, enquired about her mother. When Carol had finished telling him about Kitty's marriage and the honeymoon cruise, Morris had pulled up a chair beside her and put a fatherly hand on hers.

'I think we've discovered the cause of your discomfort . . .'

Rachel had told her she was neurotic.

'. . . there are *two* babies.'

Wait till she told Rachel!

'One was behind the other. Because of the way they are lying it wasn't obvious before.'

'Twins?' Carol said, only just taking it in.

'Think you can manage two?'

With Debbie and Lisa and Mathew that made five.

'Would you like a glass of water?' Morris said.

He had tried to call Alec but the surgery number was engaged. Then Carol had a better idea – she would go down to Godalming, it wouldn't take long on the train – and break the news to Alec herself.

She had never thought that she would get used to Godalming, to life outside the London streets, but now, as the train approached, she realised how much she missed the rural peace, the delicate air, the walks with Alec and the children in the grounds of Charterhouse with its spring daffodils, its summer magnolias, the car-park 'Pay and Display' outside the supermarket where she did her weekly shopping, the shops – Pepperpot Cards, Bookshelf Bargain, and Caprice (Gifts) – where she was known. The Queen Anne house, progressing slowly in the hands of the dilatory builders, would not now be ready until after Christmas. Carol could hardly wait.

Jessica had been a godsend. According to Alec there were no pains to which she would not go to select a finish or secure a fabric she had set her heart on. On the one occasion Carol had met her, in her hard hat and riding gear, striding through the bare rooms with her ideas and her enthusiasms 'That would look simply super!' and her 'Absolutely not!' Carol had realised that the extensive decorations were a great deal more than she was able to cope with and had been happy to leave the decisions and the running around entailed in Jessica's capable hands. More than she missed Godalming, Carol had missed Alec. Not the physical relationship – due to her uncomfortable pregnancy there had thankfully been little lately, of that – but the daily intimate contact, sharing the nuts and bolts of their lives. She had written a poem eulogising married love which she would send to Kitty when it was published.

She put a surreptitious hand on the front of her expandable dungarees beneath which her two babies lay intertwined. 'Be fruitful and multiply' the Torah commanded. She and Alec had certainly done their duty in that direction. In others, too. Often Carol wished her father was alive to see Debbie and Lisa's command of Hebrew, their knowledge of the Biblical stories and understanding of the festivals as taught to them by a Miss Wiseman who had retired to Guildford and had come over weekly to Peartree Cottage. Josh – apart from the lip service he paid to the religion to support Sarah's conversion – had turned his back on Sydney's teachings, and Rachel was interested only in Israel, her views about which had alienated her from Josh. It made Carol uncomfortable. With her mother away she felt, as the oldest daughter, responsible somehow for the family and did not like the constant bickering and dissent.

It was ridiculous really. They were all in the same boat, having babies, and there should have been a pleasant atmosphere, a sort of jolly togetherness, instead of which, until her forced incarceration at Hettie Klopman's, Rachel would not visit Carol when Josh was there and Josh didn't want to meet Rachel – whose behaviour towards him he found offensive – and Sarah wasn't too keen on talking to Rachel because Josh was upset, and Patrick, taking Rachel's side, thought it better that the two of them kept well away from one another. Kitty would not have stood for such nonsense.

Carol could see both points of view. She appreciated that although there were those, like her brother and sister, who cared vehemently, deeply, blindly, about issues, she seemed never herself to hold strong opinions about anything. Her shilly-shallying extended to her mother's marriage. She wanted Kitty to be happy. It had been no fun, she could see, being a widow, but she wasn't at all sure about Maurice Morgenthau. Firstly he was too old. Secondly they did not share a common background. Maurice had seemed a gruff sort of fellow, uncouth in a way, not like her late father with his impeccable manners. It was done now. She hoped Kitty wouldn't live to regret her decision.

Godalming. The familiar station with its hanging baskets which in summer were ablaze with busy lizzies and geraniums, its ticket office, 'Take Off for France' and 'Day Trips from London'. It felt like coming home. In the station yard, peaceful as she remembered it, flooded with the pallid winter sun, there were no taxis. Carrying herself carefully, heavily, mindful of the jutting stones, she started to walk down the hill and through Mint Street, taking the short cut past the DIY centre and the Salvation Army with its weathered proclamation: 'Jesus said I am the way and the truth and the life. No one comes to the Father except through me.' As she progressed warily along the High Street where the disposition of the shops was inscribed like a litany in her head, she glimpsed her reflection, rotund and cumbersome, against the seductive arrangements of wares in the sun-glinted windows.

At Alec's hotel the receptionist in her glass booth was on the telephone: '. . . I paid £28 for the operation – it was the biggest stone they'd ever seen – and when she came round they said 'What sort of food does she eat? – ' which Carol thought was rather strange until she realised that the girl was talking about her cat.

She put her hand over the receiver while she told Carol that Alec was neither in the bar nor the restaurant, in fact if she wasn't mistaken she had seen Dr Caplan go out half an hour ago, then waved dismissively and went back to her call. Although she was hungry, having expected to lunch with Alec at the hotel, Carol decided to walk, slowly, which was all she was capable of, up the hill to the new house where she guessed she would find him supervising the position of an electrical outlet, or the crazy paving on the broad terrace outside the dining-room into which, at Jessica's suggestion, they had installed picture windows. She glanced in the shops, not hurrying, savouring the news that she carried. She wanted to tell it to the passing pedestrians with their baskets, to proclaim it in the Godalming streets.

The door of the Queen Anne house was open. Outside it she was relieved to see Alec's Volvo – his stethoscope on the seat, and the sign on the windscreen 'Doctor Visiting' – and Jessica's Land-Rover with its chrome mascot. In the hall which smelled of new wood, particles of dust, floating in a beam of sunlight, followed her in from the street. The house was taking shape. Half closing her eyes she could imagine it, now that the steels and the joists were in place, occupied by herself and Alec and Debbie and Lisa and Mathew and the two babies, not like Peartree Cottage where there hadn't been room to move.

In the quiet she moved silently across the ground floor. They were installing a country kitchen which was being made by Jessica's local craftsmen out of yew. The pipes – essential services – were still being laid. Open-ended, they traversed the floor and protruded from the walls. From the sitting-room Carol looked out at the pecking blackbirds on the neglected lawn. On the staircase, curved and romantic, down which she would sweep like Scarlett O'Hara – when she was no longer pregnant and like a barge in full sail – an electric drill and a neat pile of workman's overalls blocked her way. On top of them she recognised Jessica's hard hat. She stepped carefully, mindful of her condition. The rooms on the first landing were empty, the plaster newly wet. They would be ready soon for decorating, the final phase. Carol's feet, in her sensible rubber-soled shoes — she wasn't taking any chances — made no sound on the hardboard with which the builders had covered the oak floor as she approached the master bedroom.

She opened the door, taking pleasure in its width and elegance. Jessica and Alec were out of sight in the dressing-room; she could hear them talking.

'Are you going to be long with those swatches? We're wasting the whole afternoon.' Alec's baritone with which she had fallen in love.

Something in his voice made Carol pause, her hand on the old-fashioned doorknob.

'How does terracotta grab you for the blinds, darling?' Jessica's clipped tones.

Carol blinked, wondering if she had misheard.

'They can be sky-blue-pink for all I care!'

'Alec! All those patterns were in order . . .' Jessica's voice tailed off.

'God, I love you.' It was Alec who spoke.

There was a silence so long that Carol thought she would faint then a low laugh, Jessica's.

'Look, you go ahead. The key's in my bag. I must wait and have a quick word with the foreman . . .'

Another silence. Interminable.

'Don't be long.' Alec again.

Jessica's sigh.

Carol shut the door soundlessly. Afterwards she could not remember leaving the house.

Chapter Twenty-one

Southbeach Oceanfront Motel
Key West
Florida   USA
5pm (I've lost track of the date)

'Dear Rachel,
'I am writing this outside our bedroom on a wooden balcony overlooking the Atlantic Ocean in the southermost city of the United States (ninety miles to Cuba!). Maurice has gone for a walk. He likes to be by himself for a good part of the day ("Solitude has two advantages, one in being by yourself and two, in not being with other people", he says some funny things) and I don't interfere. There was so much going on, on the "Song of Norway" – I've got my "I'M SHIPSHAPE" sun visor and tee-shirt for the Walk-a-Thon (see photo, that's me with the dumbells) – that there was only time for postcards, so now that I've got a moment I'll try to gather my thoughts together. It seems so long since the wedding (I was broken hearted you weren't there, once I'd got used to the idea you were coming) and the flight to Miami – which is like New York, Hackney and Haifa rolled into one – where we picked up a car and drove to Palm Beach.

'Imagine walking about on the set of "Dynasty" – where every way you turn you bump into a Joan Collins or a Linda Evans, designered down to the last eyelash – and you have Worth Avenue. Our suite at the Breakers Hotel, which Maurice had booked for the first two nights, was the size of my entire flat back home and made me feel like a cross between Marilyn Monroe and the President of General Motors. Maurice wanted everything to be nice so I didn't say anything, but it wasn't really "me". The whole trip neither, really, even the ship with the bands and the streamers when you went on board and the plastic grass on deck with the steward going round with his tray of Piñā Coladas. It certainly wasn't Maurice.

'Key West is different. It's very relaxed – you go around in shorts all day (I'm getting to be a real American grandmother) – even to a restaurant. Our motel is right on the beach and we spend the day reading, walking and swimming from the little jetty. I don't go out far because Maurice doesn't take his eyes off me – it was the same in the ship's pool, he used to stand on the side holding my bathrobe – I think he's afraid of losing me. The sunsets here are indescribable and every evening we drive out to the fishing pier, where they catch the sardines, to watch the colours in the sky as the sun goes down beneath the water and the light fades.

'To get back to the cruise. The first night out, the Eastern Airlines passengers' luggage hadn't arrived. One woman was very upset, she had nothing to wear but her travelling clothes, so I lent her something for dinner and we became quiet friendly. Her name is Rose and she comes from Washington.

'Our first port of call was the island of Grand Cayman (Big Crocodile), shaped like a footprint in the sand. We arrived in the early morning and went ashore by tender because of the Coral Reef. We had a quick look round George Town (450 banks!) where I bought two angelic hand-embroidered dresses for Debbie and Lisa, black coral cuff-links for Josh and Alec and Patrick, and necklaces for you girls, before catching the bus for the green turtle farm. I could have done without the turtles! Tiny hatchlings to 600 pound giants displayed in large round tanks. If I was a marine biologist I suppose I could have raised some enthusiasm (apparently Prince Philip went crazy about them), but as it was, although some of the patterns on the shells were quite pretty, the turtles seemed uninteresting creatures and left me cold and I wasn't sorry when we left for the Buccaneer Beach Party at Seven Mile Beach. There were organised sports – Egg Throw and Volley Ball – for the energetic, but you know me, I couldn't wait to get into the water which, without exaggeration, was aquamarine and indigo. They set up lunch in two large tents and we ate it at a wooden table on the beach in the shade of a casuarina tree, our feet on a carpet of pine cones. I tried to believe that you were coming up to winter and that the days must be drawing in, but England seemed so far away.

'Jamaica was exciting. You should have seen the hummingbirds, Rachel, with their green and black heads, hovering in front of the hibiscus. Of course we couldn't see everything in one day so we chose the tour of Ocho Rios and Dunn's River Falls where the kids stripped off to climb the waterfall. You should have heard the shrieks! Apparently it's not as difficult as it looks on the photo but rather them than me! Maurice and I took the easy way, down the steps in the shade of the banyans, to the beach. When we reached the bay a Jamaican child no older than Mathew sidled up to me and wanted to hold my hand. Maurice took my photograph with him (against a background of the Falls) and you can see by the little boy's smile that it really made his day.

'Cozumel, off the coast of Mexico, and one of the Mayan holy places, was something for Maurice who loves anything to do with the past. We went on a rickety bus to an archaeological site dating back to the early classical period. I enclose a snapshot of Maurice (doesn't he look cute in his shorts and long socks and baseball cap?) listening, lost to the world, to the guide. After the ruins we drove south to the tropical gardens (250 different species of plant) and I swam again (I'm brown as a berry) this time in the Chancanaab Lagoon.

'The photograph where we're all sitting round the table with red eyes (from the flash, our waiter took it) is the Captain's Gala Dinner – hence the balloons – which was followed by a masquerade. Rose went as a bowl of fruit. After that it was back to Miami, arriving in the early morning. I had to clear immigration because of my British passport and it was quite sad exchanging addresses with our new friends (Maurice stayed in the cabin and told me to tell them goodbye) although I don't suppose we shall ever see any of them again.

So far since we've been here in Key West we have taken the Conch Tour Train round the island, climbed to the top of the lighthouse and been to the Sponge Market and the Shell Warehouse (I've bought a beautiful encrusted box for Bette Birnstingl). Tomorrow we're going to the Hemingway House – I've promised to send Ed a postcard – and the Geiger Mansion where Audubon (Birds of America) studied the wildlife native to the Keys.

'When I think that if Addie Jacobs hadn't slipped on the ice and broken her ankle I wouldn't have gone to Eilat alone, and if I hadn't gone to Eilat I wouldn't have met Maurice, and if I hadn't met Maurice . . . What I'm trying to say in my clumsy way is how unbelievable it is that I am sitting here in this paradise feeling so very happy (I am quite recovered from the "episode"), waiting for Maurice who has made it all possible. He says that when we get back to New York I'm not to dream of walking around alone, that he'll take me shopping in the car, but although I'm very apprehensive I won't let him.

'I worry about you often, Rachel – sometimes I don't think of anything else. I hope you and Josh have stopped your silly nonsense. I know Hettie will take good care of you. Give her and Herbert and Mrs Klopman and all the others my love. As always, Mummie (Kitty Morgenthau!).'

'I guess I should carry you over the threshold,' Maurice said as they stood outside his apartment with their luggage.

'You'd have a job,' Kitty said, waiting while her new husband unlocked the door.

Joe had stacked the letters in neat piles on the sofa. At a quick glance Kitty recognised one from Carol, one from Beatty, one from Hettie Klopman and one from Josh.

'Nobody ever writes me,' Maurice said. 'Why don't you go ahead and read your mail while I see to the cases?'

Kitty sat on the sofa and picked up the letter from Carol. It was hard to believe that she had been away for three weeks which had passed as if in a dream.

'Ain't but one road there and one road back,' their cruise table-companion Chuck had said when he'd heard that they were driving to Key West. 'Best sport fishin' in the world . . .'

'We don't fish,' Kitty said.

'. . . Mutton snapper, ballyhoo, barracuda, sharks, tarpon, bottom fishing for grouper . . . take you fo'er hours. Back in the old days would've tooken you twelve hours, if you made the ferry on time, if there weren't a hurricane. An' be sure an' stop at the Green Turtle, everyone knows the Green Turtle.'

'Ain't but one road there and one road back.'

Chuck had been right about the road. Alone with Maurice, just the two of them after the distraction of the ship, Kitty had enjoyed the drive through the chain of islands which stretched from Biscayne Bay on the mainland to the Dry Tortugas in the Florida Straits. The first part of the journey had been disappointing as they passed mile after mile of liquor stores, boat rentals, motels, realtors and Highway Patrol stations, then suddenly they were slipping between the Atlantic ocean and the green Gulf waters, cruising without warning high over the ultramarine ocean on Seven Mile Bridge. Maurice switched on the radio: 'A Stranger in Paradise', 'My Heart Cries for You', and 'Lili Marlene'.

Kitty had never been so happy. As far as her new relationship with Maurice was concerned, about which she had been so apprehensive, she need not have worried. She had forgotten, or blotted out, the importance of physical happiness between a man and a woman, the bond that it creates.

As they slipped silently through the changing landscape with its grey pelicans swooping overhead, its snowy egrets, Maurice covered her hand with his and they joined in with the tunes: 'I Love You for Sentimental Reasons' and 'Sentimental You'.

'Happy?' Maurice said.

There was no need for a reply.

'I told you it would be alright.'

And it was.

Kitty realised suddenly that, as Maurice had suggested when he'd asked her to come to New York, she was living for herself, for Kitty Shelton – Kitty Morgenthau, she would have to remember – and was neither worrying about Rachel and Carol and Josh and the grandchildren with their problems, nor the vicissitudes of the Day Centre, nor the problems of her sisters-in-law or her neighbour, Addie Jacobs, for whom life never seemed to go smoothly, but had a peace and silence in her head, a quiet acceptance (with Maurice by her side) of the here and now. She recognised it, at the same moment as she did its transience, as happiness.

'Never look for happiness,' she recalled her late mother's voice. 'It will land, like a butterfly, on your shoulder.' Kitty put a hand to the top of her arm.

'Cold?' Maurice said.

She shook her head.

Blue Crab, Stone Crab, Garlic Crab, Raw Bar, Conch chowder, Seafood . . .

'I'm on the sea-food diet,' Maurice – who would be in his element in the keys – had said when they'd first met, 'I see food and I eat it.'

Kitty had come to terms with her new husband's dietary predelictions which at first, having lived so long with Sydney, had shocked her, but she had learned to close her eyes to Maurice's aberrations.

The Southbeach Oceanfront Motel, where they paid in advance for their room and carried their own bags past the swimming-pool and ice dispenser and the Coca-Cola machine at the foot of the wooden stairs, was not a place which Sydney (fussy about where he stayed) would have chosen. He would not have dined on Lobster Marquesa in 'Louie's Back Yard', walking back beneath the stars along Duval, lunched at 'La-ti-da' where the waiters, dressed in pink, flaunted their homosexuality, or relaxed in the evening bar at 'Papa Hemingway's'.

Her two husbands were as different as it was possible to be and Kitty realised that there was no question about not loving either of them. Now, back in New York, in Maurice's apartment – her apartment, Maurice was going to redecorate it and move his paintings back to the studio – reading the letters which too quickly, too abruptly, brought back the real world, it was hard to believe in the lazy Key West days, the tropical Southbeach nights with Maurice. Reading her letters she doubted already if the Military Museum with its display of artefacts with which Maurice had been fascinated, the Sponge Market and the Shell Warehouse where she had bought the box for Bette Birnstingl had ever existed outside of her imagination. Until he came into the room with the cases, which later Joe would take downstairs, she almost wondered if she had imagined Maurice himself. He sat beside her among the discarded envelopes on the sofa and she noticed, for the first time, now that they were back, the depth of his tan.

'Kitty, what's wrong?'

She looked at her sunhat on the easel where Maurice had hung it, at its red and yellow ribbons, as if to reassure herself of her respite from the world before she came to meet it head on.

'Carol's had twins, Rachel's no better, Alec wants a divorce, and Beatty's got a lump!'

Chapter Twenty-two

Carol, her movements slow, her eyes red with weeping, opened the letter with its familiar writing, its New York stamp. At this nadir of her life, the tribulation with which for the past few weeks she had been living, she missed Kitty, needing someone to direct her, someone to tell her what she must do. Glad as she was to see the letter however, for which she had been waiting, if the truth were known it was Sydney for whom at this moment she most sorely pined. Kitty was loving, practical, sympathetic, but it was her father who had known about the rightness of things, who did not prevaricate, was not afraid to mete out justice when justice needed to be done. He would have known what to do about Alec, how to cope with a situation in which Carol, in her most extravagant dreams, had never imagined herself.

With Debbie and Lisa at the school which had accepted them on a temporary basis, Mathew at the zoo with Aunty Beatty – who liked to have something to take her mind of the tumour which had been discovered in her breast, about which she did not question the doctors too closely – and her babies, Poppy and Sara, out for their morning walk with their nanny, Carol allowed herself, as she did over and over, to relive the afternoon at Godalming when, a winged messenger, she had carried to their prospective father the news about his twins. Night and day, as at a scab, she picked at the memory – taking perverse delight in the pain, the release of fresh blood – knowing the wound would never heal. Sometimes the revisitation began with Morris Goldapple and his revelation of the news of the two babies, sometimes with the beam of dusty sunlight through which she had walked in the hallway of the Queen Anne house. What a fool she had been. 'Jessica thinks picture windows for the dining-room.' 'Don't trouble to look for fabric for the girls' rooms, Jessica will sort something out.' And all the time Alec had been . . . She could not bring herself to use, not even in her head, the expression which had become common usage.

She didn't know what she had been expecting. She'd known Jessica was in the house, had seen her car outside with its equine mascot, her hat on the stairs. The exchange was recorded in her head. She kept playing it over and over: 'How does terracotta grab you for the blinds, darling?' 'They can be sky-blue-pink for all I care . . .' 'Alec! All those patterns were in order . . .' 'God, I love you.'

He had loved her once, had reiterated his vows solemnly beneath the marriage canopy before he broke the traditional glass. She remembered the wedding. 'How goodly are thy tents, O Jacob', the welcoming psalm which had filtered through to the Bride's Room as she waited, with Kitty fussing round her, to go into the synagogue. 'Blessed be you' as she leaned against Sydney so distinguished in his morning suit for the trembling journey up the aisle. The covenant of wedlock, delivered in Alec's firm voice: 'Behold, thou art consecrated unto me . . . according to the Law of Moses and of Israel.' Afterwards he had signed the declaration: '. . . I faithfully promise that I will be a true husband unto thee . . .' to which, in turn, she had plighted her troth, 'in affection and with sincerity'.

A lot of words, empty and meaningless, which as far as Alec was concerned had ended with an interior decorator in Godalming. Neither of them had noticed her as she left the Queen Anne house. She had made no sound as she retraced her steps down the dusty staircase, past Jessica's hat, across the littered hallway and out into the midday winter sun.

She did not see the 'Commissioners for Oaths', the 'Conservative Club', the 'Fine Art Galleries', with the pastels of dogs with mouths full of game, the shoe repairers, the 'Coal, Corn and Seed' merchants which in summer offered bar-b-q brickettes. She walked past Boots and the Health and Diet Centre and Woolworths and W.H. Smith and the Electricity Showroom and Shopper's Paradise with its Ivyleaf butter on special offer. If there were custard tarts and iced buns and scones and imitation wedding cakes in the window of La Boulangerie she did not see them. She did not see the Midland Bank with its service till, nor Angel Court with its bookshop, nor the Salvation Army missive: 'Jesus said I am the way and the truth and the life. No one comes to the Father except through me.' She did not stop until she came to the station, indeed had no recollection of how she reached it, and it was there, on the seat beneath the hanging baskets which in summer were ablaze with busy lizzies and ivy leaf geraniums, that she had her first contraction.

It was ironic really. She who, aided and abetted by Morris Goldapple, had planned her confinement so meticulously, orchestrated it in every detail to ensure her oblivion, minimise the pain, had given birth wide awake in the cottage hospital, in the ambulance almost, in a maelstrom of shouted instructions and running feet and whooshing trolleys and clanging doors and rushing waters and body-splitting agony and slithering satisfaction. Afterwards, when it was quiet, and she had expended every atom of energy of which she was capable, more even, she had for a moment understood what Rachel had been rabitting on about in her vehement defence of natural childbirth, known that without the travail there would not have been the glory, without the descent into Gehenna not the exhaltation – as if she had been involved in the supreme act of love – then the memory of what had precipitated the birth had come flooding back and her triumph had become ashes and her achievement turned sour.

She had not wanted to see the babies on whom, indifferently, she had bestowed the first two names on her list, had turned her head away when they presented her with them, refused to give them her breast. When she finally agreed to acknowledge them they were strangers, duplicated reminders of what she felt to be her public disgrace.

Alec had been to see her. 'Carol . . .'

'Don't "Carol" me.'

She would not let him touch her. Would not talk to him. It was Josh who had come to take her home with the dark Poppy and the red-headed Sara whom she handed over like two featherweight parcels to the nanny.

Alec followed her to London. She could not deny him access to his children. He addressed her frozen face, her turned back. He made no secret of his feelings. He spoke of marrying Jessica who was already married. He wanted a divorce. Sometimes Carol was glad that her father was not alive to witness her humiliation. In the absence of her mother the family rallied round, even her Aunt Leonora and Uncle Juda who rarely involved themselves, but no one could get through to her. She hugged her suffering to her, mourning her marriage so summarily demised. Sometimes, somewhere, a voice whispered, citing her inadequacies, her inability to communicate with her husband as she would have liked. She did not listen to it. She wrote a poem about hurt and perfidy, and a letter to her mother in which she poured out her heart, waiting eagerly for a condemnation of Alec which would scorch the airmail paper, in reply.

'Darling Carol,
'To say I was shocked at your news – Alec, I mean, not the two babies – is to put it mildly. I didn't sleep for nights. You are a mother yourself and you must know how heartbreaking it is to see your children unhappy, you would rather be unhappy yourself. You must be feeling simply terrible (you always were a sensitive girl), especially just now after the birth when one often feels down in the dumps.

'First about the babies. The bad can wait. You can't imagine how happy I was (there have never been twins in our family) and how excited that this year I will have four instead of three new grandchildren. Poppy and Sara, what sweet names. One dark like you, and a red-head like Alec. I can't wait to see the photographs. So glad the nanny has turned out well – you'll have your hands full. Pleased too that Aunty Beatty is helping out, it will do her good, take her mind off herself.

'About the other. I can't say I'm not shocked. I've always loved Alec like a son as you know, thought very highly of him, as did your father who was a good judge of character. Carol, you're not going to like this. I'm not going to tell you what a wicked, terrible man he is and that you must have nothing more to do with him. Alec – correct me if I'm wrong – has always been a good husband, a good companion, a good father, a good provider. Something has gone wrong (I don't mean the interior decorator), I mean somewhere along the

ine and I don't know how to say this, you know I've never inter-
fered, but it's usually in the bedroom. It must seem like the end of
the world for you and that your life is finished (you must have had a
terrible shock, too) but believe me, darling, these things happen.
Even in the best regulated families. You'd be surprised. I could tell
you a thing or two about people whom you know. Life is not all
"ups" and roses round the door, and nobody's perfect even if it seems
that way and if it's what your father led you to believe.

'I'm not being disloyal to Sydney but you know that he had very
high standards which were sometimes, given the frailty of human
beings, unreal. I know how you must feel, believe me. I don't think
that Alec really wants to marry this Jessica either (how could he with
such a lovely wife and family?). Apart from wrecking several lives
(Alec's not like that) I'm sure that she's just a passing aberration
which he has to get out of his system. It must have been lonely for
him in Godalming with all of you in London and this Jessica around
all the time. I'm not making excuses for him. What I'm trying to
say is that although it can't seem that way at the moment, given
time, and goodwill on both sides, which I'm sure there is, things
will sort themselves out, blow over, and you will forget that it's all
happened. Don't tell too many people, later on you might be sorry.
Another thing. They have these experts now who help with mar-
riages when relationships go wrong. I don't say it's going to work
but, if you could persuade Alec, you could go together to a
counsellor who might help you work things out. Don't think,
Carol, that I'm being unsympathetic – you must feel as if the
bottom has dropped out of your world – just realistic.

'I don't want to bore you with my problems, you have more than
enough of your own, but since I came back from Florida I've been
getting these terrible headaches (they started the first night I was
back) and Maurice has made an appointment at the hospital – he
thinks it could be to do with the concussion. I don't think it's
anything to worry about. The worst thing is going out in the streets
– I'm absolutely terrified (alone I mean) and think that everyone is
going to attack me or snatch my handbag.

'Maurice sends his love and agrees with me about Alec. Happiness
is not given away with green stamps. Sometimes you have to fight
for it. I'm glad that you have Rachel and Josh to talk to. There's no

need to be alone. Perhaps if the two of them have something else to think about they'll forget this silly Israel business. I'm sure they're really on the same side although they're both too obstinate to see it. I'm not too happy about being here while at home this one's not speaking to that, and that one's fighting with the other. Life's too short for all that quarrelling and as Maurice says you shouldn't confuse the opinion with the man.

'I hadn't meant to go off on a side track. This letter's really about you and Alec. I can only advise you to try to keep your commonsense (of which you've always had plenty) and above all your dignity. I am convinced that in years to come you will look back at this painful time and put it into its proper perspective. I know you can't do that now. Don't try. Be angry. It's natural. But don't make any hasty decisions. Write as much as you like and I'll write back. Maurice says I spend my life writing letters. It's second best. We are busy arranging Maurice's apartment for the two of us but you don't want to hear about that now. I'm so sorry this should have happened to you, my thoughts are with you day and night, believe me.
Mother.'

'What news from Carol?' Maurice said.

Kitty looked up from the stack of letters which had arrived from England. They had been back from Florida for two weeks and she had to look at the photographs of herself in her sunhat at Dunn's River Falls or Maurice against the Mayan ruins to be convinced that they had been away at all. Maurice was at his easel, painting her portrait. While not exactly flattering, Kitty had to admit that Maurice had captured an essence of her, a distillation of her thoughts. If she looked at the likeness of herself, in bold strokes of apricot and grey, she could well imagine that she was about to say something to Rachel or to Carol, and she recognised the expression on Maurice's conception of her face. She was a good model. Unless it was essential she no longer went out in the mornings by herself or with Bette Birnstingl, preferring to avoid the threatening streets, and stayed in the flat with Maurice, reading or writing her letters to Tschaikovsky's Violin Concerto (which always made her think of home and her children) or the Haffner, or knitting for the twins.

She could no longer complain about the heat. She was not looking forward to a New York winter such as Bette had described for her. She was not looking forward to anything. Since coming back from Florida she had had difficulty in summoning up any energy, seemed to have lost her *joie de vivre*. She was not ill. She still had the headaches, quite unbearable at times, which had started the first night they had been back, but Maurice had taken her to the hospital where they had investigated her *ad nauseam* but found nothing which could account for them.

'There may still be some remains of intracranial bruising which doesn't show up,' the neurosurgeon had said. He advised her to take life quietly for a while and to come back to see him in a month if she was not better. Privately, she had not told Maurice, she was beginning to think that despite the investigations, the blow to her skull had been more traumatic than it had appeared. It wasn't only the headaches; at times her hands shook, she had difficulty in writing (her last letter to Carol had looked quite peculiar, as if it had been written by an old woman), and when she walked she seemed to have trouble moving her legs. Bette had wanted her to see her own doctor, she had this marvellous man, but Kitty, not wanting to upset Maurice, did not want to start all the tests and everything with somebody else.

Picking up Carol's letter, casting her eyes over it to answer Maurice's query, Kitty realised that for the first time since she had been a widow, she had someone with whom to share: her worries over Carol, her anxiety about Rachel, her concern about Beatty's lump.

'Alec's still besotted,' she said, 'Carol says he's gone completely mad. When she talks to him about the children, he doesn't want to listen.'

'Infatuation,' Maurice said, half closing his eyes as he added a brushful of madda to Kitty's hair. 'It's a form of insanity.'

'Will he get over it?'

Absorbed with his palette Maurice worked in silence for a long while. At one time Kitty would have thought he had not heard what she said. Now she knew better. She had opened the letter in Sarah's writing and read it before Maurice said: 'Time will tell.'

'Listen to this,' Kitty said, 'from Sarah.'

'Dear Kitty,

'I know that you have had more than enough to think about with your unpleasant experience and its consequences, your wedding and honeymoon, and Carol's twins – they really are adorable – and the unfortunate business with Alec, but I thought you would be glad to know that having completed the formalities I can say, like Ruth before me, that "your people" are now "my people".

'Thanks to Rabbi Magnus and Mrs Halberstadt I have at least fulfilled all the requirements of the Beth Din. They tested me on my knowledge of Hebrew and my familiarity with and willingness to observe the laws of Judaism. They could not of course look into my heart, but had they done so they would have found a religious soul which has at last found its proper expression. As you know, Josh did not want me to convert. Did not care whether I did or not. Now that it's all over I can see, and it's the best bonus of all (more than worth the two years hard grind), that he was speaking with his head and not his heart, and how important it is to him that when his son is circumcised it will be as though God is still speaking to him, just as he spoke to Abraham in Canaan nearly four thousand years ago.

'We went out for dinner to celebrate and Josh gave me a tiny gold star of David (Rachel had a good laugh when she saw it) to wear round my neck and for the first time in my life I feel that I belong. I told my mother that the deed was done, and although she knew about it all along she was not at all pleased. Apart from your family, whom she met at our wedding, she knows few Jews. Politically her sympathies, as they always have been, are with the Arabs. I quoted Amos to her: "And I shall plant them (my people of Israel) upon their land, and they shall be no more pulled up out of their land which I have given them" but she was not impressed.

'I am sorry to hear that when everything was going so well for you in New York (Florida sounded heavenly) you are not feeling well. I am sure it is the result of the mugging. These things have a knock on effect and can last for a long time.

'Did you know that in classical Hebrew the same word is used for "to know" and "to love?". That one can only love, therefore, what one knows; anything strange or remote can neither be held dear nor cherished. Satisfying the authorities was, I am sure, only the beginning of a commitment to a system of values unique in character, enduring in continuity and relevant at all times which will be the birthright of the son shortly to be born to your fond daughter-in-law, Sarah.'

Chapter Twenty-three

In the King's Arms, at the table at which they had first met, Alec sat opposite Jessica over the ploughman's lunch which neither of them had touched.

'When are you going to tell him?' Alec said.

'I'm waiting for the right moment.'

'You've been saying that for weeks.'

It was over a month now since their incriminating conversation had been overheard by Carol. The Queen Anne house was in the final throes of decoration – wallpapers and paint, about the colour and design of which nobody any longer cared – and would shortly be ready for occupation although its future, once so rosy, was in abeyance. Jessica said that if she divorced her husband, despite her beloved horses, she would not care to remain in Godalming. Alec, whose livelihood was in the High Street, had little choice.

He was aware that in the village, his association with Jessica had not gone unremarked. It was patent in the regard of his patients whose glance was no longer direct and who pointedly avoided their customary enquiries after Carol. Alec did not care. He surprised himself. He who had been devoted to, inextricably tied up with, every aspect of his wife and family, scarcely gave them a thought. He was oblivious to the gossip which he knew followed him as he made his house-calls – waiting only for doors to shut behind him – to the havoc he was creating in Jessica's marriage, to the devastation in his own. He was sorry for Carol – he did not like to see her with her red eyes, her swollen face, her lumpy body not yet recovered from the birth – but he loved Jessica as he had never, with hindsight, loved his wife. He could contemplate no future that did not include Jessica's presence. Josh, who unbeknownst to Carol had come to Godalming as emissary, had said he was mad, he probably was, but in Jessica he had stumbled upon the complementary half of his divided self and would not let her go.

'You've had weeks.' Alec looked into eyes that were neither grey nor green.

'You're not worried, are you?'

'I just want to be sure of you.'

'Aren't you?'

Alec cast his mind back over the past few months: the guarded telephone exchanges; the hours at the riding-stables, ankle deep in straw, where Jessica had introduced her mounts, Shamus and Bianca; the afternoons in the cottage where he had knelt to remove the crop from Jessica's knee length boots before pulling them off and making lazy love, urgent love, selfish and unselfish love, lighthearted, passionate, in-love and loving love. He tried, in this respect, not to compare Jessica with Carol, with whom love, even at its best, had always been restrained. Jessica, prodigal, emotional, physical, was a woman whereas Carol seemed not to have completed the transition from childhood to maturity. Life with Jessica, would never be dull.

Josh had upbraided him with the children – Debbie, Lisa and Mathew – who in a sense had always been Carol's, just as she had belonged to her father when he was alive, and to whose memory she was faithful now that he was dead. He tried not to think about the twins. The financial burden, he did not delude himself, was going to be heavy. The Queen Anne house would have to be sold. Alec did not care. He would make life as easy as possible for Carol who, with nothing to keep her in Godalming, would probably prefer London and the family to which she was so attached. He would live in a garret with Jessica. He might even give up medicine. There had been idle talk, in each other's afternoon arms, about a horse-drawn carriage in Ireland, romantic notions of a fresh start on the other side of the world. Life, for Alec Caplan, had unexpectedly blossomed and with Jessica at his side he was convinced that anything was possible.

He'd had a letter from his mother-in-law, from Kitty in New York, had it still in his pocket. He had expected nothing but recrimination but found it imbued with understanding. In it she implored him not to act in haste. Looking at Jessica in a black polo-neck sweater against which her skin took on a Rubens' luminescence, he knew that if he took all the time in the world it would make no difference. He was sorry for Carol. He would do everything within his power to make life easy for her and his children, but Jessica was something he was both unable and unwilling to fight.

'Jessica Caplan,' Alec said, trying it out on his tongue. 'It used to be Cohen. How does it grab you?'

Jessica took his hands in hers, caressing them.

'Like everything else about you.'

'What are you waiting for, then?'

'He won't know what's hit him,' Jessica said of her husband. 'He's going to be very hurt.'

Carol sat nursing her babies, responding in kind to the changing grimaces that passed involuntarily over the tiny faces, ten delicate fingers curled tightly round her own. Just as at first she had wanted nothing to do with her twins, now she would not let them go. She sat, for hours sometimes, as if she had never had a child before, not tiring of the trusting eyes searching her own, the tiny legs – deceptively fragile – in perpetual motion, the gossamer cheeks, the nacreous ears. How soft their heads, one sable, one Titian. Silk' or satin. She swaddled them in their shawls, knitted – the second one post haste – by Aunty Mirrie, and swayed them back and forth as if by the movement she could assuage her hurt.

At the table Debbie looked up from the letter she was writing to Kitty in New York.

'When will our house be ready?'

'I don't know,' Carol said, pulling a shawl more tightly.

'Why doesn't Daddy ever come?'

'He's very busy.'

'He's got a rota.'

'He'll come when he can.'

'He used to come every weekend.'

'I told you, he's busy.'

'Did you and Daddy have a quarrel?'

'What makes you think that?'

'I heard you. In the bedroom.'
'You shouldn't eavesdrop.'
'I didn't. We heard in the sitting-room. Me and Lisa. I don't like it when you shout.'
'Get on with your letter.'
'When can I see my new bedroom?'
'When it's finished.'
'When will that be?'
'I'm not sure.'
'You promised by the Christmas holidays.'
'The builders are very slow.'
'I don't like it here.'
'It's bathtime.'
'I haven't finished my letter.'
'Finish it tomorrow.'
Debbie sat defiantly at the table.
'Didn't you hear me?'
'I want my daddy,' Debbie said.

Despite the fact that her blood pressure seemed now to have returned to normal, Rachel was still at Hettie Klopman's. They had been about to move to Putney when Herbert, who had been complaining of indigestion all week, had woken in the night with chest pains which had been diagnosed as a minor coronary thrombosis, for which he was prescribed bed rest, and Hettie had urged them to stay.

'He could be ill for ages,' Rachel said, 'we can't live here forever.'
'Just a couple of weeks,' Patrick said.
'To please your mother.'
'Is that so terrible? She's looked after you all this time.'
'If it is a couple of weeks. I'm not having my baby in this house.'
'I didn't say you should. They feel safer if I'm around.'
'Blackmail.'
'He could have another coronary.'
'Are you going to stay home all day from the hospital?'
'You know what I mean, Rache.'

* * *

Kitty put up a double fold of white card, engraved in black copperplate, on Maurice's bookshelf.

'What's that?' Maurice, his head on one side, was thumbing through his record collection.

'A wedding invitation from my nephew Norman.'

'He's the one who's marrying that South African girl?'

'Sandra. He's waited long enough. He looked after his mother, my sister-in-law Dolly, until she died, then Sandra came along and scooped him up. They're getting married in December. I'll send a nice present – not that they'll need anything. Sandra's a little heiress. Rabbi Magnus is officiating at Sydney's synagogue – funny, I still think of it as Sydney's. We'd all given up hope for Norman.'

'Emperor?' Maurice straightened up, the record in his hand.

It was one of her favourites. 'I thought I'd go to bed,' Kitty said.

'At eight o'clock?'

'My head hurts.'

The pattern of their evenings had changed. Although Maurice tempted her, La Forza del Destino or Boris Godunov (sung in English to make her feel at home) at the Met, or dinner in Little Italy, which she had always enjoyed, Kitty no longer wanted to go out. She declined all his invitations and, tired and listless, hardly bothering with dinner, went earlier and earlier to bed. Although all the hospital tests had proved negative, Maurice was worried about her. He was not the only one.

Ed, who was now dating Bette – to the chagrin of Mort who had lost out – had brought her *The Dangling Man* and *Dubin's Lives* to read, in hopes of enticing her back to class which she no longer attended; Bette, who lectured Kitty at length about looking after her body and combating disease, now went to class on her own. Mort had bought a scrabble board and had taught her to play but her heart wasn't in it and whenever he challenged the words she had made, she did not really care. As she grew increasingly disinclined to cook, Herb, who came almost every night, had taken over the kitchen. He made special dishes in an effort to stimulate her appetite – Chicken Cacciatore and Baked Alaska – which Kitty only picked at to please him.

Tonight, Ed's birthday, the four of them had gone to a show but Kitty, feeling she could not sit through it, had declined the invitation. In her bedroom, her's and Maurice's, redecorated with the help of Bette Birnstingl who had used a ribbon and bow design in shades of nectarine and peach (romantic without being frilly), Kitty got into bed looking forward to an evening spent re-reading her letters to the accompaniment of the Beethoven which came from the sitting-room. Bed was the only place that she felt comfortable, where she was able to rest her weary limbs and her constantly aching head.

At the moment her greatest worry was Carol. It was no joke to be abandoned with five small children. Although Kitty had written twice to Alec, she seemed to have had no luck in getting him to change his mind about leaving her eldest daughter. At moments such as this she wished Sydney was alive. Happy as she was with Maurice it was Sydney, with whom she had brought up her children, who would have known what to do. Thirty odd years, she supposed, could not easily be discounted. A lifetime together had forged her relationship with Sydney and because there was no shared memory bank she could not expect, hard as they both might try, such understanding, such rapport with Maurice. That she loved him there was no question, as Maurice loved her, but it was different. Neither better nor worse, but different. You could not have everything and she had much to be grateful for.

Rachel, still at Hettie Klopman's, was her next problem. Although Kitty told herself, in all honesty, that among her children she had no favourite, perhaps because she was the youngest she had a special feeling (despite the fact that she had always been a renegade) for Rachel, and found it hard to convince herself that her own baby was about to give birth to a child. After what she had read about toxaemia in Maurice's encyclopaedia, Kitty would be relieved (although Rachel had assured her that she was now better) when the child was safely born.

Sarah, whose confinement was to be at home – how the pendulum had swung! – would have her own mother in attendance. What was it she had said in her letter about 'to know' and 'to love'? Kitty loved Sarah as her own daughter and the letter had touched her deeply. Josh, who had never managed to live up to his father's expectations of him – which had always distressed Kitty – deserved a little happiness. She wished that he would stop this silly backbiting with Rachel and realise that life was too short for vendettas and that there was room for more than one opinion in the world.

Beatty was her latest worry. She had been having radiotherapy for her tumour but it didn't sound as if it was terribly successful. According to her last letter – in which Beatty's terror had leapt from between the lines and Kitty recognised the loneliness and hopelessness of widowhood after a lifetime of having someone to care – they were taking her into hospital for a mastectomy, the success of which in combating the disease seemed to be in some doubt. Sydney, as the head of the family – although he was not the oldest – had always been responsible for his sisters and they looked to Kitty now that he was dead. She made up her mind to write a long letter to Beatty in the morning, probably – she always woke these days in the small hours – while Maurice slept.

Preoccupied, Kitty did not hear Maurice come into the room. He brought her a cup of tea – which he had learned to make to her liking – as he did every night, and putting it on the table next to her sat down on the bed. Seeing him look at her Kitty put a hand selfconsciously to her fading scar.

'Headache?'

'Not worse than usual,' Kitty said.

'You know something, Kit?'

Kitty waited. She loved the way he said it: 'You know something, Kit?'

'I've never given you a wedding present.'

Kitty had not given Maurice one either. In the excitement of the event and the planning of the trip to Florida she had quite forgotten.

'I'd like to give you one now.'

She looked about his person but could see no gift-wrapped package, no box.

'How would you like to go to Norman's wedding?'

Kitty looked to see if he was serious.

'I'm going to take you back to England, Kit. There's no reason I can't paint there.'

Chapter Twenty-four

Kitty, belonging to the 'pull yourself together school', had never held any truck with illness which was psychosomatic – she had had long arguments with Patrick about it – but she had to admit that from the moment that Maurice had announced his intention of taking her back to England, her symptoms, headaches, fatigue and listlessness, had disappeared like magic. She told herself that it was because she had something definite to do, something on which she must concentrate her mind, but she knew that it was not really so. On the morning following Maurice's announcement – his welcome wedding present – she had woken early but her dawn alertness held a different quality to that which she had been experiencing since her return from Florida. There were plans to be made about which they had talked long into the night. The move was to be permanent. Maurice was to sell the apartment, wind up his affairs, pull up his post-war roots such as they were, for Kitty.

That it was a considerable sacrifice she knew. Having been the victim of one catastrophic upheaval in his time, it was not easy for him to start again. 'A new life at my age,' he had said, and when Kitty told him how much she appreciated his decision to take her back to England, to relinquish such semblance of belonging that he had created in New York, Maurice had replied that 'Nothing was written in marble or in stone'. He would miss his friends. Despite their apparent dissimilarities, Maurice and Herb and Ed and Mort had forged a relationship, an interdependent quartet which, beneath its flip exterior, Kitty found touching to behold. The three of them had at first been disbelieving.

'I'll keep an eye on the place for you, Mo, while you're away,' Herb had said.

'I'm not coming back.'

Kitty could see that Maurice was choked, perhaps had not realised until that moment the robustness of the bond that existed between the members of the poker game.

'I have to see my grandchildren,' Maurice said.

It was the most beautiful thing Kitty had heard.

'So what about the game?' Mort said. 'What about Tuesday and Thursday nights?'

Maurice had not answered. There had been nothing to say. Kitty could see how hard it was for him. In the weeks that followed, Herb and Ed and Mort had stood around – watching Maurice pack and dispose of his superfluous possessions – humming defiantly as if what they could see before their very own eyes was not really happening, or looking on helplessly, their hands in their pockets, like lost souls. That they revered Maurice was obvious to Kitty, who had not really thought about it before. Although none of them said anything, they made her feel guilty as she read the hurt, the silent accusation, in their eyes.

'You'll write?' Herb said.

He was addressing Kitty and from the tone of his voice she realised that in her short time in New York, she too had somehow become important to the poker game and that in her turn she was going to miss the 'boys'.

'You must all come and see us,' she said brightly, knowing full well that the bond forged in Maurice's apartment, was unlikely to survive transplanted to England.

'Sure,' Herb disappeared into the kitchen, 'sure.'

Bette Birnstingl took the announcement of Kitty's impending departure as a personal affront.

'You're making a big mistake,' she said when Kitty told her of Maurice's decision. 'He's not going to like it.' She had put her finger on the very thing which had been worrying Kitty. Suppose Maurice were miserable in England? Suppose he hated the people, the way of life, the climate? Suppose he could not paint? She weighed it against her own happiness, her craving for her family – to have those about her whom she loved – and decided that it was a chance she would have to take.

'I'm going to miss you, Bette,' Kitty sighed. And it was true. Tuesday nights not spent gossiping with Bette in her apartment with its 'disappearing' closet and 'floating' staircase would not be the same.

'Why don't you marry Ed?' she asked, realising with amusement that her own romance had exercised Bette when she first came to New York and that now the boot was on the other foot.

'Ed's a great guy,' Bette said. 'We have a real fun time, but I couldn't say he's my ideal.'

'I sometimes wonder whether one shouldn't think so much about ideals but consider available alternatives,' Kitty said.

Bette stared at her friend.

'You know, Kitty, that's the wisest thing anyone's ever said to me? What will I do without you?'

It was strange, Kitty thought, how the depth of their mutual understanding had little to do with the duration of their friendship. Leaving Bette was going to be a wrench.

'We'll write,' she said pragmatically.

Bette smiled. Kitty read her all the letters from England. 'I won't have you to share the letters with.'

'Marry Ed,' Kitty repeated. 'It's no good being on your own.'

Maurice packed his books personally – the surrogate family through which he had managed to keep sane over the years – not trusting them to the shippers. Already Kitty was planning how to accommodate them in her flat. He refused to take his paintings, the dark and personal prisms through which he had expressed in a black catharsis of oils his past life.

'I'll start again,' he said.

And when Kitty looked at him doubtfully as he placed only his easel, some empty canvasses, his palette and his paints into the chest left by the removal men, he put his arm around her reassuringly.

'It'll be a new beginning. Michelangelo, Goethe, Rembrandt, Victor Hugo, Titian, Kant, Rabelais, all did their best work well after middle age.'

He packed his portrait of Kitty and the record collection to which they had done their courting. The more cheerful Maurice was as he went about his arrangements the more Kitty, who was not deceived, realised how much her husband was giving up for her.

* * *

'What news of your mother?' Herbert said. He lay in bed while Rachel, painstakingly knitting a grubby white vest, kept him company.

Apropos of the state of Rachel's wool which snaked over the carpet Herbert had already told her the story about the textile showroom where in the men's room there was a large notice: 'Please wash your hands before touching the pastels.'

The boss had surprised one of his employees coming straight out of the toilet and into the showroom. 'Moishe,' he says, 'you didn't see the notice? "Please wash your hands before touching the pastels"?'

'Who's touching the pastels,' Moishe says, 'I'm going to have my lunch!'

'She's coming home,' Rachel said, unable to keep the triumph from her voice.

'Did you hear the one about the husband who came home and said to his wife, "If you only learned to cook we could sack the housekeeper," to which his wife replied, "And if you only learned to make love we could sack the chauffeur."'

Rachel smiled. It was no worse than the rest of Herbert's jokes on to which she realised now he displaced his anxiety over his heart condition. Putting down her knitting she retrieved his eiderdown from where it had slipped on to the floor, and adjusted the pillows behind his head. His normally ruddy face was overlaid with a greyish pallor.

'Comfortable?' She sat down again heavily in the chair and picked up her needles.

'I make a living.'

When he realised that his father's condition was not improving, Patrick, considering it unfair to Rachel, had offered to take her to the Putney flat. Paradoxically she, who had never cared for life in Winnington Road, had opted not to go.

'Your father likes to have me around,' she said. And it was true. Although her relationship with Hettie was still abrasive – there being no aspect of child care on which they agreed – she had grown fond of Herbert with his addiction to the news on the television at the foot of his bed, every bulletin of which he would scan for its Jewish content, his bottomless fund of stories which were frequently neither topical nor particularly amusing. Together, while Hettie was out – glad to have Rachel to keep her husband company – they commiserated with each other over Israel.

'When the good Lord said, "I will give the land unto your seed", unfortunately he didn't provide a timetable. Tell me, Rachel, how is it that what is so obvious to you and me is to so many others like a closed book? Even Hettie only pretends to go along with me because she's afraid I'll have another heart attack.'

'What most people don't realise,' Rachel said, 'is how tiny Israel is, no bigger than Switzerland, smaller than Wales. They're absolutely amazed when you bring it to their attention.'

'It's hardly surprising,' Herbert said, 'when you think of all the confusion there is over Northern Ireland.'

'Have you told him?' Alec said to Jessica, meaning her husband as he joined her in the newly painted drawing-room of the Queen Anne house.

'What do you think of these for the conservatory?' Jessica said, offering him a copper tile.

'I don't give a damn,' he said, capable of thinking of nothing but their future life together, how it would be.

'When are you going to?'

'When he comes back from Bahrain.' Jessica, on her knees, studied a sample of material, peacocks and exotic flowers.

'You didn't tell me he was away.'

'I must have forgotten.' She held the fabric at arm's length, her head tilted to one side.

'Look, Jess – ' Alec pulled her to her feet – 'you're not changing your mind?'

Jessica leaned back in his arms and caressed his hair. He pulled her hand away.

'I'm not one of your horses.'

'I say beautiful things to my horses . . .'

'You haven't answered my question.'

'I stroke them when we're alone, like this, and like this . . .'

'Jessica!'

'I run my hands along their flanks, feel the muscles beneath my fingers . . .'

'Jess . . .'

'Put my face close to theirs, whisper in their ears . . .'

'Be serious for a moment.'

'I've never been more serious. Shall I tell you what I say to them, in the mornings, just the three of us, standing on the straw, nobody there? Come closer and I'll tell you, oh, the secrets, Alec, the wonderful secrets, the ineffable mysteries I share with my horses . . .'

Alec knew that no matter what the obstacles he would never give Jessica up.

In Kitty's flat, with Carol and the children, the situation seemed less straightforward. It was as if he were two different people, with two different lives and no way he could reconcile them. Debbie, her arms round his neck, pulling at his heart strings, Lisa's lisping account of school, Mathew's plea from the floor for assistance with his Action Man, fogged the image of Jessica, muted her ever present voice. Face to face with Carol things were harder still. She tried to keep him away from the twins as if by looking at Poppy and Sara, holding them in his arms, he would contaminate them.

'I wish I was dead,' Carol said.

And Alec's heart went out to her, once so particular like her mother about her appearance, now so untidy, so unkempt.

'You mustn't say things like that.'

'There's nothing to live for.'

'How about the children?'

'What do you care about the children?'

'I care,' Alec said.

And he did. There was room in his troubled heart still for Carol and his children but his feelings for Jessica, the passions which had blinded him, a sudden and total eclipse, consuming and possessing him, had effaced them all.

'Are you going to meet your mother at the airport?' Sarah said to Josh who was reading a letter from Rachel.

'My sister's mad,' Josh said. 'She accuses me of implying that there is a comparison between the actions of the Nazis and those of the Israeli government.'

'Did you?'

'Not at all. I did refer to "Ayatollah Begin" . . .'

'Josh!'

'It was a joke.'

'It's not a joke to Rachel.'

'She says that I've taken it upon myself to preach Christianity to the Gentiles and turn the other cheek but that if the Jews want to preserve their independent state they have to fight for it . . .'

'"Even the High Priest Phineas took a spear in his own hand and personally struck down evil doers." Is Rachel going to the airport?'

'Not if I'm going.' Josh put the letter back into its envelope. 'She says I'm an antisemite!'

Chapter Twenty-five

Rachel was alone with Herbert Klopman when he died. He liked her to sit with him. He did not care for Hettie's fussing and the presence of old Mrs Klopman, who still treated him like a small boy, made him agitated. Rachel, with her knitting, did not bother him.

'What time does your mother arrive?'

'Eleven o'clock.'

'A man goes to a restaurant and he's forgotten his watch. He calls a passing waiter and asks him the time. "Sorry, sir," the waiter says, "you're not my table!"'

'Josh is going to meet her.'

Herbert raised his eyebrows.

'I'm not going. Not if Josh is. He still refuses to put blame where it belongs . . .'

'I see that Reagan's going to rebuild and train the Lebanese Army so that it can maintain internal security . . . You can bet your bottom dollar they'll be at each other's throats again as soon as the Israelis pull out.'

Rachel concentrated on her needles. She was looking forward to seeing Kitty – although she was not so sure about Maurice – but she was not going to the reunion dinner that Carol and Sarah had planned. She would see her mother tomorrow, on her own, preferably without Maurice. It was quiet in the house. Despite the central heating, the room in the winter light seemed chill.

'It's cold outside,' Rachel said. 'Would you like me to shut the window?'

'Will that make it any warmer outside?' Herbert said, with no enthusiasm, putting a hand to his head.

Rachel closed the window, looking out on to the grey street, the neo-Georgian mansions on the other side reflecting the Klopmans' own. 'Are you all right?' She adjusted the rug over her father-in-law's feet, which were always cold these days, and sat down on the bed with her knitting, casting off the stitches on a navy blue bootee. She would ask Hettie to buy her some scarlet ribbon.

'A bit faint,' Herbert said. 'Which reminds me. There was this woman fainted at the theatre. "Get me a doctor!" she moans from the floor. A doctor, a good-looking fellow, rushes over to help. He's just feeling her pulse when the woman sits up and beams at him: "Oy, doctor," she says, "have I got a girl for you!" Rachel?'

'That's me.'

'Did I ever tell you the one about the Jap who was walking up and down Fifth Avenue trying to find Tiffany's?'

'No,' Rachel lied.

'There was this Japanese man walking up and down Fifth Avenue looking like crazy for Tiffany's . . .'

Rachel severed the navy-blue wool with her teeth.

'. . . He stops this little old lady . . .'

She was quite proud of her bootees, even if one had turned out to be slightly larger than the other. They were not at all bad for a beginner.

'. . . and says, "Excuse me, Ma'am, I wonder if you'd be kind enough to assist me? I've been up and down this street a hundred times but I can't seem to find Tiffany's . . ."'

Rachel thought she would make a vest next with the rest of the navy-blue wool. She was really getting the bug.

'. . . the little old lady pokes the Jap in the stomach with her umbrella . . .'

He had embellished the story since the last time.

'. . . "Tell me young man," she says . . .'

Rachel put the bootee in the supermarket carrier which served as a knitting bag.

'. . . "Pearl Harbour you found" . . .'

Rachel waited for the punchline.

'"How come you can't find . . ."'

Herbert had his eyes closed.

Rachel waited.

'Tiffany's,' she prompted.

Herbert's lips did not move.

'"How come you can't find Tiffany's?"'

His hand was very cold.

Rachel had the impression that the room was suddenly empty. She stood up and as she did so a headache, worse than any she had had before, gripped her skull, lights flashed, brightly, painfully in her eyes and her stomach knotted tightly with pain.

The last thing she remembered was old Mrs Klopman, with her bent head, coming into the room.

Kitty, who had always been terrified of flying, was becoming a seasoned traveller. The fact that she was not consumed with terror as she had been on her first trip to Israel – which seemed a lifetime ago – was due, she felt, not so much to the flying hours she had now put in as to the presence of Maurice by her side. He was such a safe man somehow, so certain of everything, but of course, after what he had been through there remained very little for him to be afraid of. As she looked at him in the aisle seat next to her, felt his warm hand on hers, she thought that his confidence was catching and that she had already, although she was still in mid-air, come home.

Exhausted as she was from the last minute hassles entailed in the giving up of Maurice's apartment and the social whirl of the past week, she was wide awake as those around her slept with the excitement of being reunited with her family. Herb and Ed and Mort and Bette and even Joe, who unable to speak had watched Maurice's departure with tears in his eyes, had not wanted to let them go, clung on to them as long as possible. Bette had thrown a party for them in her apartment at which Maurice, surprisingly, had been the life and soul, and Kitty thought what a pity that they were leaving just when he and Bette looked like becoming friends.

Herb had prepared a farewell dinner for them in Maurice's kitchen, serving, to Kitty's amusement, her own chopped liver recipe (now included in his culinary repertoire), followed by Breast of Chicken Sauté à la Herb (sherry, palm hearts and shallots) accompanied by a *Marbre de Legumes* which had entailed a labour of love to do with layers of zucchini and kohlrabi and small leeks and little green beans and red peppers and beef bouillon (painstakingly made with beef shank and vegetables), assembled in a mould and refrigerated overnight, followed by the Pecan Pie with Caramel Sauce which was his *pièce de résistance*.

Mort had treated them all to the best seats at '42nd Street' and Ed – at ridiculous expense, Kitty thought – had taken them to dinner at Laserre at which he had announced his engagement to Bette Birnstingl. It had been a night to remember, the apotheosis of her stay, during which she realised with surprise what a good time she had had in New York, about which she had at first been so apprehensive, and how very much she was going to miss her transatlantic family.

By the day of their departure the elation engendered by the celebrations had subsided. Herb and Mort, and Ed with Bette, had wandered miserably among the packing cases and while she and Maurice nervously put together their last minute things the conversation was desultory. Mort produced a bottle of whisky and dispensed it into the rinsed out breakfast cups.

'To good times,' he said, raising his to his lips.

'*Bon Voyage*,' Herb said.

'*Auf Simchas*.' Ed looked at Bette.

'*Le Hayim*!' There was a break in Maurice's voice. Kitty did not underestimate how much he was giving up for her. She had had a taste in the past months of what it meant to uproot yourself.

As she put her coat on, Bette had shed a tear. She handed Kitty a package. 'To remember me by.'

'Did you think I'd forget?' Kitty said as they embraced. Bette's gift-wrapped parcel lay on her lap together with the *In Flight* magazine at which, too busy with her thoughts, she had not even glanced.

She untied the ribbon, took the small box from its paper. A piece of costume jewellery, two entwined hearts in gold, winked in the reading light.

Kitty put the brooch in her lapel and Maurice, who she had thought was sleeping, fastened it for her, brushing her face with his lips before leaning back in his seat.

There was no sound in the side-room they had given Rachel. Her body was weightless, seeming to be one with the mattress. She was not dead. She noticed her hand on the counterpane and that there was something strange about it, then that it was not her hand that was unfamiliar but the fact that the bedclothes, the thin cotton hospital blankets, lay flat. There was no bump. She turned her head, half a turn. A cradle, sloping, at an angle. Her absent thoughts made a halo outside her head. One by one, with difficulty, she gathered them in. There was one to do with Tiffany's, and Herbert – such an old joke, she must have heard it a hundred times – and old Mrs Klopman. An ambulance siren. Her nephew Mathew had referred to the sound as the 'nee-naw' when he was an infant, running in fear whenever he heard it to bury his head in Carol's lap. Nurses with wavy faces, advancing and retreating. Pre-eclampsia. They kept repeating it. Pre-eclampsia. And caesarian section. She'd tried to tell them that her name was Rachel. Klopman – waiting for the reaction – that her notes quite categorically stipulated *natural* childbirth to the accompaniment of 'Ten Green Bottles', encouraged by Patrick, her labour partner.

Patrick had come. And gone. She did not remember any 'Ten Green Bottles' yet she could see her toes beneath the counterpane. The cradle. Beside the bed. Belonged to her. Mrs Klopman. Mrs Klopman. You have a beautiful daughter. Ridiculous. You couldn't call a girl Sydney. What then? The decision entailed more than the bestowing of a name. It included the act of creating images and symbols, interpreting perceived reality, telling a personal and communal story. The cradle was still. Quiet. Panicking, Rachel raised herself on her elbow. Her stomach was stiff, sore. There was a bundle. Gritting her teeth, she lifted it on to the bed.

A great delirium consumed her. An almost embarrassing ecstasy as she looked for the first time at her child. Daring, she raised the bundle to her face, kissed the cheek, the long eyelashes – Patrick's – unfolded the minuscule fingers with their papery nails, looked for the first momentous time into the speculative eyes of her daughter. It was a moment of understanding: that every mother contains her daughter in herself, and every daughter her mother, and every woman extends backwards into her mother, and forwards into her daughter. In that instant she understood Kitty utterly for the first time, and knew exactly – for her womb contracted achingly – how she would feel when her daughter left, unthinking, with her knap-back on her back, for the world. Life, Rachel thought, was spread out over generations. She would call her daughter Rebecca, after the matriarch Rebecca, Sidonie (for her father), Hephzibah, 'My pleasure is in her', as she recognised with every fibre of her being, every nerve ending, that it would be.

Putting her child to her breast Rachel realised, with sudden clarity, that there were decisions to be taken, choices to be made, and that life as she and Patrick had known it would never be the same again.

In the Visitors' Room – the dog-eared magazines long time expired, Maurice motionless by the window – Kitty, still in her travelling clothes, waited to see Rachel. For the umpteenth time she went over in her mind the jumbled events of the past hours. As soon as she had seen Josh's face as he waited by the barrier, hemmed in by the airport crowds, she had known that something was wrong. They had come straight to the hospital. Maurice had been wonderful. He had explained to her about pre-eclampsia. Kitty bombarded him with questions. Could it have been avoided? (She blamed herself for going to New York.) Should Rachel have eaten better? Shouldn't the doctors have spotted it earlier? Maurice said that as far as he knew – and he was not an expert – the condition had to do with the body's immune system, and that the word itself meant 'before a fit', which was what, as far as Kitty could in her jet-lagged mind make out, had happened to Rachel at Hettie Klopman's. The swollen legs had been a precursor.

Kitty blamed herself. She had told Rachel enough times to be sensible like Carol, to put herself in the capable hands of Maurice Goldapple. It wouldn't have made any difference, Maurice said, but Kitty had had her own theories. Anyway, thank God, everything had ended well and she had a new granddaughter whom, when they had once more checked Rachel's blood pressure, she would be allowed to see.

She had come home with a vengeance. The shock about Rachel – her heart had turned over – then the news about Herbert Klopman. The reins of her life were in her hands before she had had time to pick them up. There was so much to do. Rachel would need looking after now; a Caesar was no joke, you needed time to recover, and she could hardly go back to Hettie's. Poor Hettie. Kitty knew, too well what it meant to be a widow. Glancing at Maurice to reassure herself, she determined that she would slowly, gently, when she had got over the first shock, take Hettie – giving her the benefit of her own experience – in hand.

Then there was Beatty. She had had her mastectomy, and every day, according to Josh, asked when Kitty was coming. Beatty was a shadow of her former self, he had said, and Kitty had understood that he was preparing her. Beatty would have to be encouraged, nourished, nursed back to whatever health was available to her.

Josh's own baby was due next, the son who was to be born in his mother's bed. Kitty didn't hold with that and doubted whether Sarah's mother – assuming she could tear herself away from Leicester – was going to be much help. She knew very well who it was who was going to do all the shopping and cooking and the running to and fro.

After that there'd be the twins, Carol would need some help, and Alec, perhaps her biggest problem. The interior decorator had taken off for Los Angeles permanently with her husband, but Carol was adamant: she would not take Alec back. There was a situation which had to be handled with the tact of a Habib, the diplomacy of a Kissinger. Kitty saw no reason why, given time and the right handling, Carol and Alec shouldn't eventually be installed in the Queen Anne house in Godalming with their growing family round them. Alec was a broken man, Josh had told her, but he would get over it. It wasn't the first time such a thing had happened. It was Carol who would need all the reassurance, all the love and support that Kitty could muster.

It was as if her time in New York, the honeymoon in Florida, had never been. As if it had been a dream and, like a dream, was fading. She had to force herself to think of Maurice's apartment, her ordeal at the hands of her assailants in the graffiti-covered street, of her surrogate family, Herb and Ed and Mort and Bette. As soon as everything calmed down (if it ever did), as soon as she had dealt satisfactorily with her quiver full of problems, she would invite Bette to stay with her, show her London – which she scarcely knew herself – as Bette had shown her New York.

There was another imbroglio: Rachel and Josh. She couldn't have them at each other's throats, not speaking, when with their new families, cousins, they would have so much to offer each other. Life was too short. That their views about Israel were diametrically opposed, she understood. So what? It didn't mean they couldn't be in the same room, couldn't speak to each other. She was a Zionist. It was a good thing for the Jewish people to return to the land of Israel, and bad for them to be scattered among the nations, for the family to be divided. There were ten, maybe fifteen million Jews in the world. Didn't they deserve a country hardly a quarter the size of Syria? Didn't the Arabs have enough countries? She would enlist the help of Maurice in resolving the delicate situation, knowing that first she would have to work on the acceptance of her new, her dear husband by Rachel. She wasn't going to put up with any friction there either.

Waiting for the nurse to summon her to Rachel, Kitty saw herself arrived from the new world, an emissary really, for her family, for Israel. If Kitty Shelton had anything to do with it, both of them, God willing, given time, would live in peace. She looked at Maurice silhouetted against the window.

Everything was possible.

She was no longer alone.